Caribbean Adventure Series

Book 2

VANISHING WATERS

A Rick Waters Novel

ERIC CHANCE STONE

2021 by Eric Chance Stone

Published by Lost and Found Publishing

Printed in the United States of America

ISBN: 978-1-7341626-3-9

First Edition
10 9 8 7 6 5 4 3 2 1

ACKNOWLEDGEMENTS

I'd like to thank my beta readers Anne Torrey, Kathy Zeller, Sherry Whitten Petrivelli, Cathy McCabe Dee, Ron Dalton, Mike Keevil, Michael Bolton, Bavette & Dennis Battern, Shari Lynne, Deb Mangold, Eric Moore, Kim-Cara Lalonde, Steve Bowman, Kathleen Eby Semenuk, David Dyer, and Chuck Springs.

I thank Bob Bitchin for all his advice and support.

I thank my editors, Marsha Zinberg and Stephanie Diaz Slagle.

I thank my graphic artist Les.

I thank my formatter Colleen Sheehan.

I thank my mentors, Wayne Stinnett, Cap Daniels and Nick Sullivan.

Special thanks to all the people who bought my first book and gave me the encouragement to keep going. I couldn't do it without y'all.

Find The Official Synopsis Music at:

GUM.CO/VANISHINGWATERSMUSICFREE

VANISHING WATERS

CHAPTER ONE

From the luminous glow of the deck lights of Rick's boat on Destin Harbor Walk, he could see her brown eyes. She stood there trembling, and she looked desperate.

"Are you Rick Waters?" she asked.

"Yes. Who's asking?"

"My name is Emily Davis. May I come aboard?"

"Sure," Rick replied, as he held out his hand to help her step onto the deck.

"Can we go inside the boat? I read about the case you solved in Texas and how you used your treasure hunting skills to solve that crime. I have something very sensitive I want to discuss with you, and voices carry over water," she said.

"No problem."

Rick opened the sliding glass doors of the Viking 55. After solving a huge case in Texas and getting paid more money that he had ever made in his life, he had purchased the yacht and put the rest into the bank. He was finally financially comfortable for the first time in his life.

She took a seat on the settee, and he pulled up a chair to sit across from her.

She was a good-looking woman with long silver hair and a smooth face, only slightly wrinkled. She didn't look old enough to have silver hair, but he had seen young girls in their twenties dye their hair silver sometimes. Apparently, it was a fad.

"You have a bird?" she asked, pointing to the cloth-covered cage.

"Yeah, that's Chief. He's an umbrella cockatoo, but he's deep into dreamland now. Don't worry, we won't bother him. Can I get you a drink? Amaretto?"

"That would be fine."

Rick poured her drink as she rummaged through her purse.

She handed him an Alabama driver's license. "As I said, my name is Emily Davis. I'm from Tampa."

He glanced over it. "This license says you're Patricia Benning from Mobile, Alabama. I'm confused."

"So am I. What I'm about to tell you will be hard to believe. As a matter of fact, if you were to tell me the same story, I probably wouldn't believe you. But it's true." She took a sip of amaretto.

Her hands were shaking and she was shivering. It was a warm evening, so it couldn't be from cold.

"Nine months ago," she began, "I went to an office in downtown Tampa to meet with a man named Hans Larsson, who used to be a co-owner of a biotech company in Zürich. I had worked with him and his former partner, Liam Furrer, in the past and was looking forward to the meeting. I'm a chemist and I developed an immunotherapy drug that was going to revolutionize cancer treatment. It had a one hundred percent efficacy rate on lab animals. I'm not just talking about on skin carcinomas or lymphoma. It worked on everything we threw at it. In other words, Rick, what I'm saying is, I think I found the cure for cancer."

Rick raised an eyebrow. "You're right, that's hard to believe."

"That's just the beginning of the story. During the meeting, three masked men burst into the office and shot Hans in the back. They threw a bag over my head and injected me with something. When I woke up, I was in a hospital, strapped to a gurney. My face and hands were covered in bandages, and both of my legs were in casts. I had no idea where I was. It felt like I was there for many months, but without windows or a clock of any kind, it was impossible to know for sure. They questioned me about every aspect of the drug, and I had no choice but to cooperate and tell them as much as I could remember. The room they kept me in was locked and had padded walls with no windows. It only had a bed, a toilet, and a shower. It was miserable and frightening. They had a team of doctors and therapists, and they forced me to do physical therapy after the casts were removed. But I was always under gunpoint."

Rick was silent for several moments. Finally, he said, "I can't even begin to imagine what you went through. It's incredibly traumatic and horrific."

Emily tightened her grip on her glass. "One day, a nurse came in and injected me with a needle," she said. "When I woke up, I was in a hotel in downtown Tampa. Beside the bed was a suitcase filled with new clothes in my size, and a purse sat on the nightstand with the Alabama driver's license and some money inside. When I went to bathroom and looked in the mirror, I nearly fainted. The person in the mirror looking back at me was not me. There was no resemblance to myself at all in the reflection. You have no idea what it's like to see someone else's reflection in a mirror. I almost felt like I was a ghost or a zombie."

"You'd be surprised, but I actually do know the feeling," replied Rick.

"What?"

"Never mind." Rick changed the subject. "How is this all possible? I don't see any scars."

"I know." She shook her head. "It doesn't make sense."

Rick studied her driver's license again. "Your license matches your description of being five-foot-five with brown eyes."

"I know, but I was five-foot-seven with blue eyes when they abducted me."

"Are you trying to tell me they shortened you by two inches and changed the color of your eyes?"

"Yes, and that's not all."

She held out her hands and flipped them over to reveal the palm side. She had no ridges on the tips of her fingers that would make fingerprints. Feigning a smile, she pointed at her perfect white teeth.

"Also, I used to have a small gap between my two front teeth. Now I have none. I went to my house in Hyde Park, but it was gone."

"What do you mean 'gone'?"

"Gone as in vanished. It was a grass lot. I kept to myself when I lived there, so I didn't really know the neighbors. I asked a guy who was trimming the hedges next door what happened, and he told me the house burned down and a guy inside was found dead. I went online and found in some news articles that the man inside was my husband. He had been shot in the head and burned. They identified him with dental records. My husband was my only living next of kin. I am an only child; both of my parents died a few years ago in an airplane crash over the Bahamas."

"So, let me get this straight," Rick said, rubbing his temples. "Your teeth are different, as well as the color of your eyes, and you're two inches shorter? You look different and your fingerprints have been altered. How?"

"I don't know. I told you it would be hard to believe."

"Hard is an understatement."

Tears welled up in her eyes. "You have to believe me. It gets worse. Even if you can somehow prove that I am Emily Davis, Emily Davis is a suspect for the murder of both her husband and Hans Larsson. The bullets that killed them both came from my gun. My husband made me get it for protection. I kept it in the nightstand beside my bed. It was registered in my name only." She let out a quaking breath and finally said, "I was framed."

"I don't even know what to say," Rick began. "So, why didn't they just kill you? Why would they go to all the effort to change you into someone else? Your whole story is beginning to sound like that movie *Face/Off.*"

Being a pop culture enthusiast and movie buff, Rick often referred to movies and used them as analogies.

"I know. That part doesn't make sense. I don't know why they didn't kill me, but I need your help to prove who I really am and that I'm innocent of murder." Emily paused and stared for several seconds at her hands, which lay folded in her lap.

When she looked up and began to speak, her eyes filled with tears. "There's something else I need to explain to you. My parents were very wealthy. I inherited their entire estate, worth over four hundred and fifty million dollars. I tried to access the money when I was finally released, but I have no way of proving I'm Emily Davis, so I'm basically broke. I can't pay you now, but if you can help me and we can get my money back, I'll pay you any price. Just name it."

"Right. Ok, how about one million dollars?" Rick said with a chuckle.

"Deal. I will pay you one million dollars if you can prove I'm Emily Davis, and that I'm not guilty of double homicide."

He hadn't expected her to take his request seriously. Rick sat deep in thought, sipping his drink and saying nothing. But when he looked into her eyes, he couldn't help but believe her.

"Why are there no scars on your face from the plastic surgery?" he asked.

"I did some research on the computers at the public library in Tampa on plastic surgery, and found some information about runway models. Some of them have their faces altered by a surgeon going in through their nose and trimming bones to streamline their face. Some have their back teeth removed to give that sunken-in look. I suspect that's what they did to me, minus removing the back teeth. They somehow changed my nose and chin and the contours of my cheekbones entirely. My eyes look different too, and if you feel back here, beneath my hairline, you'll feel a small ridge." She touched the spot with her fingertips. "That's the only incision mark I could find. Unfortunately, all that proves is that maybe I was vain and wanted a facelift."

"Ok, well it sounds more believable. I guess science and plastic surgery have come a long way since *Face/Off*. What about your height?"

"I can't figure that out. All I know is I'm shorter than I was before."

As Rick sat there pondering, she watched him intently. She was obviously hoping he'd come around.

"Where have you been living and how much money did they give you?" he asked.

"Until today, I was staying in the hotel where they left me. It was booked and paid for through yesterday. There were two thousand dollars in my purse and a pre-paid debit card with another two thousand dollars on it."

Rick studied her face and tried to read her body language. After a few minutes, he got to his feet and said, "Ok. Against my better judgment, I'll help you. The facts don't make sense, but at least I can tell that *you* believe it really happened."

She jumped up and hugged him.

"I can't begin to thank you. This is the first time I've had any hope."

"No pressure, right?" said Rick.

"The first thing I did once I was free was go back to my lab, but I found the place ransacked. I think my security key code to the lab still works. Maybe you could start there?"

She wrote down the key code and handed it to Rick. "When you go there, look behind the inside door. My lab coat is hanging there and I left some money the pocket. It was for a delivery I had coming in which I never was able to get. In my hast and distress, I forgot about it and left fast. Use it for expenses."

"Where is the lab?" he asked.

"It's in Clearwater. I'll give you the address."

"Ok, I'll start there. Also, give me the address of your house. Or should I say, the grass lot where your house used to be."

She wrote down both the addresses and thanked him.

"Oh, yeah, one more thing. With no identity, I have no credit, so I got this prepaid phone. Here's the number," she said.

"Thanks," he said. "I forgot to ask, where are you staying, and do you need a ride?"

"No, I'm staying just across Highway 98 at the Village Inn of Destin. I took a one-way flight and Uber'd here in hopes that you would take my case," she said.

He walked her to the dock. "I'll do everything I can to help you," he said.

After giving him a long glance and a quick nod, she walked off in the direction of the parking lot and vanished into the night.

CHAPTER TWO

Rick stayed up later than he'd liked rehashing the story Emily had told him. He wanted to get up early and head down to Tampa. He thought about driving, but it would take six or seven hours to get there, so he decided to book a flight instead and rent a car when he got down there. He texted Jules, hoping she was working a late shift at the casino.

Hi Jules, Rick here. Are you still planning to visit Florida on your vacation? Instead of Destin, how about Tampa?

Hi Rick, I'm actually in front of my computer now. Let me check. I can use my reward miles, so I don't think it matters.

He smiled to himself. This might work out well, since he could possibly see Jules, and get paid for the trip. He'd met her in St. Croix while working on his last case and fallen hard. Now they were in a long-distance relationship and he really missed her.

> Rick, there are plenty of available flights into Tampa. I'm so excited. Can you pick me up or should I rent a car?

> You book the flight and I'll pick up you up. I'm working a case there but we can catch up and have some fun. Sound good?

> Sounds great! Hang on and I'll book it now and email you my confirmation.

> Okay, Jules. I'll look for it.

The next morning, when he woke up at about 7:15, his first mate, Johnie McDonald, was already in the galley frying up some bacon. Chief was sitting on top of his cage, munching on a red grape.

"Good morning, Johnie. I see you've found Chief's favorite treat."

"Yeah, he loves those things. We're getting along just fine."

"That's good, because when I hired you, remember I said you might have to bird sit? Well, that needs to happen today. I have to fly to Tampa. I don't want to hassle with putting him on the plane. I'd rather him stay here."

"No problem. I'll just chill on the boat while you're gone. How long will you be?"

"I'm not sure. Could be a while."

"We have a charter next week—will you be back?"

Rick frowned. "Crap, I forgot about that. I guess I'll have to cancel the charter."

"Wait a sec. I know a guy who could run the boat while you're gone. He covered another boat I mated on once. He just charges a $125 daily flat rate. It's definitely better than cancelling the charter. You don't want to get that reputation right out of the gate, eh?" Johnie smiled, flipping the bacon in the pan.

"You're right. Give him a call. I have to run to the airport soon."

"Let me drive you so you don't have to pay for parking."

"Ok, that'll work."

Rick was lucky to have Johnie, a fellow Texan. They'd met at the message board not far from where the boat was now docked. Johnie had recently retired and was looking for something part-time. In his previous life, he'd worked as a master diesel mechanic on a drag race team and had developed a software plugin that increased horsepower to the point that it was banned by the National Hot Rod Association. After the chance meeting, Rick had hired him on as a first mate/engineer, and Johnie had installed the plugin on both of the Mann engines on Rick's yacht. It made an indescribable difference in performance and horsepower.

Johnie was turning out to be not just a valuable first mate, but also a hell of a cook. His eggs and bacon were always fried and seasoned perfectly. His grits were as good as Rick's mama used to make.

After quickly packing a duffel with his .38 inside in a flight case, and a backpack for his laptop and other electronics, Rick shoved the new passport he'd recently ordered into his front shirt pocket. Then he sat down to eat breakfast.

"Sit down, Johnie. Let's eat together. I wanna go over a few things before I take off."

"Sounds good, Rick."

Johnie made himself a plate and pulled up a chair across from Rick.

"Remember those gold bars I found when searching for Fletcher's treasure?"

"Yeah, boss. Why?"

"Well, I was thinking, after this case maybe we can take *Nine-Tenths* down to the Keys and follow up on the riddle I showed you. You know, the one I found in that bottle with the bars."

Johnie grinned. "I love the Keys! You say the word, and we will go. I'm always game for an adventure."

"Yeah, it might lead nowhere, but I have to follow up on it."

"I agree."

Once they finished eating and Chief was back in his cage, Rick told him goodbye. Johnie loaded Rick's bags into his car, and they headed to the airport through Fort Walton as Rick went over a checklist of routine maintenance Johnie had scheduled for the boat. He was thorough. Rick's boat, *Nine-Tenths*, would be in good hands while he was gone.

The plane pushed back from the gate a little early and made good time in the air, touching down after one stop in Atlanta. But the rental car counter was busy; ten people stood in line in front of Rick. While he was waiting for his turn, he texted Johnie to let him know he'd arrived and to check on Chief. His mate let him know that everything was great and that his buddy, the captain, had agreed to work their charters while Rick was gone.

At least the boat will be making money while I'm gone, he thought.

Rick had originally reserved a midsize car, but when he got to the counter, they were all out and offered him a free upgrade to an SUV instead. He took the keys and plugged in the addresses for both the grass lot where Emily's house supposedly used to be, and the lab in Clearwater. The GPS routed him to the grass lot first.

The route would take him to Hyde Park first, then back onto I-275 and onto State Route 60, also known as the Courtney Campbell Causeway. It wasn't rush hour, but it was Sunday, so the traffic could still be bumper-to-bumper. As he scanned though the channels of the radio, he picked up mostly country stations and one Latin one. It made him think of Jules. He turned up the music and rolled down his windows to let in some fresh air.

He was starving by the time he got to Hyde Park half an hour later. When he spotted an A-frame sign on the sidewalk outside a small restaurant advertising fish tacos, he quickly parked and then grabbed a table by the street. A waiter brought him a menu with a little dragonfly on the cover and the name Bartaco.

"Three Baja fish tacos and a mojito tinto," Rick told the waiter. He wasn't sure what the tinto was in the mojito, but it was made with Flor de Caña rum and that was good enough for him.

He devoured the tacos in no time and then finished his mojito. The GPS placed the location of Emily's former house only a few streets down and to the right. Since he already had a parking spot, he decided it would be better to walk.

On the way to the lot, he noticed how wealthy and non-diverse the area was. A white Lamborghini was parked on one corner, and a few steps later was a Ferrari. It was the whitest place he'd seen in a long time and it made him a little uncomfortable. It almost felt like a movie set, similar to the village up near Destin in Seaside, where the movie *The Truman Show* had been filmed. He walked down South Dakota Avenue and took a right on Bayshore Boulevard to what was known as Historic Old Hyde Park. The street was lined with two-story mansions. Money!

When he arrived at the address Emily had given him, he found exactly what she had described: a simple grass lot. The grass was trimmed and it sat between two opulent homes with high-end imported cars in each driveway. A Latino man was mowing the grass in a yard a few houses down. He was the only non-white dude he'd seen in this neighborhood so far. Rick approached him and waited to be noticed. The man looked at Rick, killed the engine, and walked over.

"Excuse me. I hate to bother you, but do you know who owns the lot next door?" asked Rick.

"No sé," replied the man. "I speak little English. Un momento," he said, motioning for Rick to wait. The man walked toward the backyard of the house.

A few minutes later, he returned with a young man.

"Hi, I'm Luis. My dad said you had a question?"

"Yes, hi, thank you. I was wondering if you knew who owns that grass lot next door and if it's for sale?"

"I'm not sure. A few weeks after the house burned down, a company came in, demolished the place, and planted sod. There never was a 'For Sale' sign on it, which is surprising, considering how few available lots there are around here. No others that I can think of. I've never seen a car there. It's kind of strange. Maybe they were having problems getting a permit from the city. I don't know."

"Ok. Well, thank you very much. I appreciate your time."

What the kid said had given Rick an idea. In the morning, he would go to the county property appraiser's building and search the records to see who owned the lot. But first, he needed to investigate the lab.

It took about an hour to drive to Clearwater. When he arrived at the address, the building was empty. The windows had been boarded up and the parking lot hadn't been swept in quite a while. The place was in complete disarray. He decided it was best to park down the street and enter on foot.

When he reached the building, he made sure no one was watching as he typed in the code on the main door. Inside, he found another keypad on a second door, so he punched in the numbers Emily had given him again. It beeped and opened. Several broken glass beakers and overturned filing cabinets greeted him on the other side.

The door was heavy and when it was open all the way, the coat rack behind it could not be seen, just as Emily had mentioned. On the rack hung a white lab coat. There was a small roll of hundreds in the pockets, so he pocketed it and continued to search for clues. The room had definitely been ransacked, but lots of valuable items still remained intact.

Whoever had done this had clearly been looking for something in particular; they weren't just there to rob the place. In the restroom, all the drawers had been pulled out and the mirrored cabinet door was open. He felt under the cabinet but found nothing. Out of the corner of his eye, he noticed something lying on the floor behind the toilet.

It was a hairbrush, and it gave him an idea. Enmeshed in the brush were long strands of black hair. After wrapping it up in toilet paper, he dialed his new client.

"Emily, it's Rick."

"Hi, Rick. Did you find out anything yet?"

"Maybe, I'm not sure. There's a grass lot where you said your house used to be, just as you said. Someone verified that a house used to be there but burned down. So far, your story is checking out. I'm at the lab and I found a purple hairbrush with paisley designs on the back. What color is your hair? I mean, what color was it before they dyed it silver?"

"That's definitely my brush. I didn't dye my hair, Rick. In the excitement to tell you what happened to me, that's the one thing I left out. My hair was jet black before they took me. I've always had black hair. I thought they just dyed it, but it's been long enough for the roots to show and they're still silver. Somehow, they changed the color of my hair permanently."

Rick's brow furrowed. "How is that possible?"

"Well, I did some research on a computer at the hotel office. There's a therapy called nano-pattern diffraction. That, along with concentrated doses of certain hormones, allowed them to age my hair follicles. They basically turned my hair old."

"This is getting stranger and stranger," said Rick. He paused for a moment. "I need you do something for me. Go to Health Street. It's a business in Destin. Ask for Karen. She will swab you and test your DNA. I'll send her this hairbrush. If it's a match, then I'll know you were here. It still doesn't prove who you are, but it corroborates your story at least. Have you ever had a DNA test done before?"

"Not that I know of," replied Emily.

"Dang. Ok, well, at least it'll help me believe your story."

"Whatever it takes, Rick. I'm telling the truth. I'll go in the morning."

Rick hung up and checked his phone for the nearest FedEx office.

After dropping off the hairbrush, Rick drove down to St. Pete Beach and checked into the Don CeSar. It was surprisingly reasonable for such a fine hotel, less than two hundred dollars a night. There was so much history attached to the hotel that Rick was drawn to it, even though it wasn't super convenient for his investigation.

It had started out as Thomas Rowe's "Pink Lady" when it opened in 1928, and after Rowe's death, it became a United States Army Air Corps convalescent center and later a VA office. Eventually, it was purchased and reopened by C.L. Pyatt and William Bowman in 1973 and, after many upgrades over the years, was listed in the National Register of Historic Places.

He asked the desk clerk for a recommendation for a good place nearby to get some seafood, and without hesitation the man asked, "Do you like stone crabs?"

"I've never had them."

"You'll love them. They're huge claws with succulent, sweet white meat inside. The best place to get them is right here at the Rowe Bar in our hotel, named after the man who originally built this place."

After processing his credit card, he handed Rick his keys and asked him if he needed help with his bags.

"That's ok, I can get them."

His room had a small, round balcony overlooking a hot tub, a rectangular pool, and a beautiful view of the Gulf of Mexico. Through the window, he could see the beach was still packed. The sun was on the horizon, and a mix of oranges and reds colored the sky.

He opened his laptop on the desk and found the address for the Hillsborough County Property Appraiser's office. It was in Tampa, so he could visit it in the morning. With that done, he listened to his rumbling stomach and made his way down to the Rowe Bar.

The restaurant was small but quaint, and the place was bustling. A mix of tourists dressed in resort-casual and businessmen in suits sipped drinks at the main bar while waiting for a table.

When Rick asked the hostess for a table, she said, "It'll be a twenty-minute wait. If I were you, I'd try the bar."

A few seats opened up as he walked into the bar, so he grabbed one of the high-top bar seats and sat down. A young, tatted-up guy placed a cocktail napkin in front of him.

"What can I get you to drink?"

"I'll have Cruzan and soda, and can I look at a menu?"

"Coming up. You can either eat at the bar or at the tables in the center, but they're full at the moment," the bartender told him, as he handed Rick a menu to peruse.

This was apparently the place to be seen. Hot girls in revealing dresses were everywhere. The guys wore enough gold bling to pay off the national debt. People-watching here was a sport.

Rick opened the menu as he waited for his drink and flipped it over to the back to read about the history of the restaurant.

Another bartender dropped off Rick's drink, a glass of water, and a happy-hour flyer. Rick only glanced at it; he knew he wanted stone crabs. He took a sip of his cocktail and enjoyed the peace.

When the bartender came back, Rick said, "In a few minutes, I'll take another Cruzan and soda, and I'd like to start with some conch fritters. What size order do you suggest for me for stone crab claws?"

"I would go with an order of jumbos for sure. That's four per order or about a pound and a half. If you want sides with it, I would suggest the roasted broccolini and truffle mac and cheese. They're to die for."

"Sold! Hook me up, my man."

The bartender nodded and walked back to the bar. A few minutes later, he returned with Rick's drink and an order of steaming hot conch fritters.

The fritters were full of conch and perfectly seasoned. Rick had had conch fritters a few times before and some-times they were more corn meal than conch, but this time they were loaded to the gills with tender, succulent white meat.

His crab claws arrived just as he finished the last fritter. The stone crabs were just how they had been described: juicy and tender white meat, with a hint of sweetness. They were served with a side of zesty aioli, which went better with the claws than he expected.

As he ate the crab, he people-watched. To him, everyone drinking and dining there seemed plastic. Putting on airs was not Rick's thing, and it made him laugh when he saw zoomers, who probably lived at home with their parents, dressed to the nines and snapping pics for Instagram.

The meal was one of the best he'd ever had and he was perfectly satisfied. Not too full, but just right. When he got the bill, he didn't blink an eye, even though it was more than he'd paid for his hotel room. The meal was worth it.

He walked back into the lobby and grabbed a bottle of water on his way up to his room. It was 9:30 p.m. but surprisingly he wasn't tired at all, so he moseyed through the hotel looking for something to do.

When he discovered that the lobby bar was lined with gold high-top chairs and spotted little wooden casks of rum high above the bar, he knew he'd picked the right hotel.

The bar was fairly empty, with only a few seats taken. Rick ordered a drink and walked out to the pool. Grabbing a seat by the window, he stared at the Gulf as he sipped his cocktail. After about an hour and a couple more drinks, he retired to his room.

This place is going in my cool book, he decided.

There was no need to set an alarm, as the Hillsborough County Property Appraiser's office wouldn't open until 8:00 a.m. He chugged some water and drifted off to sleep.

Early in the morning, a noise in the hallway woke him up as some tourists clumsily tried to get into their room after an all-night rave. It was 6:20 a.m., so Rick got up.

He wasn't hungry enough for the restaurant buffet and decided instead to head to a little midtown coffee place he knew called the Bula Kafe. It wasn't too far and his schedule was pretty loose. Besides, he preferred something with a little local flair and it was on the way to the appraiser's office.

Once he'd arrived and grabbed the end barstool, a bearded young man in a coral tank top greeted him from behind the tiki-inspired bar.

"Hi, I'm Conner. What can I get ya?" He had a tattooed left arm, two light-blue face piercings, and a nose ring.

"I'll have a large coffee with two Splendas."

"No problem," said the kid.

After a few minutes, Conner brought out Rick's coffee and another small cup half filled with some brown liquid. Rick hadn't ordered it but assumed it was their version of Kahlua and cream.

"What kind of cream is this?" asked Rick.

The kid laughed and said, "It's not cream, dude, it's Kava. And the first one's on the house, my man."

"What the hell is Kava?"

"It's a Fijian drink. Trust me, you'll like it."

It was a little early to be drinking, but what the hell?

Once he finished his coffee and Kava, he drove to the appraiser's office, but realized on the way that his face was numb. He looked in the rearview mirror as he touched his face, but couldn't feel it.

Crap. What the hell was in that Kava?

It was only 9:45 a.m. when he arrived. Thankfully, the Kava was starting to wear off. He parked and headed toward the appraiser's office. When he stepped inside, he was the only customer in the place.

"How may I help you, sir?" asked the overweight woman behind the desk.

"I need some information about a property in Hyde Park."

She handed him a clipboard and a pen. "You probably could've found out what you needed for free online. Is it a private address or public?"

"Well, it used to be private, but I'm not sure now."

"Ok. Fill this out and bring it back to me. The fee is one dollar per printed page."

Rick sat down, filled out the form, and returned it to the lady. After a moment, she handed him a printout from her computer, and he sat back down to read it.

The paper said the property was originally owned by Emily Davis. Eight and a half months ago, it had been converted from a single-family residence to commercial status. The ownership details corroborated Emily's story. The time frame listed was two weeks after the house burned down, which meant that Emily would have been in the hands of her abductors during that time.

The tax lien was listed as an address in Grand Cayman. That didn't surprise him. Lots of rich folks sheltered money in the Caymans. He needed to call Emily.

Rick studied the printout for a while and asked the woman if there was any other public info he could obtain on the address. She snatched the paper from him and looked it over.

"No, this paper represents all the public records we have on the property. Are you trying to buy it?"

"I'm just getting the info for my friend, Emily."

"If you want more info, I suggest you talk to the owner. Looks like the lien is in Grand Cayman... Wait, Emily Davis? I didn't notice the name when I printed it. I know Emily Davis. She has several properties in the Tampa area and always comes here in person to do her business." She frowned, shaking her head. "It's a shame what happened to her husband."

"What happened?" asked Rick, as if he didn't know anything.

"A few months back—actually, two weeks before Emily came in and converted the property to commercial—her house burned down and her husband was murdered."

"Emily came in person?"

"Yeah, I was working that day and I remember it vividly. She came in with all the documents filled out already. She paid with a cashier's check from a bank in Grand Cayman. I thought that was odd because she always banked with Sun-Trust, a local bank. When I told her how sorry I was to hear about her husband, she looked shocked that I knew. She acted like she didn't know me. I figured she was just upset over the recent death and house fire and not being herself. I haven't seen her since that day. She usually was in here fairly often, dealing with all of her properties."

Rick's mind was racing. "I see. When she came in, was there anything else about her that seemed strange?"

"No. Other than her demeanor, she was the same old Emily. I did notice her hair was a bit shorter but didn't think anything of it."

"Ok. Well, thanks a lot. You have a great day."

"You too," she said, shifting her attention back to her computer.

Rick stepped out of the office and called Emily. She picked up on the second ring.

"Emily, it's Rick. You need to tell me what's going on. I just left the appraiser's office in Tampa, and the woman there told me that you personally came in and changed the property over to commercial, and paid with a check from Grand Cayman."

"Rick, I've never been to Grand Cayman. What was the date stamped on the property document?"

Rick pulled out the printout. "March 14th."

"I was abducted March 1st, so there's no way that was me."

"Yeah, that's what I thought. It couldn't have been you, even though she said you came in often."

"That's true. I always used to pay my taxes and do my other business there in person. I don't like doing it online. That same woman in appraisals has been working there for years. But the last time I was in that office was in January."

"Ok, well someone who looked like you paid in person with a check. I need to find out more. I'll keep you posted."

He hung up, his mind still going over everything he knew. Who would've come here pretending to be Emily Davis? He suddenly remembered seeing video cameras in the appraiser's office. He needed to see the tapes on those cameras. But breaking into a government office would be no easy task. It was the only way, though, as those tapes were not public record.

The appraiser's office was on the bottom floor of a high-rise on East Kennedy Boulevard, an extremely busy street. Rick headed back to his hotel and used the appraiser lady's advice about checking a property online to see what he could find out about the office. On a government website, he found that blueprints of most properties were available. The blueprints he downloaded showed that there was only one main door on the cone-shaped building. He then pulled up a photo of the entrance door on Google maps and could clearly see several security cameras in place. Mentally, he listed what he'd need to get inside: a black jogging suit with a hood, black running shoes, a paint gun, a cordless drill with carbide tips, a black duffel, and a hole-saw bit.

It would have to be done after dark, and he would have to get in and out fast. A hardware store and a mall were nearby. After buying the necessary items, he went back to the hotel to wait.

By now it was almost 7:00 p.m. and dark outside, so he put on his jogging suit over his street clothes and headed down to the lobby. It was the first time he'd worn anything other than boots, except when he was on his boat, in a long time; the running shoes felt strange on his feet.

As he walked out to the street, the valet asked him if he wanted him to bring around his Tahoe, but he declined.

"You shouldn't go out jogging wearing all black. Someone might hit you," said the valet.

Thinking fast, Rick said, "I'm going to a gym."

"Oh, ok. Have a great workout."

Rick flagged down a cab and gave the cabby an address three streets down from the government building. He chose a cab over Uber so there wouldn't be any paper trail.

The man dropped Rick off, and he paid in cash. "Keep the change."

"Thanks, man."

The streets were fairly empty except for a few homeless guys. As he approached the front of the building, Rick looked around, pulled his hood over his head, and pulled the strings tight, leaving just enough room to peer out with one eye.

After making sure no one was around, he retrieved the paint gun from the duffel, took aim at the first security camera, and fired. It was a perfect shot. With all three cameras covered in paint, he pulled out the drill and approached the door. At the top left corner, Rick placed his drill with the hole-saw bit attached and drilled. When the hole he'd made was big enough for him to put his hands through, he reached in with an electric wire crimp and squeezed the crimp on each wire leading to the door alarm. Once he crimped it, the circuit was complete, and the alarm wouldn't go off when he opened the door.

After changing the hole-saw bit to a half-inch carbide bit, he drilled through the door lock. In less than thirty seconds, the guts of the lock became exposed. He reached in with a pair of pliers, pulled out the locking mechanism, and opened the door. With his head down and hoodie still in place, he took aim and directly hit all the interior security cameras with a triple shot of paint from the gun.

Then he headed to the back of the room, where he found the hard drive for the cameras. They were backed up on the Cloud, so they only stored about thirty days' worth of video. What he really needed was the footage from nine months back. Scanning the room for storage, he spotted a large metal cabinet. Inside, he found what he was looking for: DVDs with dates of each month. He scrolled though the discs until he got to the right month.

There was no time to copy the DVD, so he just took it. A spindle of blank DVDs sat above the recorder. He took out a blank one, wrote down the same date on it with a Sharpie, and stuck it back in the paper sleeve. He placed it back with the others, in the correct order, and was about to exit when he noticed a flashing question on the computer screen.

Log off?

Whoever worked there last had forgotten to log out of the computer. It was still signed into the system. He clicked *NO* and the screen came to life. Once he found the search button, he typed in the address of Emily's burned-down house. All the non-public info of the sale and reclassification to commercial was there.

There was no time to read it all, so he right-clicked and selected *Print All*. He cast a quick glance at the time on the monitor. He had been inside the building eight minutes already, and even with the alarm disabled, he knew he couldn't hesitate. As soon as the last page printed, he shoved it into his bag and headed for the front door.

The door opened just as he reached for the handle. Rick froze.

He was face-to-face with a security guard. The guy's hand gripped his holstered gun. With no time to think, Rick tossed the duffel toward the guard, who instinctively tried to catch it. The weight of the bag moved him back a foot, and Rick lunged out the door.

With his right foot, Rick swept the legs of the guard out from under him. He fell backwards onto the sidewalk. The duffel was still on top of him, blocking his view, so Rick pulled out his .38 and said, "Freeze!"

The guard flung the duffel off him before slowly raising his hands. His eyes were wide.

"Flip over on your stomach," ordered Rick. The guard complied, and Rick wasted no time reaching down and pulling the gun out of the man's holster. He tossed it back into the office and then put his .38 to the back of the guy's head.

"Don't be a hero. Close your eyes and count to one hundred and you'll live."

The man was shaking with fear as he began to count. Rick took off around the block and into an alley. He ripped off the black jogging suit, then grabbed the printout and DVD from the duffel and tucked them inside his shirt. After tossing the duffel into a dumpster, he slowly and calmly walked back to the street.

When he rounded the next corner, he spotted a cab across the street and waved him down. The driver did a quick U-turn and pulled up next to Rick.

"St. Pete Beach, please," Rick told him with an easy smile.

"You got it."

Rick had the cabby drop him off at the Gulf Key Motel, which was just a few blocks from the Don CeSar. Back at his hotel, Rick sat down at the lobby bar and ordered a

Diet Coke. A dark-skinned Latino girl was washing glasses behind the bar. She reminded him of Jules. So, after he finished his Diet Coke and paid the bartender, he stepped outside and called her.

"Hey, it's Rick."

"Rick who?" Julie responded, laughing. "I'm so glad to hear your voice. How are you? Qué pasa?"

"Guess what? I'm in Tampa—well, St. Pete Beach, actually—at the moment."

"Really?"

"Yep. After I talked to you, I picked up a job down here."

"How long will you be there?"

"I'm not sure, but it could be quite a while. You're still coming to Tampa, right?"

"Yes, I'll be there in five days."

Rick smiled. "Perfect. I'm sure I'll still be working the case then, and if not, I'll just hang out until you get here. I can pick you up at the airport. Have you bought your ticket yet?"

"Yes, I'm on American Airlines. I'll send you my itinerary. Hang on."

A few second later, Rick's phone whistled and the confirmation popped up on his screen.

Juliana Álvarez Castro. American Flight 227. Arrives 12:00 p.m.

Rick tried not to laugh. "Ok, Fidel, I'll be there to pick you up. I'm so glad you're coming. There's so much to tell you."

Jules laughed again. "Me too, Rick. I'm ready to party like it's 1999. You have to take me dancing. I've been working a lot of doubles."

"It's a date. See you soon. I'll be waiting for you."

Feeling both relieved and excited, he headed toward the elevators. Once inside his room, he pulled out the printed property paperwork and began to go over it.

The property, it said, was owned by Emily Davis and the zoning had been changed from residential to commercial. It was slated to become a parking lot, run by a company called HiTow out of Grand Cayman. An odd thing to put in the middle of a residential neighborhood.

He popped the DVD from the surveillance cameras into his laptop. After a few minutes of searching, he spotted a black-haired woman matching Emily's description. That section of the video was date-stamped the same as the printout. When the second camera switched to the face, he froze the DVD and created a screenshot. After emailing it to his phone, he forwarded it to Emily with the text, *Is this you?*

Within minutes, Emily responded: *It certainly looks like me, but I've never worn hoop earrings.*

Rick leaned in and zoomed the photo larger.

Sure enough, hoop earrings.

Another camera view came up next, and Rick again froze the screen. As he zoomed in, he saw a purse with the brand name NKY on the side. A quick Google search told him NKY was a Grand Cayman brand only sold at Camana Bay.

Gotcha!

Rick texted Emily back.

Are you sure you've never gone to Grand Cayman?

I've never even thought about it.

Ok, thanks Emily. I'll be in touch.

Another text popped up. It was Jules.

Yay, I got some more shifts covered for an extra week. Will that work?

Rick texted her back.

That's a big, Texas-sized ten-four!

Huh?

Yes, it will work. Sorry I forgot you don't speak Texan, just Mexican.

Hey, now! I'm Colombian.

*I know, just kidding, see
you soon.*

She texted back.

Xxoo

Rick grabbed a tiny bottle of Crown Royal from the minibar. They didn't have any Cruzan or Mount Gay, so it would have to do. He drank it straight from the bottle and let out a big sigh. The evening had been one successful whirlwind.

He called Johnie next. He picked up on the third ring.

"What's up, Rick?"

"Hey, Johnie, how's everything on the boat?"

"It's all good. I changed the oil today and all the filters, including the water separators. The engines are sounding better than they ever have. That charter is tomorrow and my buddy is going to sleep on the settee tonight, since it's such an early start."

"Nonsense, let him crash in my cabin. The bed is more comfortable, and we want him to be happy and keep covering these charters. Now, where's Chief?"

Johnie held his phone up to Chief's cage and clicked on FaceTime. The bird started to bounce up and down and raise his crown.

"Hi, Chief! How ya doing, buddy?" Rick asked affectionately.

Chief bobbed up and down and flapped his wings a few times while Rick spoke to him.

After they hung up, Rick grabbed another tiny bottle of Crown and downed it before ordering room service. He'd had enough excitement for one day and just wanted a burger and some sleep.

CHAPTER THREE

The next few days went by quickly. Rick continued his investigation and followed up on some leads about HiTow in Grand Cayman, but didn't find anything promising yet. Before he knew it, five days had passed and he would be picking up Jules in a few hours.

Her flight would land at noon, so Rick woke up early and hit the gym. After a brief workout and hot tub session, he returned to his room and made a cup of joe.

He sipped on his coffee and daydreamed about picking up Jules and bringing her back to the hotel. Since she had never been to Tampa, he thought it might be best to let her do a little sightseeing first, if she wasn't too tired from her flights.

A wooden display rack in the lobby was filled with brochures, so he went down and began to browse through them. He wanted to stay away from tourist traps but still be a tourist. It would be great to go where the locals went.

The concierge saw Rick browsing and walked over. "Hi, can I help you with some excursions?"

"Yeah, my girl is coming in today and I want to take her to some locals' spots and then maybe someplace romantic for dinner. What do you suggest?"

He thought for a second. "Ok, I would start at John's Pass Village. They have some of the best people-watching on the planet! You can have lunch on the boardwalk and then take her shopping."

"Sounds good. Any other places we should check out?"

"After John's Pass, maybe head over to Splash Harbour Water Park. Does she like waterslides? It's geared toward kids, but I had a blast there with my son. After spending the day there, you'll feel more invigorated than you ever have."

"Well, she's a kid at heart," replied Rick. "What do you suggest for dinner?"

"How adventurous is she?"

"I think she's up for just about anything."

"Ok, then I would take her over to Madeira Beach Marina. You can catch a private dinner charter there. I have a buddy who runs a beautiful, fifty-foot catamaran. He'll take you out. The boat does a sunset dinner cruise for $600 for up to six people."

"Can I charter it for just the two of us?" asked Rick.

"Let me call him and see what his bookings are like."

Rick waited as the man called his friend. He came back a few minutes later and said, "He has no one booked tonight. If you want the boat, he'll do it for five bills."

"Book it, Dano," said Rick, handing him a credit card.

The concierge got back on the phone and gave his buddy Rick's card and info.

"Make sure he has some Cruzan on board. Oh, and some aguardiente," said Rick.

"Ah, a Colombian girl, huh?"

Rick nodded and smiled, then headed into the hotel café for a quick breakfast. He was excited to see Jules and couldn't wait to pick her up at the airport.

He still had a couple hours left until she landed, so he went back to his room to try to find more information about HiTow in Grand Cayman. It was listed in Grand Cayman as a real estate development company with holdings in the US, the Caribbean, and Switzerland.

"Switzerland, that's interesting," he thought out loud.

He dug a little deeper and found out they were under the umbrella of a conglomerate out of Zürich called LaufeRänne LTD, which owned a bunch of smaller companies. LaufeRänne translated into two words in English: Walk Run. The conglomerate held several companies in Zürich, including a big pharmaceutical company called NoahTech. Their biggest seller was a cancer drug known as Revacizumab, a similar drug to Avastin, the world's top-selling cancer drug.

There was a possible motive. If Emily's immunotherapy drug were ever released, it would crush the sales of Revacizumab, crippling the profits of NoahTech—which, according to public records, was by far the most profitable company under the umbrella of LaufeRänne LTD.

It was all starting to make sense, but what still bothered Rick was the fact that'd gone to so much trouble to change Emily's identity. Why not just kill her?

After pondering the case a while longer, he called Emily. "Hi, Emily. It's Rick. Is there anything else you can remember about the time you were held hostage? Anything you overheard or saw that seemed strange or memorable?"

Emily thought for a second. "Well, I heard someone speaking a foreign language outside my door a few times."

"Do you know what language they were speaking?"

"It sort of sounded German? It was definitely European. I didn't think anything of it, as I've worked with so many Europeans over the years. Plus, Tampa is full of European tourists. I heard that language often."

"Could it have possibly been Swiss German?"

"Maybe. Wait. I do remember hearing the same phrase quite often, usually after they fed me dinner and left the room. It was '*gueten abig.*' At first, I thought they were saying, 'Groom it big,' which made no sense to me."

"Say it again?"

"*Gueten abig.*"

Rick typed it out phonetically, Grewton Ahbig, and then added the word Swiss in the search bar of his laptop. The words *gueten abig* translated into Swiss German for *good evening.*

"Ok Emily, thanks. I may be on to something. How many people knew about your cancer drug trials?"

"Only myself, my husband, and Hans Larsson, to my knowledge."

"Phew, ok. This is big. We just need to figure out why they changed your identity instead of just killing you. That's a big piece of the puzzle that doesn't fit."

"I agree. Thanks, Rick. I'll let you know if anything else pops into my head. My time there is mostly a big blur, if I'm being honest."

Rick tapped his fingers on the desk, thinking. "Have you ever been hypnotized?"

"No. Why?"

"There's something known as hypnotic regression therapy. What they do is put you into a trance. It's supposed to help you remember things that are deep inside your brain. Would you be up to give it a try? It might unbury something that could help us."

"If you think it will work, I'm game. I'll do whatever it takes to prove who I really am. Oh, I got the DNA results back, by the way. The hair on the brush matches me, just as I told you. I'll email the results to you."

"Ok, Emily. Stay put and let me do some research and I'll get back to you."

After hanging up, he typed quickly on his laptop. An online search for hypnotic regression therapy revealed a man named T.C. LeNormand based out of Houston. His center was ranked as one of the best in the country. That gave Rick an idea.

It was time to call Possum, his old treasure-hunting buddy from Houston. His real name was Michael, but all his friends knew him as Possum because he loved George "The Possum" Jones's music so much.

The phone rang twice before Possum answered.

"Hey, Rick! What's happening?"

"Hey, Possum. I have a question for you—a few, actually—and a favor to ask."

"Shoot, buddy."

"Have you ever heard of hypnotic regression therapy?"

"Is that where they hypnotize you to try to help you remember things you may have blocked from your past?"

"Exactly!"

"Well, I know it's not a science, but I've also met a few people who swear by it," replied Possum.

"I used to think it was all hocus-pocus, but after what I saw in Haiti, I'm more inclined to believe anything these days," said Rick.

"True dat!"

"Listen, Possum, I'm working on a new case and it's pretty freaky. My client is in Destin, but I want her to see a guy over at Houston Hypnosis. I'm going to fly her to Houston. Can you pick her up and keep an eye on her? I'd feel better if she stayed with you. Her name is Emily Davis—sort of."

"Sort of?"

"It's a long story, but when she lands at the airport, you'll be picking up Patricia Benning. It'll be way easier for her to explain the whole deal to you. Trust me, as weird as it is, I think she is telling the truth. Maybe you'll spend some time with her and feel her out for me?"

"No problem, Rick. *Mi casa es su casa*, always."

"Look, I scored big on my last case and I'm doing pretty good financially now, so I insist on paying you for your time on this one. I know you don't need it, but let's just do it to keep things on the up and up. How does two hundred dollars a day to be her babysitter and gopher chauffeur sound? Hey, that rhymes!"

"Haha! No problem bro. Just forward me her flight info and I'll be there."

"You're the best, buddy. I don't care what they say about you."

Rick looked online for flights and then called Emily back.

"Hi again. I've found a very qualified hypnotherapist in Houston. I want you to fly there, and a friend of mine named Possum will pick you up and take care of you for a few days. Take a pic of your driver's license so I can book your flight.

I know you're low on money. Stop by the boat and I'll have Johnie give you some cash for spending."

"Whatever you think is best, Rick. I don't know how to thank you."

"If this all pans out, you can thank me then," said Rick.

Next, Rick called Johnie and instructed him to take a thousand dollars out of petty cash and give it to Emily. He agreed without question and they hung up.

It was time to head to the airport, so Rick called the front desk to bring his SUV to the lobby doors.

As he drove to the airport, visions of Jules in that sundress he loved raced through his mind. It had been a while since he had seen her. At a red light, he waved over a guy selling roses from the median, gave him ten bucks for a bouquet, and set the flowers on the seat.

He got a spot in short-term parking and decided to walk up to gate area exit to meet Jules there. His phone whistled as she texted him, saying she was on the ground. He texted her back and said he was waiting for her.

As people started coming out of the gate area, he spotted her. With the flowers behind his back, he waved and grinned at her. She waved back and almost began to skip as her pace picked up. When she got closer, he pulled out the roses. Tears welled up in her eyes as she took them and embraced him. They hugged for an eternity, and she kissed him.

"God, I have missed you!" said Jules.

"And I've missed you! Do you have any bags to pick up?"

"Just my carry-on."

"Perfect. Are you tired, or do you wanna go do some sightseeing?"

"I'm not tired; I'm wired." She laughed. "I napped a little on the flight. Let's do something fun!"

"You're so cute and sexy too!" He gave her a squeeze with one arm.

Jules rolled her eyes. "Well, flattery will get you everywhere, Rick."

They walked to the parking lot, and Rick put her bag in the back seat. They hugged again and kissed. She smelled so good. He couldn't believe how much he'd missed her.

"Where are we going?" asked Jules.

"I think it would be fun if we went to John's Pass for lunch. It's a gorgeous day and it's supposed to be an open-air place, great for people-watching. Sound good?"

"Sounds super good. I'm famished. I skipped breakfast today."

"Ok. Well, let's see if we can get some chow into you."

"You are a country boy, aren't ya?"

"Yep. You can take the boy out of Texas, but… Well, you know the rest."

Jules laughed and squeezed his hand. It was so good to feel her touch again.

They pulled up to a public parking spot, and Rick paid for a couple hours. Hand in hand, they strolled in the sun toward John's Pass, listening to the Gulf waters lapping the shore and the seagulls laughing as they flew overhead. Rick pointed to a beautiful flock of gulls above the palm trees, gliding lazily toward the beach.

"Hear that? Those are black-headed gulls. They have a unique call that differs from other gulls, almost a laugh," Rick told her.

"Too funny!" said Jules. "Where do you want to eat?"

"Wherever you want; this is your day. What are you in the mood for?"

"How about something very local?"

"You read my mind."

They meandered along the boardwalk, assessing all the different outdoor cafés and restaurants as staff stood outside trying to hand them menus.

Jules pointed at a place. "There! Let's eat there! Sculley's Waterfront. I love the name and I haven't had seafood in a while. Plus, we're near the water, so it must be fresh!"

"I'm down. Let's do it."

A hostess greeted them and seated them at an outside table in the sun with an umbrella for shade. Rick pulled the chair out for Jules to sit down.

"Aren't you being so romantic? I love it, but you don't have to. I'm a sure thing, remember?" said Jules with a wink.

Rick laughed. "You deserve it, Jules. I love taking care of you."

She blushed and welled up a little, then took Rick's hand and held it to her face. "You are so special, Rick. I'm so glad we met."

He smiled deeply at her. "So are you. It was fate."

They both opened their menus and at the same time said, "Let's get a mojito!"

"You owe me a Coke," said Rick.

"Huh?"

"It's an old expression people use when they say the same thing at the same time."

"Oh, ok. Well, how about I'll pay for your mojito instead?"

"Deal!"

Rick ordered two mojitos and an order of conch fritters as an appetizer.

They sipped on their drinks and grazed on the fritters, touching hands, looking into each other's eyes, and hardly noticing the Gulf directly in front of them. They were too busy drinking each other in, and that was just fine by Rick.

"I'm in the mood for scallops," said Rick.

"I want fish!" replied Jules. "I'm gonna go with the pistachio-crusted grouper."

"I think I'll try the scallops and tequila-lime shrimp."

"Ooh, sounds interesting!" said Jules. "Can I have a taste?"

"Of course you can, babe."

After lunch, they walked hand-in-hand to Rick's Tahoe and hugged a long time by the door.

"Where to now, Rick?"

"Waterslides, baby, waterslides. Did you bring a suit?"

"Oh yeah, and I think you'll approve," said Jules with a devious smile.

He grinned. "I can't wait."

He drove north on Gulf Boulevard, the slow route, as Jules scoped out all the tourist shops and the beach along the way. That was one thing Rick loved about Jules. She was more of a window shopper than a spender and was more interested in looking at Rick than shopping. It was as if nothing else mattered and she didn't have a care in the world; she just wanted to be with him.

They found a parking spot and went into the water park to change into their beachwear. Rick put on a pair of swim trunks and a tank top, then stepped out of the men's room and waited for Jules.

She sauntered out and did a spin to show off her outfit. His eyes widened. She was wearing a sexy thong bikini and a cover-up. Her parts were in all the right places.

"You look gorgeous, babe."

She flashed him an appreciative smile. They put their street clothes into a soft bag Jules had brought and held hands as they walked to the first slide. But they found a couple of open lounge chairs and opted to grab some sun first.

"Can I get you something to drink?" he asked. "Water, juice, soda, beer?"

"They have beer here?"

"I would think so. On the map, I saw a place called the Cruzan Rum Shack."

"Do they have Presidente?"

"I'll find out. Lie back and chill, and I'll go get us a couple drinks."

When Rick returned with the drinks, Jules was all stretched out on the lounge chair, the sun glistening off her tanned skin. He couldn't take his eyes off her.

She noticed and smirked. "What's wrong, cat got your tongue?"

"Uh, no. I was, uh, thinking about something."

"Do tell."

"I was thinking how lucky I am to be sitting here with such a beautiful woman."

"Flattery *will* get you everywhere!" Jules reached over, took Rick's hand, kissed it and held it to the side of her face. It felt as if they had never left each other way back in St. Croix.

While they hung out on the lounge chairs, Rick told Jules more about the case he was working on.

"I have a special surprise for you for dinner this evening."

"That's awesome, Rick. I can't wait to hear, but let's slide."

Hand in hand, they headed for Smuggler's Run, a forty-two-foot slide with twists and turns. There were a lot of kids in the park, but Jules didn't mind. She was having as much fun as they were. They rode every slide available multiple times and then headed for the lazy river. It was Rick's favorite thing because it reminded him of the spring-fed Comal River in Texas, where he would float with a cooler as a teenager. After an hour of floating, kissing, and catching up, they toweled off.

"You wanna head to the hotel and get cleaned up for dinner?" asked Rick.

"Sounds good. Is it close?"

"Pretty close. Just over in St. Pete Beach."

They arrived thirty minutes later.

"This is a beautiful hotel, Rick."

"I know, right? I've always wanted to stay here, and I know you're a history buff like me. There's a lot of history here."

Rick told her all about the Don CeSar's flowery past in the elevator as she listened intently. When they reached his room, he opened the door and set Jules's suitcase on the stand. She opened it, took out a sexy black dress, and hung it in the bathroom.

"I'm gonna hop in the shower, or do you want to go first?" she asked.

"No, you go ahead."

While Jules was in the bathroom, Rick sent a couple of emails. She came out wearing one of the hotel robes.

"Your turn."

Rick took a quick shower and also grabbed a robe. When he came out, Jules had pulled the covers down on the bed and was lying there with a devilish grin on her face.

"We already had lunch. I was thinking it was time for dessert," she said.

"Well, if I knew you were on the menu, I'd never leave the hotel."

She laughed and pulled up the covers for Rick to climb in. They began to kiss tenderly and sweetly, their bodies a perfect fit for each other. They made love and held each other afterwards for what seemed like an eternity. Rick didn't want to leave now. Just rinse and repeat.

"Tell me about the surprise tonight," said Jules.

Rick looked at his watch. "Oh crap, we better get dressed."

They both hopped up and pulled on their clothes.

"If I tell you, it won't be a surprise."

"Ok, fair enough. But am I at least dressed right for the occasion?"

He looked her up and down. "You in that dress works for any occasion."

She smiled and kissed him on the cheek. "I love you."

Rick was taken aback by that, as Jules had never said it before. But almost without hesitation, he said, "I love you too, Jules."

Jules's eyes were filling up again. Rick knew she meant what she said, and for the first time in his life, Rick felt like he meant it too.

"Let's just love each other," she said. "There are no rules. I know we both lead different lives, and I don't expect anything from you and never want to influence your choices. So, yes, I love you, Rick Waters, and you're just gonna have to get used to it."

Rick wrapped his arms around her and held her tight.

"I could definitely get used to this. Let's go to dinner, baby."

CHAPTER FOUR

Jules climbed up in the Tahoe in her lovely evening dress, a shawl under her arm, and buckled in. Rick shut her door, walked around to the driver's side, and fired up the SUV bound for Madeira Beach Marina.

The air was crisp and clean, and the smell of the Gulf wafted into the Tahoe like a welcoming friend. Rick kept the windows down for the short drive. Jules smiled every time she looked over at him; she seemed content and happy.

She reached over and patted Rick's knee as he drove. He was smitten with her.

When they reached the marina, he could see the fifty-foot catamaran side-tied by the fuel dock. The crew hustled as they moved about the deck, getting everything ready.

"We're here," said Rick.

"Are we eating at the marina?" asked Jules.

"Nope, we're eating on that." Rick pointed out the beautiful Leopard catamaran with the name *Dremi* painted on its hull.

Jules's eyes lit up. "Ay, Dios mio, we're going out on a boat?"

"That's right. Not just any boat either, but a private yacht. Just you, me, and the crew tonight."

Jules jumped out of the passenger side and ran around to Rick's side. When he opened the door, she threw her arms around him, put her head on his shoulder, and hugged him tightly.

"Thank you, Rick. I don't know what to say."

"It's my pleasure. Now, let's go have some fun."

Jules grabbed his hand and pulled him toward the boat the way a dog pulls its owner on a walk to a tree.

"Permission to come aboard?" Rick asked the captain at the helm on the flybridge.

"Permission granted, sir, and welcome aboard *Dremi*," said the man behind the wheel. "Please take your shoes off and I'll come down and introduce the crew."

The captain climbed down from the flybridge as one of the crew handed Rick and Jules each a glass of champagne. The captain stuck his hand out to shake Rick's.

"Hi, I'm Frank, the captain, and this is Tanya, the chief stew. On the bow wrapping lines is Chris, our engineer."

"The name's Rick, Rick Waters, and this is my girlfriend, Juliana."

Jules looked at Rick in a deer-in-the-headlights sort of way. He had never called her his girlfriend before. Her shock transformed into a sweet smile.

"How'd you come up with the name of the boat?" Rick asked the captain.

"I didn't—the owner, Craig, did. He lives in Peru and owns a hardwood export business. He named the boat after his two daughters and combined their names, Dreandra and Emily, to come up with *Dremi*."

"Wow, that's interesting. So, what's on the agenda today, Cappy?"

The captain smiled. "Please call me Frank, if that's ok. We're not formal here."

"No worries, Frank. What's the plan?"

"That's up to you guys. We can do whatever you want for the next two and a half hours."

"Can we sail or do we just motor?"

"I like the way you think, Rick. Let's raise some canvas!"

The captain climbed back up to the flybridge, and Tanya offered Rick and Jules some bacon-wrapped scallops on a silver serving tray. They each took one and devoured it.

"Damn, those are good," said Rick.

"I know, right?" said Jules. "So tender and sweet, with a hint of garlic at the end. I love them. I want this recipe!"

"No problem, I'll jot it down for you," said Tanya as she stepped back into the galley to retrieve more champagne.

"The boat is so pretty, Rick," Jules said, taking in the beautiful lines of the vessel. "Thank you again for doing this. I'm overwhelmed."

"You are worth it, babe," said Rick, putting his arm around her.

The captain fired up the twin Yanmars as Chris untied the lines from the dock. As they slowly motored toward Clearwater Bay and John's Pass, the captain steered the boat in the direction of the John's Pass drawbridge. He timed it perfectly, as the bridge was opening upon approach.

The engineer walked back to the stern. He was a small guy, but carried himself as a big one. He stuck out his hand

and shook Rick's with vigor. With a warm smile, he asked Rick where he was from. Rick told him Texas.

"Texas, huh? Well, everything's bigger in Texas, they say. I'm from New Jersey—Egg Harbor Township just outside of Atlantic City," said Chris.

"Egg Harbor? Is that where they make the boats of the same name?"

"It used to be," replied Chris. "The company was established in 1946 but they're out of business now. The original owner, Russell Post, started Post Yachts over in Massachusetts, after he sold Egg Harbor. You've been to Egg Harbor Township?"

"I've been through it, on my way to Atlantic City to throw some bones," said Rick.

"Ah craps, huh? That's the only game I play in the casinos whenever I go, which is rare. We should shoot some dice together sometime," said Chris, as if they were longtime friends.

"Sure, Chris, I'd like that."

Chris clinked his bottle of water against Rick's champagne glass and toasted,

"Cheers, big ears."

Rick didn't have big ears, so he assumed it was something Chris always said and laughed. He liked Chris immediately. The engineer handed him a business card and told him his cell number was the same number as on the card. Rick stuck it in his pocket and turned his attention toward his surroundings.

The marina sat about as close as any marina could get to open water. They were in the open Gulf in less than fifteen minutes.

The sun was beginning to sink lower in the sky, and the wispy cirrus clouds were ablaze with color. A stunning sight. As they watched the sun slowly make its way to the horizon, the captain pointed out a pod of dolphins dancing on the bow.

Pulling her phone from her purse, Jules asked, "Can I?"

"Of course, but be careful. One hand for the boat and one hand for you," said Rick, as she walked toward the bow to take some photos.

Rick followed her with a drink in one hand and another bacon-wrapped scallop in the other, ignoring his own advice. The water was incredibly calm, with barely a ripple, and the gulf looked like a giant lake. There was little chance Rick would fall overboard, and he was about as sure-footed as a mountain goat anyway.

Jules snapped photos of the bottle-nosed dolphins playing inches from the bow, spinning and breaking water. They were amazing creatures, riding just ahead of the waves made by the deep V of the twin hulls.

"Are y'all ready for dinner?" yelled the captain above the wind.

"You ready, Jules?" asked Rick.

"Sure, sounds good."

They both made their way to the salon and sat down on the silky white leather couch wrapping around the elegant, high-gloss mahogany table. In the center of the grandiose table was a decorative arrangement of white roses, carnations, and lavender Peruvian lilies, accented with baby's breath, seeded eucalyptus, and assorted greenery.

Tanya approached the table and asked, "Aguardiente for the lady?"

Jules looked up in amazement. "Sí, I mean yes, please. How did you know I liked aguardiente?"

"Ask your handsome boyfriend," answered Tanya with wink.

When Jules looked at Rick, he shrugged. "I have a memory like an elephant. When you told me about your homeland and culture, you spoke with such passion. How could I forget?"

"Aw, you are so sweet to remember."

"What will you have, sir?" asked Tanya.

"I'll try the aguardiente, with a side of Flor de Caña and one ice cube just in case," Rick said with a laugh.

"You probably won't like it, Rick," Jules warned him.

"Hey, I'll try anything once."

Tanya brought out the drinks and set salads in front of them. The butter lettuce was crisp and fresh, adorned with Castelvetrano olives, Spanish Manchego cheese, and chives. They dug in immediately.

"What do you think of the aguardiente, Rick?"

Rick smiled politely, then slid the glass toward Jules with a wince. "I hope you're not offended, but I'll stick to the Flor de Caña."

She laughed. "I told you, you wouldn't like it!"

"Wine with the entrees?" chirped the stew.

"Yes, please," replied Rick.

"Red or white?"

"Yes, please," replied Rick with a chuckle.

"Well, that actually makes sense," said Tanya, "since we're serving surf and turf tonight."

Both Rick's and Jules's eyes lit up at that comment.

"Do tell," said Rick, as they both finished off their salads.

"Instead of tell, how about I show?" asked Tanya, approaching the table with the main dishes.

Sitting atop each fine china plate was a one-pound, savory Maine lobster tail, swimming in lemon butter and garlic, and garnished with finely chopped fresh parsley. Beside it was a tender six-ounce filet mignon brushed with olive oil and topped with a twig of rosemary and a large garlic clove. Grilled broccolini and a nice helping of red potatoes sprinkled with Parmesan came on the side. A meal fit for a king.

Tanya set down both a glass of Duckhorn cabernet sauvignon and Tobin James "James Gang Reserve" chardonnay. Rick studied the bottles. He wasn't a big fan of most chardonnays but really enjoyed the Tobin James.

"What else could we ask for?" said Rick.

They both ate the perfectly prepared meals, drank wine, laughed, and talked through the entire meal. It was a perfect dinner.

Just when they thought it couldn't get better, Tanya cleared the table and set down two forks and a molten chocolate volcano cake that could only be described as colossal.

"It's my own twist on the famous recipe," declared Tanya. "Try it and see if you can figure out my secret."

Rick cut a huge piece, plopped it on his side plate, and pushed the cake toward Jules to try.

"So, girls are chocoholics, huh?" she asked sarcastically.

Rick just looked up her and smiled as he drove a piece of the cake into his mouth. He chewed slowly, looking up at the ceiling, trying to decipher the secret inside the cake. He let it sit on his palate for a few seconds.

"I taste sweet, salty, and wait...spicy. Could it be cayenne pepper?"

"Oh my God, you got it," said Tanya, clearly impressed. "No one ever guesses that. It's subtle but there at the end."

"Well, I grew up on the border of Texas and Louisiana. We use cayenne pepper on almost everything," explained Rick with a laugh.

"Winner, winner, chicken dinner," said Tanya as she refreshed both Rick's and Jules's wine.

"Shall we raise the sails?" asked the captain as he stepped into the salon.

"Indeed, my man, let's do it," replied Rick.

Rick and Jules stepped onto the back deck and climbed up onto the flybridge. The view was even better, and the sky was getting dark as the twinkling stars began to make their grand appearance. There was no moon and the sky was clear. Soon the Milky Way would be visible for all to see.

"Night sailing!" said Rick, slapping his leg in approval. "I've made several yacht deliveries in the Caribbean and always choose the 2:00 a.m. watch so I can see the stars in the heavens," he whispered to Jules.

"That sounds amazing. Maybe one day I can do a delivery with you."

"I'd like that."

Once the sails were raised tight to the top of the mast and jib, the captain turned the boat into the light breeze and killed the engines.

"Oh, the canvas can do miracles, just you wait and see," sang Rick quietly as Jules listened and smiled. "You know what my favorite part about sailing is, Jules?"

"What?"

"The silence. There's something magical about the sound, or lack of sound, I should say, once the engines are turned off."

"I agree. It's so romantic."

Jules put her head against Rick's chest and held him tight. They stayed in that embrace for ten minutes. It felt so right. The boat sailed on for an hour, and then pointed into the wind to drop the mainsail and roll in the jib. The captain reluctantly fired up the Yanmar diesels, and they spun around to head back toward the shore. It had been a beautiful sail.

Once ashore, Rick tipped the crew, each one separately, and swapped cell numbers with the captain, sure he'd book another charter.

As they waved goodbye to the crew, Chris made the gesture that he'd call Rick and pretended he was throwing dice. Rick gave him a thumbs-up. They'd play craps together one day soon.

Rick and Jules hopped back into the SUV and let out a sigh at the same time. The night had been perfect and didn't seem like it could get any better.

"Where to, Jules? It's only nine o'clock," Rick said.

"I want dessert!"

"We already had dessert."

"Not the kind I'm talking about," said Jules as she rubbed Rick's knee.

He smirked. "Oh, that kind. I'm in like Flynn."

"Huh?"

"Never mind. It's an old saying referring to Errol Flynn, an Australian actor, meaning, I'm on the same page, let's do it."

"Ah, I understand," replied Jules. "So, what are we waiting for?"

On that note, Rick started the SUV bound for the Don CeSar. It was going to be a night to remember.

When they got to the room, Jules stepped into the bathroom and came out wearing a black silk nightgown. She looked stunning. Rick kissed her and held her tight.

"Can you call room service and order us some port wine?" asked Rick.

"I'm on it," she said, picking up the hotel phone.

Rick cleaned up as fast as he could. The wine arrived just as he came out of the bathroom dressed more comfortably. Jules offered him a full glass.

She put on some soft music and dimmed the lights. The table had some electronic candles sitting on it, and Jules looked divine in the glimmer of their glow. Rick took a sip and kissed her hard. She put down her wine, loosened the front of her nightgown, and Rick put his arm inside the nightgown around her waist. He pulled her toward him and onto the bed, his mouth on hers the whole time.

They made love for hours, playing and kissing, rubbing and caressing each other. It felt different than before, maybe because they had exchanged I love you's, or maybe because it just felt so right. They fell asleep in each other's arms.

CHAPTER FIVE

The next morning, Rick was awakened by a phone call from Possum.

"Good morning," Rick managed, his voice still hoarse from sleep.

"Rick, it's Possum. Sounds like I woke you. Sorry, man."

"No worries, five hours sleep is too much anyway," said Rick with a half chuckle. "What's up?"

"I got the results back from Emily's hypnotic regression therapy."

"Really? Tell me more," said Rick.

"Well, it's incredibly interesting. She told the doctor that I was her brother and she wanted me in on the session. He didn't seem psyched about it, but he agreed. I used my GoPro to record the whole thing. I've already emailed you the files. It's mind-blowing."

"Ok I'll fire up my computer after we hang up," said Rick.

"Not once did she talk about murdering her husband or Hans Larsson, but she did repeat almost the same exact story she told you. She also gave some insight into her abductors that we didn't know before. I took the liberty of transcribing the entire session and included it as a searchable pdf that might be helpful to you."

"Possum, you're the best."

"I know. You can pay me later," he said with a laugh.

"Anything else you want to add?"

"Yes, I have a friend at the University of Texas, Houston, Department of Diagnostic and Interventional Imaging. He used a new imaging machine similar to an MRI, only higher tech, on Emily. There are perfectly healed hairline fractures on her tibia and fibula, as if they were cut with a bone saw. It's highly likely she's telling the truth about them making her shorter. This is some serious *Face/Off* shit."

"No kidding," said Rick, running a hand through his hair. "I think about that movie all the time because of this case. Thanks, Possum. Keep a tab running for me, and I'll take care of you."

"Rick, I ain't worried about that. Just figure this case out. Let's get the bastards who did this to her. She comes across as strong, and she is strong, but deep down she's fragile. She's been though a lot. I've set up some therapy sessions for her with a friend of mine who deals with PTSD. She helped me a lot after, you know, what happened to my wife."

His wife, Jennifer, had been murdered three years ago. The official report was that she had been the victim of a mugging gone bad. Neither Rick nor Possum believed that, though, but the case had gone cold. The only thing taken from her was an ancient treasure hunting book she had bought on eBay, which she'd been very excited to show to Possum. She'd never gotten the chance. All Possum knew was that the book was about an ambiguous, sacred gem-stone, worshipped by a tribe in South America.

"Say no more, Possum. Do whatever you think is best, man, and one day we'll catch that son of a bitch who killed her. I give you my word."

They hung up and Rick inched out of bed, trying not to wake up Jules. She rolled over and moaned, but fell back asleep. She looked so peaceful sleeping there that Rick didn't want to leave, but he had to. Picking up his computer and wireless headphones, he stepped out onto the terrace.

He opened the pdf file so he could read along with the recording, and opened a can of Coke as quietly as he could. He wanted coffee but he was afraid the machine would wake Jules. He propped his feet on the opposite chair and hit the "play" button on his laptop.

Rick read along as the video played. The file was clean and clear thanks to the high quality of Possum's GoPro 4K Hero Black. Possum was a high-tech redneck who always had the latest gear. He was the one who had turned Rick on to many of the gadgets he used for his P.I. work, including the GoPro.

"Good morning. It's Jan 23rd, 9:00 a.m., I, T.C. LeNormand, will be asking Emily Davis a few questions in hopes of helping her recover her memory. She is already in a hypnotic state and lying on the couch directly in front of me."

The video focused on Emily.

"Emily, can you hear me?"

"Yes."

"Good. What is my name?"

"You are T.C. LeNormand."

"That's correct. I would like to ask you a few simple questions to create a baseline. Is that ok with you?"

"Yes."

"Ok, Emily, what is your last name?"

"Davis."

"Where have you lived for the past several years?"

"I lived in Hyde Park, a suburb of Tampa."

"What do you do for a living?"

"I'm a research chemist, and I work with grants to create immunotherapy cancer drugs."

"Where is your laboratory?"

"It's in Clearwater, Florida."

"Do you still work there?"

She labored to make a response. Her eyes were twitching as if she were in REM sleep. After a minute, she said, "My lab was broken into and I was abducted."

"Who abducted you?"

"I don't know, but they were from Switzerland."

"How do you know that?"

"Because I recognized the accent. It was similar to Dr. Hans's."

She began to wiggle uncomfortably on the couch, her eyes moving faster than before.

"Who is Dr. Hans and where is he now?"

Her hands were shaking and she looked as if she was beginning to convulse.

"He is Dr. Hans Larsson. He and I were working together on releasing a new cancer treatment, but he was killed by my abductors."

"Did you kill your husband, Emily?"

"No, they did. They did it all."

"Who's they?"

"The ones who abducted me and did all the surgeries on me to change my appearance."

"What color is your hair?"

She hesitated, as if afraid it was a trick question, and then said, "Black. No, wait, silver now. They changed it."

"How did they change it?"

"I'm not sure. With some sort of hormone therapy, I think."

Rick made marks on pages that he wanted to reference back to as he watched and read along. *She's either telling the truth or the greatest actress of this generation*, he thought.

"What cancer treatment were you working on with Hans?"

"It was an immunotherapy drug. It could revolutionize cancer treatment."

"What do you mean revolutionize? Was it effective?"

"It had a one hundred percent efficacy in animal trials. We were about to begin human trials when I was abducted."

"Emily, are you saying you found the cure for cancer?"

"Yes, I believe I did. I was ready to test humans so we could make certain it worked, but all the signs were pointing to yes."

T.C. looked over at the camera, in Possum's direction, shaking his head in amazement.

"Emily, I'm going to step out of the room for a moment. Just relax and I'll be right back and we will continue."

She didn't respond. T.C. waved at the camera, gesturing for Possum to follow him into the hallway.

"This is groundbreaking info and I know I must adhere to doctor-patient confidentiality, but this could change the future of mankind."

"I know, and I know I can count on you to keep this to yourself, right?" said Possum from behind the GoPro.

Possum's hand appeared, holding out a bundle of cash. T.C. looked down, pushed Possum's hand back out of sight, and said, "Look, just put that away. I'm a man of science and I don't need your money to keep quiet. What I do need is for you to find the people who stole Emily's cancer treatment and make sure she's able to bring it to market. My mother and brother both died from cancer. I bet there's not a single person in the building who hasn't been affected by cancer directly or indirectly. I'm on your side, and you can count on my discretion."

"Thank you, T.C. I believe you," replied Possum.

They proceeded back into the exam room. T.C sat down on the chair next to Emily, and the movement of the GoPro showed Possum was sitting back down too. Emily hadn't moved.

"Emily, are you with me?" asked T.C.

"Yes, I'm here."

"Ok, is there anything you can remember about the Swiss people who abducted you that might help us find them?"

She lay there in silence for a minute, then said, "I heard them on the phone one time, and the conversation became heated. I heard the main abductor say that he didn't want to go to Grand Cayman again. He was cursing loudly and switching back and forth between English and Swiss German. I couldn't hear the other side of the conversation, but I heard Liam agree that Grand Cayman would be the best place to store it."

"Emily, you said Liam. Is that the name of the man in charge?"

"Liam?" Her brow furrowed. "It can't be. I've worked with Liam before. I was so drugged up, maybe I misheard it. But as much as I don't want to admit it, I remember his name. One of his nurses called him that and he scolded her and told her no names, not realizing I could hear."

"What were they planning to store in Grand Cayman?"

"I can't be sure, but I think it's my cancer treatment," she said.

"Why Grand Cayman?"

"I heard them whispering outside my door one time and I put a plastic cup to the door so I could hear. They talked about a lab under the estate on Seven Mile Beach."

"Where exactly is the estate?"

She looked like she was thinking hard. "I'm not sure, but I heard them reference the west bay. One of them was worried about the tourists at the...the Cobalt Coast Resort, I think it was called. Liam told him they've had the lab next door for years and no one's ever suspected a thing. So, it must be next to the resort."

"Emily, you're doing a great job. Can I ask you a few more questions? These may be tough ones."

"Yes, go ahead."

"Did you kill your husband, Emily?"

"No, I loved him. We had our issues but I *did* love him."

"Who killed your husband?"

"I don't know."

"Do you suspect the Swiss?"

"Yes!"

"Why?"

"Because other than myself and my husband, Hans Larsson and his ex-partner Liam were the only people who knew I had discovered the cure for the worst disease of mankind. I think they—Liam and his company, I mean—wanted to release it themselves or squash it because it would hurt their profits."

"What profits?"

"NoahTech's profits—they make Revacizumab, a top cancer drug."

"So, you think the people who abducted you and killed your husband and Hans are affiliated with NoahTech?"

"No, I think they are NoahTech."

T.C.'s mouth was as wide open as his eyes. He glanced in the direction of the GoPro.

"Ok, Emily. I'm going to count down from three to one, and you will awaken and feel rested and calm. You will retain the memory of everything you told me today. Are you ready?"

"Yes."

"Three, two, one."

With that, Emily's eyes opened and she calmly looked over at T.C. "When do we start?" she asked.

"We're already done."

She lay there for a minute, then sat up, staring at the ceiling.

"Wow. I don't remember you putting me under, but I'm remembering a whole bunch of new stuff about what happened to me," she said, rubbing her forehead.

"Do you want to jot some of it down? I can get you a scratch pad," said T.C.

"Yes, please, while it's fresh in my mind."

T.C. walked out of the room and soon returned with a yellow pad and a pen. He handed them to Emily.

Waving his head toward the door and glancing at the GoPro again, he said, "Let's give her some space for a few minutes."

The footage followed him out of the room, as Possum gently closed the door on his way out.

"I've done many sessions like this before, but nothing has come close to this one for details. They usually say yes or no or murmur a few words. She was almost cognitive. I thought she was acting at first, but the graph shows she was clearly unconscious during the entire exchange. I'm flabbergasted," said T.C. as he rubbed his hands across his face.

"It was incredibly helpful to the case. I can't thank you enough," replied Possum.

"Finding Emily's drug and the guys who did this will be thanks enough. Just let me know if there's anything else I can do."

"I'll let you know for sure, T.C."

The GoPro stayed in one spot in the hallway, as Possum waited for Emily to finish writing stuff on the pad. After about twenty minutes, she called for Possum through the door. The camera moved back inside the room, showing Emily standing up and holding the pad out.

"I wrote down everything I could think of."

"You did great, hon," said Possum.

Once he'd watched the entire recording, Rick scrolled though the files sent by Possum and found one called "yellow pad."

When he opened it and began to read, he saw all the same info Emily had opened up about during the session. Nothing new—until one line gave him pause. It said: "Liam Furrer is in charge." She hadn't said his last name during the session.

He smiled to himself. Finally, he had a lead.

Rick typed the name into Google, and the first thing to pop up was NoahTech. Liam was the chief chemist and CEO at NoahTech. He had started the company in Switzerland with his best friend, Noah Rechsteiner, in 1977. Back then it was called RezepCorp, but they later changed the name to NoahTech. Noah had died of undetermined causes just before the sale of the company to the conglomerate LaufeRänne LTD for five hundred million francs in 1982. In his will, he'd left his 51% of the shares to none other than Liam Furrer.

After an hour of exhaustive research, Rick found that Liam still held 73% of the shares of NoahTech.

There was the motive.

The only part of the puzzle that still didn't fit was why they hadn't just killed Emily. Why go to all the trouble to change her appearance and then let her go? It troubled Rick, and he couldn't wrap his brain around it.

He heard Jules stirring in the bed, so he went over to sit down beside her.

"Good morning, beautiful. How are you feeling?" he asked.

"I feel amazing!" said Jules with a yawn.

"You want to go to Grand Cayman today?"

"Grand Cayman? Are you joking?"

"Nope. I got a lead on the case and need to follow it up, but I want you with me. You wanna be my Watson today? Watson, as in Sherlock Holmes and Watson," he added when she looked a little confused.

"Oh, as in *The Adventures of Sherlock Holmes*. I read that book in high school. Sounds like a blast. When do we go?"

"As soon as I can book a flight. Why don't you order some breakfast and I'll see what I can find?"

"Sounds like a plan, Sherlock." She laughed.

CHAPTER SIX

Jules ordered room service as Rick looked up flights on his computer. He found a nonstop on Cayman Airways leaving Tampa at 2:20 p.m. and arriving in Grand Cayman at 4:10 p.m.

He smiled. *We'll make it there for happy hour.*

It was 9:15 a.m. There was plenty of time to make that flight, so Rick booked it. He was surprised how cheap it was for a same-day flight.

Rick finished his coffee and began to pack his duffel bag. Jules was already packed and in the shower. While he waited for her, he called Johnie to update him and check on Chief and the boat.

"Hi Rick, what's new?" said Johnie.

"You tell me. Anything new happening up in Destin?"

"Well, we got three more charters this week. I got a call for a private charter for one couple, so I up-charged them twenty-five percent. I hope that's ok."

"Sure, that's fine. Do whatever you feel is fair. Consider it your boat while I'm away," replied Rick.

"Never. I'm just your trusty mate and mechanic," said Johnie with a chuckle.

"Nonsense, you're more than a mate and mechanic. Hell, I ought to make you a partner."

"We can talk about that someday, Rick. Right now, I'm happy and in no hurry."

"Ok. How's Chief?"

"He's the same ol' Chief. He gets excited when kids walk down the dock; he's really good for business. One of the charters I booked told me they booked it because their kids loved Chief so much and they felt comfortable bringing them on the boat. He's worth his weight in gold."

That reminded Rick of the tackle boxes under the settee. "Any bottom-fishing trips?" he asked.

"Nah, all trolling. I did have a guy interested in doing a bottom trip, but it's not confirmed yet."

"Ok, well don't use the weights in the tackle boxes under the settee. They're keepsakes from my grandfather's collection and only there for good luck."

"I understand. I'll head over to Half-Hitch and get some leaders, hooks, and weights," said Johnie.

"Sounds good. Listen, I got a new lead on the case and I'm heading to Grand Cayman today. I don't think my cell will work there, but I can call with Wi-Fi and should have access to internet and email while I'm on the island."

"No worries. I'll hold down the fort here."

He was saying goodbye when Jules came out of the shower in a pair of white shorts and a black tank top. She looked gorgeous and all Rick wanted to do was take her clothes off, but they needed to get to the airport.

I can't wait until after happy hour, he thought.

Rick quickly showered and shaved, then threw on a pair of fishing shorts and a Henley t-shirt. The steam from the shower took out all the wrinkles and he was glad he didn't have to iron it. He loved his Henleys.

Rick called the valet and had his rental pulled up to the front of the hotel. He'd already booked a room and dive package at the Cobalt Coast Resort. He couldn't wait to surprise Jules with a PADI Open Water Scuba Course, so she could get certified and do some diving with him. Though, as he put the key in the ignition, it occurred to him that she might already be certified.

"Jules, have you ever gone scuba diving?"

"No, I've always wanted to, though. I've done a lot of snorkeling. Why?"

"Just curious. The resort I booked us in Grand Cayman does a free *Try Scuba* in the pool in the afternoons. I thought it might be fun for you," he said, trying not to give away his surprise.

"I'm game." She smiled. "Let's do it."

They boarded the flight at 1:50 and got a row to themselves. Rick ordered a couple of beers from the flight attendant after take-off. The flight was smooth and they ended up drinking three beers apiece, so they were perfectly primed for happy hour once they landed.

At the car rental plaza, Rick sweet-talked the girl behind the counter into a free upgrade to a Ford Explorer. He hated little cars and there was no need to start driving one now.

"Where's a good happy hour?" he asked. "We're staying at the Cobalt Coast Resort. Is there something along the way, maybe on the beach?"

The girl pulled out a local map and circled five spots with happy hours. One jumped right out at Rick. Lone Star Bar & Grill. It was right on the way, and happy hour was from 4:00 to 7:00 p.m. According to the girl, they had the best brisket in town.

"Sold!" said Rick.

He put their bags in the back of the Explorer and headed down West Bay Road next to the beach. Not long after they had been driving, he saw the sign for Lone Star Bar & Grill.

"Are you hungry, Jules?"

"Hungry and thirsty!"

"Have you ever had brisket?"

"No, but I've heard of it. What is it exactly?"

"It's a Texas favorite and I absolutely love it. It's tender beef slow-cooked over a smoker, and when it's done right, it will melt in your mouth," he told her.

"You make it sound like food from heaven."

"Well, it's food from Texas, and that's about as close to heaven as it comes, in my opinion—next to you, of course."

Jules blushed and kissed Rick on the cheek.

They stepped inside and were greeted by a nice local who sat them at the edge of the open-air restaurant. It wasn't on the beach, but they could still see it across the street.

Rick ordered a Caybrew, a local beer brewed at Cayman Islands Brewery. Jules opted for a Lone Star signature margarita. He also ordered some brisket and an appetizer of Big Bang nachos.

The order of nachos was huge, and he almost wished he hadn't ordered them. But the brisket came out fast, so they mixed the two together and put pieces of tender brisket on their nachos. It was a great combination.

Rick switched to water, while Jules slowly finished her giant margarita. She said she was buzzed, but Rick felt fine and assured her he was good to drive.

They drove along West Bay Road and passed many dive shops and bars on their way to the Cobalt Coast Resort.

"You want to go to Hell, Jules?"

"Qué?"

Rick laughed out loud. "Hell. It's a neat little place on Hell Road. It really looks like what hell on earth would be. It's pretty interesting." He had gone diving on Grand Cayman years back and visited Hell before, so he knew it would blow her mind.

As they continued on Hell Road, Rick pointed out a red shanty on the side of the road that read, *Welcome to Hell*. It was a small gift shop with a devil cut out of plywood standing next to the street.

They got out and walked around the back of the small shop, not really wanting any souvenirs from Hell. Rick pointed out the limestone rock formations, eerily similar to what hell might look like. Someone had placed a metal devil in the middle of the formations, which made the place seem even spookier.

Jules tugged on his arm. "Ok, Rick, I've seen enough. Let's go. It gives me the creeps," she said, wincing a little.

"No problem, we can go. It is pretty awesome, though, right?"

"Yeah, I have to admit it's amazing, but I wanna see the water."

They hopped back in the Explorer and backtracked through Hell a little, then followed the GPS to the Cobalt

Coast Resort. Grabbing their carry-ons, they went inside and checked in. As they headed up to their room, they heard a local guy playing steel pans by the pool.

"Can we go to the pool, Rick?" asked Jules, perking up.

"Sure, we can do whatever you want."

Once they got to the room, Jules put on a one-piece. Rick grabbed his swim trunks and a couple of towels, and they headed back down to the pool. It was a beautiful night and there weren't many people there. The resort had a huge scuba program and the boats left early, so most of the guests must have already retired for the evening. Rick hadn't booked a trip for first thing in the morning because he wanted to do beach dives first and wasn't sure how tired they'd be from the trip. This wasn't just a vacation, after all; he was here to do some recon on NoahTech.

The pool water was chilly at first, but they got used to it fast. Jules wrapped her legs around Rick with his back against the side of the pool and kissed him.

"Thank you, Rick. I'm having a great time."

"So am I. Tomorrow I'm gonna do some beach dives and you can do the Try Scuba program." He hesitated, then grinned. "Ok, I can't keep it a secret any longer. I booked you a PADI Open Water One Scuba course. It starts at 2:00."

"What is Patty?" she asked.

"No, it's PADI with a D. It's an acronym, P.A.D.I., which stands for Professional Association of Diving Instructors. I booked you some scuba lessons."

Jules's eyes lit up. "Oh my God, really? Like I told you, I've always wanted to dive! Thank you, thank you!" She hugged him again.

"Well, the waters in Grand Cayman are some of the best in the world and the diving here is phenomenal," he said, stroking her wet hair. "I didn't want you to miss out."

"I can't wait to start," she said.

"You're gonna need some dive gear, so in the morning, while I'm on a beach dive, go to the dive shop at the resort and tell the guy you're doing a course. He'll set you up with all the stuff you need. Just charge it to the room. Get a dive light too. I want to take you night diving once you're comfortable."

"Ooh, night diving! Sounds scary."

"It can be a little intimidating at first, but you'll see things at night you'd never or almost never see in the day, including octopus, sharks, and my favorite sea creature, nudibranchs."

"Sharks?" she asked, her eyes widening with fear. It was as if she hadn't heard any of the other names he mentioned.

"Don't worry. It's mostly nurse sharks and black tip reef sharks. They won't bother you at all," he reassured her.

"I won't promise anything. Let's see how my diving during the day goes first."

"Fair enough," said Rick. "You ready to hit the hay?"

"Not just yet, but I am ready for dessert."

"I read you loud and clear, Jules."

CHAPTER SEVEN

Rick and Jules woke up at the same time. Rick made some coffee in the room and stepped outside to check the weather. It was a beautiful, clear day. Even though it was early morning, a few people were doing beach dives off the end of the pier, and two nearly identical dive-boats were docked and being loaded up with divers and gear.

It had been a while since Rick had gone diving. He wanted a refresher before going out again.

"Jules, I'm gonna head down to the dive shop, check on your class today, and see about renting some gear for myself for a beach dive. Do you want to come?"

"Can I just lie here a little longer?" she asked, yawning.

"Of course you can, sweetie. I'll bring us some bagels and the green tea you like."

"Thanks. You're so thoughtful."

Rick brushed his teeth and splashed his face with water. After throwing on a baseball cap, dive shorts, and a tank top, he kissed Jules on the forehead and headed down to the dive shop.

It was a nice shop and several of the employees had an accent that sounded like Kiwi. Rick had been to New Zealand several times, back when he worked for the airlines and could fly for free, so he recognized it right away.

"You wanna go diving today? It's a beauty, eh?" commented a man behind the counter.

"Name's Rick Waters," he said, stepping up to the counter. "It's been a while since I've been diving, but I wanna get back in and get wet."

"Sounds good. I'm Curtis," replied the man, offering his hand.

Rick shook it. "Do I hear a bit of an accent there?"

"Do you? I'm from Manitoba," Curtis told him.

"Canada, eh?" asked Rick, trying to make a gentle joke.

"You betcha."

"What on earth brought you all the way from the Great White North to Grand Cayman?"

"You hit the nail on the head when you called it the Great White North. I was sick of the snow."

"That makes sense. I'm not fond of it either. I don't ski, I hate snowmobiles, and I don't need to look at snow to drink a beer by a fireplace," said Rick with a chuckle.

"How long has it been since you last went diving?"

"I'd say about six years?" Rick said, trying to remember.

"Six, eh? You have a dive buddy today?" asked Curtis.

"Nope, but my girlfriend is signed up for the afternoon open water course, which I believe takes three days, right?"

"That's true, chum. It starts at 2:00 p.m. in the classroom and they get wet in the pool around 4:30 p.m., when they practice taking off their masks underwater and putting them back on."

"I remember those days when I did my first course," said Rick, smiling at the memory.

"Are you PADI or NAUI?" asked Curtis.

Rick pulled out his NAUI Rescue Diver card and handed it to Curtis.

"NAUI Rescue, eh? Impressive," Curtis remarked.

"Yeah, back in the days of the dinosaur I considered becoming a dive instructor and owning a shop one day. Then I found out they don't make much money. No offense."

"None taken. I don't do this job for money; I do it for my sanity, so I can get away from the damned snow."

"Fair enough," replied Rick.

"Ok, so one of the best parts of my job is that when someone shows up solo, I have to buddy up with them for safety. We don't allow solo diving here. When do you wanna get wet?"

Rick thought for a second and said, "How about 10:30? I need to grab some breakfast for my girlfriend and me first. I also need to rent some gear."

"Try on this mask," offered Curtis, handing him a Scuba Pro mask from under the counter.

Rick pushed it onto his face and looked downward—the mask stayed on.

"That looks perfect," said Curtis "You about six feet?"

"Six-one," said Rick.

"Ok, no worries. I'll grab everything you need for your size and set it aside. I'll meet you back at the shop at 10:30. Sound good? Oh, do you want a dive skin?"

"Nah, I like to dive in shorts and a t-shirt. I hate wetsuits and I'm not fond of skins, really."

"Me neither. The water temp is around seventy-nine today, so we don't really need one. You might get chilled if we do multiple dives, though."

"Ok, Curtis, see you back here at 10:30."

Curtis nodded and started putting together the gear for Rick.

Rick grabbed a couple of bagels, bananas, and a green tea from the buffet and headed back to the room. When he saw the à la carte prices on the menu, he was glad he'd purchased the all-inclusive dive and meal plan offered by the resort. Jules was still in bed when he got back, reading a Wayne Stinnett novel.

Rick set the tray on the bed, then spread pineapple cream cheese on the bagels and handed Jules her tea.

"Mmmm, it smells so good!" She set her book aside to take a sip. "How was the dive shop?"

"It's fantastic, and I met a nice guy from Canada named Curtis who's gonna be my dive buddy this morning. He's also teaching your class this afternoon."

"I can't wait. So, he's nice, you said?"

"Yeah, he's a real laid-back dude. You'll enjoy his class, I'm sure."

"I hope so." She smiled.

It was 10:15 when Rick kissed Jules and left for the dive shop. She was content to sit in bed and read for a while, especially since she had a bit of a hangover and felt like being lazy.

"You ready to splash in?" asked Curtis as Rick walked back into the dive shop.

"Ready as I'll ever be. Anything interesting to see down there?"

"Yeah, there's the usual stuff, but since you're going with me, I'll take you off the beaten path." Curtis grinned mischievously.

Rick grinned back. "Killer. I'm stoked."

The twin dive boats had already left the dock, and two divers were donning their gear at the end. By the time Rick and Curtis walked down there, the divers were already in the water. Rick paid close attention as Curtis explained the gear, which had advanced over the years. No longer was there a dive belt with heavy lead weights attached, like he was used to; now there were pockets on the buoyancy compensator holding bags of lead BBs that locked into place. The Scuba Pro BC also had an Air2 instead of an octopus, the backup regulator Rick was used to using. But he liked the idea of the octopus being directly connected to the BC.

After a quick safety check, they took giant strides off the end of the pier. The water was cold for a few seconds until Rick got accustomed to it and then it felt invigorating. The visibility was far beyond a hundred feet, and he could see the reef clearly below. Curtis motioned him to follow him toward the drop-off a few hundred feet from the dock.

For Rick, this was not only a dive, but also an opportunity to do some recon on the house owned by NoahTech just two buildings away.

They dove to the right along the drop-off, and Rick followed Curtis as he pointed out all the different sea life. A friendly squid came right up to Rick's mask, as if to say hello. His colors changed as Rick blew bubbles toward him; he was pulsating and looked almost neon. A small nurse shark lay near them with its head stuck under a ledge.

A turtle leisurely swam nearby as Curtis took photos. Rick had been keeping count of his kicks since they'd taken a hard right on the drop-off. He motioned to Curtis that he needed to surface, and the two slowly ascended to the top.

"I need to adjust my mask and make it a little tighter. I was having trouble down below."

Rick handed the mask to Curtis to adjust the straps. With his buddy's attention on the mask, he studied the shore and cased the house he planned on breaking into soon.

From all indications, the house looked vacant. It was a large structure, with a pool overlooking the rocky beach and aqua-blue ocean. Rick would jog by it later on while Jules was in her dive class and scope out the front, to make sure there were no cars in the driveway.

He was about halfway to the house from the pier, so he knew, depending on current, that he would need to kick seventy more times to be directly in front of the house. His plan was to do a night dive and approach the rear entrance under the shadow of darkness. He was sure there would be a security system and cameras, but he would be prepared for any scenario.

After Curtis finished adjusting his mask, they both gave the ok sign and dropped back down to the ledge. Rick spent the rest of the dive actually enjoying himself and put the house out of his mind for a while.

The fan coral waved a welcoming hello as the waves moved them to and fro. Brain coral sat atop mountains of thousand-year-old reef, as blennies and yellow damsels darted in and out of their hiding places. Parrotfish nibbled on coral, creating sand as they munched away.

Thousands of silversides moved in unison as a large tarpon swam dangerously close to the school, and a giant stingray flew inches from the sandy bottom looking for breakfast.

Curtis motioned Rick closer to show him something—a deep cavern with a small entrance at the bottom of the ledge. Curtis turned on his flashlight, and Rick followed suit.

They squeezed through the rocky crevasse and entered a large, dark room. Inside the cavern, they found a school of yellowtail snapper, while glass fish danced in the reflection of the flashlights. Rick had dived Trinity Caves once before, made famous in the movie, *The Firm,* but he'd never seen this one. It was even more spectacular than the others. Rick was glad Curtis had taken the initiative to show it to him.

Curtis pointed at his gauge, indicating they were getting a little low on air, and made a thumbs-up sign that it was time to surface. Rick still had 750 pounds of air left, but knew by the time he ascended he'd be below 500, which was the danger zone for divers down below.

They rose slower than their bubbles, keeping a close eye on the dive computers on their wrists. Once at the surface, Rick pulled his mask down around his neck and looked around. They were directly in front of the house owned by the Swiss abductors.

"Who owns that house? It's huge," asked Rick.

"I'm not sure. I believe it's someone from Norway or Sweden or something. They're rarely there, but I met a couple of them at the resort bar once—I sometimes pick up a bartending shift. They had European accents, and they weren't staying at the resort. When I asked them how they'd ended up at a bar all the way on the west end, they said they'd walked over from the house two doors down."

"Were they nice?" asked Rick.

"Nice enough, I guess. The tall guy seemed intense and kept looking at his watch and iPhone. They drank a couple of rum punches, dropped me a twenty, and left while I was turned away filling the ice bin. I haven't seen them since."

"Hmm. Interesting," Rick commented, as they both began to kick on their backs toward the resort. The current was light, and they made it back easily in a few minutes.

After rinsing the gear and setting it aside, Rick asked Curtis if he could store his gear for him for a night dive the next day.

"No worries. You need a buddy again? I love night dives. If I wasn't working, I'd join you. I can set you up with one of our other divemasters."

Rick had forgotten about the resort policy for always needing a dive buddy. Thinking fast, he said, "That's ok. I have friend who's gonna meet me here from Georgetown. He has his own gear, but can you put aside two tanks for us?"

Curtis hesitated, then said, "Well, I'm supposed to see his dive card before I release a tank. Does he have a lot of experience?"

"Oh, yeah. I've dived hundreds of times with him in Mexico. He's staying over at the Sunset House. I guess I could have him bring a tank from there," Rick said thoughtfully.

"Aw, don't worry about it. What's his name? I'll jot it down and make up a NAUI number for him. We don't get many NAUI divers here. It's almost all PADI- or SSI-trained divers. No one will notice."

Rick gave him a name, then pulled out a twenty from his dry bag and handed it to Curtis. He tried to wave it away, but Rick insisted, and eventually he took it.

"Thanks, Rick. I appreciate it. If I see you after class, first round is on me."

"Sounds good. Thanks for the dive, and thanks for showing me that cave. You're a great underwater tour guide."

"My pleasure." Curtis shook his hand and then turned his attention back to the dive gear.

Rick rinsed off by the pool and jumped in, making a huge cannonball. The warm water invigorated him. He did a few laps, then dried off and went back up to the room to see how Jules was doing. She was probably famished. It was 12:30 and Rick's stomach was growling.

Jules was sitting in a hotel robe on the balcony with the sliding glass doors open to let in the breeze. She was still reading.

"Nice cannonball, Louganis," she said with a smile.

"You saw that?"

"Not only did I see but I heard it. I think half of Grand Cayman heard it," she added and broke into a laugh. "I'm just teasing you, Rick. It was very graceful."

"Ok, now I know you're full of it." He grinned. "You hungry?"

"I could eat a horse."

"Well, will a cow do instead? Let's go into town and grab some lunch at Agave. I hear they have incredible street tacos."

"I love street tacos!" she said enthusiastically.

Rick quickly showered, threw on a robe and grabbed some shorts and a t-shirt out of his duffel bag. Before he could put on his clothes, Jules moved to the couch, opened her robe, and whispered seductively, "Do you think I can have dessert before lunch?"

"Jules, you never cease to amaze me."

Rick dropped his robe and they made love on the couch. They held each other for a few minutes afterward, before Jules suddenly broke their silent embrace.

"Let's go eat some cow!"

They drove toward Georgetown with the windows open, letting the ocean breeze fill their senses. On North Sound Road, they pulled up to Agave and walked inside. The place was bustling with folks in business suits on their lunch hour, and some in jeans.

Grand Cayman was famous for offshore banking. Although the little island was only twenty-two miles long and eight miles wide at its widest point, it boasted over two hundred banks. To say there was a lot of money in Grand Cayman was like saying Babe Ruth hit a few home runs.

Rick and Jules were lucky to catch two people leaving the bar and grab the two stools they'd just vacated, against the side wall. Every table was occupied and the restaurant had a waiting list.

The drinks looked amazing, and Rick was thinking of ordering a couple before he remembered that Jules had her first scuba class that afternoon.

"Since you've got a class today, Jules, how about a horchata instead of alcohol? It's like sweet rice milk," said Rick.

She gave him an amused look. "I'm Latina, remember? I know horchata well, even though it's from Mexico."

They both ordered street tacos. Rick got two beef and one tequila shrimp, pan-seared and deglazed with Tequila Ocho Plata, red sauce, and topped with sweet and sour slaw. Jules went for straight cow—three of them. They also ordered a molcajete bowl filled with queso and barbacoa, and a side of tortilla chips.

"Mmm," said Jules as she finished her last taco, licking the sauce off her fingers. "This was a good choice."

Neither one felt overstuffed. They both felt just right.

Rick drove back to the resort and got Jules set up for her class. Since Curtis was teaching, they chatted a little before class, bragging to the students about how great their morning dive had been.

Once class started, Rick went back to the room and threw on some jogging shoes. He grabbed his micro binoculars and put them in a case he usually wore around his biceps to carry his iPhone when he jogged.

Making sure several employees saw him, he stretched in the front lobby, then waved at them and patted his belly as if he needed to lose weight. It was all an act. He jogged out of the hotel to the street and took a left. Within a minute, he was directly in front of the suspects' house. Then he jogged backwards and did a 360-degree spin, making sure no one was in the area.

He bent over to tie his laces, which were already tight, and slipped the binoculars out of the case. As stealthy as a he could be, he scanned the house. No cars were parked in the driveway, and several newspapers were piled near the front door. It had been a while since anyone had been there.

A car started coming up the street, so he did his fake stretch routine and kept his face out of view. He was turning around to head back to the hotel when he spotted the mailbox. Quickly, he took several letters out of the box and shoved them into his shorts. He was back at the hotel in a couple of minutes, then walked around the north side and entered from the rear, avoiding the front desk.

Once back in his room, he put the envelopes on the desk and opened his computer. It was time for some sleuthing.

CHAPTER EIGHT

The sun was already warming the room when the alarm went off the next morning. Jules rolled over and wrapped her legs around Rick's. He stroked her black hair and kissed her gently. They were in love, but both too tired to fool around.

"Wanna grab some breakfast?"

"Yes, I could use some energy food."

They got dressed and strolled down to the eating area. Bagels, fruit, eggs, bacon, and ham were set out on a buffet table, along with various cereals, milk, and the usual starchy treats all good resorts lavished on their guests.

Jules grabbed two large glasses of orange juice for herself and Rick, while he scoured the buffet, trying to decide what to eat.

"Feel like health food today?" he asked her.

"Hell, no, I'm on vacation. I'm getting a pecan waffle," she replied, studying the à la carte menu. Since they had an all-inclusive package, they could eat from the buffet or order off the menu. It was nice to have a choice.

Rick scooped some eggs onto his plate and nearly made them vanish with all the bacon he laid on top of them. He grabbed a bowl of grits with tons of butter and sugar and set them on the table, then waited politely until Jules's waffle arrived.

He drank his O.J. fast, saw they had fresh spinach and kale juice on the menu as well, and ordered two glasses in case Jules wanted some.

When she saw it, she turned her nose up at it.

"Good, more for me," said Rick jokingly.

After they finished breakfast, they both felt stuffed and decided to burn some of it off with a nice swim. Jules wore the new skin she'd bought in the dive shop over her bikini, and Rick threw on board shorts and a rash guard shirt. They both wore aqua socks, walked to the end of the dock, and jumped in together, holding hands.

The two dive boats had already left for the morning trip. A few divers were milling around the shop but weren't on the dock yet. Rick and Jules had the ocean to themselves.

They swam along the shore to the northwest and around the point, which was a little more than half a mile. Once they rounded the corner, they saw a sign that said Dolphin Discovery Grand Cayman. Jules's eyes lit up.

"Can we come back here and swim with the dolphins?"

"Why come back? Let's just go now. We're already in our swim gear."

He reached into the Velcro pocket of his board shorts and pulled out a clear dry bag with some cash and a credit card inside.

Jules's eyes widened. "You think of everything!"

"I like to be prepared. I mean, can you imagine if we finished our swim and wanted a beer but had no money? We could die of thirst!"

Jules laughed and wrapped her arms around Rick, nearly dunking him under. They carefully climbed out of the water onto the rough coral shoreline, trying to avoid scratching themselves.

Once in the parking lot, they air-dried a bit before approaching the ticket counter. Rick bought Jules the Royal Swim package. It was thirty minutes long and included the famous foot push, where two dolphins would push her from the soles of her feet up through the water surface. There were no cruise ships in town and no one waiting, so Rick tipped the trainer fifty bucks and got him to let Jules go out for an hour instead. He also included the photo package free.

It was noon before they finished.

"You wanna swim back or walk?" he asked her.

She twisted her mouth. "I think I've had enough water for a while. Let's walk."

It was a short walk back to the resort and when they arrived, Rick had a message and text from Johnie. The text looked urgent.

Call me ASAP!

"Crap, I think there's something wrong with my boat. I need to call my first mate."

"No problemo. I'm gonna hop in the shower. I hope it's nothing serious."

Rick stepped onto the terrace and sat on one of the chairs, opened a Diet Coke, and called Johnie.

"Johnie, it's Rick. What's up?"

"Are you sitting down, Rick? This is serious."

Rick sat up stiffly in his chair, suddenly concerned.

"Just spill it, Johnie."

"Ok, I was calibrating the tachometers this morning and I put Chief out on the stern like I do sometimes. You know how he loves the sun and the kids on the Harbor Walk?"

"What happened?"

Rick swallowed hard, afraid of what he would hear next.

"Well, everything was fine. I hooked my computer up to the boat's interface on the flybridge and starting running a diagnostic, glanced down at Chief, and he was happy as a clam. I revved the engines a little to get a baseline reading and was studying the chart and concentrating. Then I climbed down the ladder to grab a better screwdriver and... he was gone."

"Gone? What do you mean, gone? He got out of the cage? His wings are clipped. How did he get out?"

"I don't know. I have no idea—that's just it. The cage was locked in the front with the padlock you had on it. The key was on my chain. All I know is he was gone. Vanished."

Rick began to hyperventilate. He pressed his hand to his chest.

Not again!

"Rick, I'm so sorry, but before you have a coronary, let me finish," said Johnie.

"You're a hundred percent sure the cage was locked?" asked Rick.

"Yes, I double checked before I climbed up to the flybridge."

"Well, you and I have the only keys... Wait. The lock is the same lock that came with the cage. When I rescued

Chief from his owner, he told me one day he'd be back to get his bird. He said it with a smile, so I assumed he was being facetious. Do you think he came on board and stole Chief?" he asked desperately.

"Please, let me finish," Johnie pleaded.

"Ok, ok! You rattled me."

"So, remember those security cameras you had me install on the boat? Yeah, well, they paid off. I reviewed the footage and saw a clue. The guy who took Chief was wearing a Half-Hitch polo shirt. I blew up one of the stills of the man and paid Half-Hitch a visit. One of the employees, Thomas, said he remembered that guy coming in asking about charters. The man told Thomas he was down from Orlando on vacation and wanted to do a half-day charter. He said he seemed odd and was only interested in one charter in particular—*Nine-Tenths*. I asked him if he bought anything. He told me the only thing he purchased was a Half-Hitch polo shirt. Thomas gave him our contact info.

"I went back to the boat and watched the surveillance video a couple days prior to Chief's vanishing, and the same man cased the boat a few times and even approached it once the day before. But he turned around and left right after I climbed down from the flybridge."

"Where's Chief?" asked Rick impatiently.

"I'm getting there, boss. You're gonna love this. I went back to Half-Hitch and explained to Thomas what the man had done and asked if he knew his name. He was reluctant to share it at first, but after I told him how much you loved Chief and slipped him a Benjamin, he got on the computer and pulled up the sales for the day. The thief had used a credit card to buy the polo shirt. His name is Kim Hess. He wasn't the smartest individual, either. I opened up Facebook on my phone and searched for Kim Hess Destin Chief. The idiot was bragging that he got his bird back and even posted a picture of him and Chief on the balcony of the hotel where he was staying. You'll never believe where he was."

"Where?"

"Emerald Grande, five hundred feet from the boat. I know one of the maids there. I went out with her a few times. I met her there and she let me into the room. And low and behold, there was Chief, sitting in a cat kennel on the desk beside the balcony. I took him out of the cage and brought him back to the boat. He was a little shaken but seems ok."

"So, what about that Kim Hess guy?"

"That's where it gets better." Johnie chuckled. "I called the Sheriff's Department and a deputy met me. He's actually the son of a friend of mine. I explained to him what happened but left out the part about me sneaking into his room. I told him I saw Chief on the balcony and coaxed him to fly down to me. He bought it. Then I told him the man's name and gave him a copy of the surveillance video. So, he went to Emerald Grande to arrest him for theft and trespassing. Once they got to the room, they found him passed out on the balcony face down next to a line of coke and an empty bottle of tequila. The cage door and balcony door were both wide open, so that helped sell the whole 'Chief flew down from the balcony' scenario. I guess Kim pulled an all-nighter—he had a hand stamp from that strip club, Sammy's. He resisted arrest and got an attitude adjustment on the top of his head. Now he's in County with too many charges to list."

"Holy shit, that's quite a story. I'm exhausted from hearing it." Rick ran a hand through his hair, trying to get his breaths back to normal. "I'm so happy Chief is ok. Next time you text me, *Call me ASAP,* and it ends well, please also let me know that on the text as well. I'm gonna need a defib if I get any more messages like that."

"You got it, boss. Chief says hi!"

CHAPTER NINE

When Jules appeared from her long shower, she must've been able to see Rick was distraught, because her eyes widened in concern.

"Oh my God, Rick, what happened?"

"Someone came aboard my boat in Destin and stole Chief. I'm still in shock, I think. The good news is Johnie got him back. It brought back some bad memories from when he was taken before," he told her, trying to hold back his emotions. "I love that little bird."

She hugged him hard. "I'm so sorry! I've never met Chief, but I know how much you love him. He sounds like a special bird."

"Here's to Chief, the bird with nine lives," said Rick.

They pantomimed drinking a toast to Chief. No more words were spoken for several minutes as they looked into each other's eyes.

Rick took a deep breath and exhaled abruptly, wiping away his happy tears. He put his arm around Jules. "Whatever we do today, let's do it in honor of Chief's amazing rescue."

They ordered room service, and Rick did his best to eat, though he didn't have much of an appetite. His nerves were rattled, but tonight, he'd scheduled the night dive so he could approach the Swiss house from the shore, hopefully undetected. It was time to man up.

"Jules, I have to do some solo work tonight on the case, while you are in class."

"Oh, ok. I wish I could go."

"I'd love for you to come, but it's far too dangerous and you aren't ready for a night dive yet. Hell, you haven't even finished class yet."

Jules made pouty lips, then smiled. "It's all good. I'll study hard in class while you're gone."

"Thanks for understanding. You're the best." He kissed her on the forehead.

After lunch, they drove into town. Rick needed a few things he hadn't brought with him on the plane. He bought a jet-black dive skin, booties and a hood, along with a large dry bag and some black latex gloves.

Jules raised an eyebrow at him. "You robbing a bank?"

"No, but I will be committing B&E tonight, breaking and entering," whispered Rick.

Her eyes got wide and her mouth made an "ooh" shape.

Rick winked at her. "All in a day's work, my dear."

"Please be careful," she said. "Promise me."

"I always am."

The house would surely be locked up and protected like Fort Knox, so he picked up some black spray paint, wire cutters, and gator clips with three-foot wires attached. He started to think of every possible scenario and picked up some carabiners with rope attached to the ends, and then grabbed a can of pepper spray in case he encountered an unexpected guard. At the last minute, he picked up some talcum powder.

"Your butt chafed, Rick?" asked Jules with a giggle.

He laughed. "Yeah, it is...but in a different way," he said, thinking of Chief. Her smile faded and she squeezed his hand in understanding.

They headed back to the resort with all the supplies. It was 5:30 p.m. and today's scuba class was at night, so Jules went straight to the classroom. Meanwhile, Rick returned to their room, filled the dry bag with everything he'd purchased in town, and added his lock-picking kit. After donning his dive skin and booties, he headed to the dive shop to get ready.

Since Curtis was getting the class settled, he just pointed toward the side of the dive shop, where he had placed Rick's rental gear and two eighty-cubic foot aluminum dive tanks.

Rick gave Jules the peace sign as she glanced over at him and smiled. She made her hands into a prayer and then blew him a kiss. Rick approached Curtis and told him, "My friend will be along shortly." Then he put all the gear into a dock cart.

"Enjoy your night dive, Rick. I put a huge floodlight in the bag and an extra handheld, just to be safe. I assume your friend has lights?" asked Curtis.

"Enough to light a football field," said Rick.

"Ok. See ya later."

"Peace out, Curtis."

Curtis closed the door to start class, and Rick pushed the dock cart to the end of the pier. After fastening one tank tightly to his BC, he put on fins and hung his mask around his neck. He glanced back at the classroom as the sun receded beneath the horizon. The door was still closed. Carefully wrapping the second tank with the rope, he fastened it to his waist and put it under his arm, then took a giant stride into the water.

He unhooked the second tank from his waist, secured it tightly to one of the pilings, and opened the valve one-eighth turn to let some air escape. He couldn't return a full tank to the shop; it might arouse suspicion that he had gone diving alone.

Counting his kicks toward the intended target, he turned to face the rocky shore and surfaced slowly, barely peering above the water. He removed his dive gear and attached it to an outcropping of dead coral on the beach.

Like a cat, he made his way to the rear fence of the house. To his relief, the fence wasn't electrified. Slowly, he scaled it and flipped his legs over in a quick motion, landing on the grass facedown. As he looked up, a shadow came toward him fast, growling and barking.

Fumbling inside the dry bag, Rick grabbed the pepper spray. A Doberman leapt toward Rick just as he shot the spray. It hit the animal's face dead center while he was in midair. He yelped and came crashing down inches from Rick, who sprayed him again. The dog yelped once more and rolled on the ground, wiping his eyes with his paws. Rick grabbed one of the carabiners and rope and lashed the dog to the fence before he could bite. The dog, blinded by the spray, couldn't react before Rick stood up and sprinted toward the back door of the home.

He pulled out the can of spray paint from the dry bag and blacked out both cameras. The back door was steel with a security magnet at the top. After pulling out a small, thin magnet and a piece of galvanized steel, he placed the steel gently between the magnet and the door. With his lock pick kit, he made quick work of the handle, and in one quick motion, he opened the door and placed the magnet on the opposite side of the security alarm.

He counted four cameras in the room. Before stepping in, he pulled on latex gloves, then dusted the air with the talcum powder so he could see long, thin lines of laser beams crisscrossing the floor. He gently stepped over each beam. They all began in the far-right corner of the large room. Once he got close to the laser source, he attached a GoPro tripod to the base of a hand mirror with no edge, and in one motion, shoved the mirror in front of the beam. The rest of the beams vanished, and he was clear to black out the cameras.

With all the cameras covered, he removed his hood and exhaled a deep breath. He was sweating under the skin. The small layer of seawater had warmed up and his nerves were raising his body temperature. He needed to calm down and begin his investigation.

The great room with an attached dining area didn't look out of the ordinary. It did, however, look Scandinavian. The hallway to the foyer revealed nothing as he shined his light. Several small bedrooms and a half-bath led to a formal living room. Everything looked normal. Nothing resembling a laboratory came into view.

A large beige rug lay under the dining table, and its far-right corner looked somewhat discolored. Frowning, Rick moved all the chairs to the side and lifted the table off the rug. He rolled back one corner, revealing a trapdoor in the floor. Lifting it up, he stuck his head inside and scanned the basement below for cameras. He counted twelve in total. A wooden drop ladder led to the floor.

His brow furrowed as he considered his options. It would be faster to destroy the hard drive recorder than to try to spray-paint twelve cameras. After dusting the air with powder, which revealed no lasers, he put his hood back on and raced down the ladder to the security recorder. It sat in a recessed, locked cabinet. He pried it open, unplugged the hard drive from the power supply, and ripped out all the RCA cables.

With all the cameras out of commission, he turned on the main lights. His eyes widened in surprise. Around him was a state-of-the-art chemistry laboratory. "Bingo," he murmured. It appeared to be far more advanced than the lab owned by Emily back in Florida, from what she'd told him. Toward the back of the room, he could see a long hallway with two rooms adjacent to each other. Going closer to inspect, he found a Judas spyhole and serving slot on each door. They had large, external sling bar locks. The locks were hanging there but not secured.

Rick removed the lock and opened the door to one of the rooms. In the center stood a hospital-style bed, with an open bathroom and shower, just as Emily had described. He pulled out his phone from the dry bag and took several photos.

Inside the other room across the hall, he discovered a full-blown operating room, complete with surgery lights above the operating table, an anesthesia cart next to a respirator, and a heart monitor machine. It confirmed once more that Emily was telling the truth about her captors changing her appearance.

Back in the main lab, he noticed several computers. They were in sleep mode, so he touched one of the keyboards. The screen came alive, but it required a password to gain access. Instead of trying to crack the password, he simply unscrewed the cases, removed both hard drives, and tucked them into the dry bag.

After taking several photos and video with his iPhone, he began to hunt for any physical evidence that could link Emily to the lab. Under the computers was a large filing cabinet. He scanned through the folders and came across one labelled "HRT." Once Rick opened it, it revealed several research papers regarding hormone replacement therapy and the reversal effects on hair color.

Another folder titled "Radiology" had several X-rays with dates coinciding with Emily's capture time. He held one up to the light and could clearly see hairline fractures in perfect straight lines across the tibia and fibula. In the top right corner, written in grease pencil were the letters "ED BEFORE." and another one read, "ED AFTER." The bone was clean and had no fracture in the first X-ray. In the second image, the fracture was visible.

The images of the femur were the same as the fibula. Written in the top right corner of each X-ray was the note, 2.54 *cm.*

He figured ED must be Emily Davis and he knew that 2.54 centimeters equaled one inch.

They shortened her two inches!

Shaking his head at the absurdity of this situation, he carefully rolled up the X-rays, wrapped them with a rubber band, and put them in his dry bag. Now what he needed was some documentation about the connection between NoahTech and Emily's cancer drug.

After opening every drawer and cabinet in the lab, he discovered a closet behind the lab coats. An Apple laptop sat on a shelf, inside a neoprene zippered bag. He pulled it out and plugged it in. As it booted up, Rick held down the "shift" key and the MacBook booted in safety mode, bypassing the password. Once he'd accessed the documents folder, he hit "Select All," then "Share," then "AirDrop." He opened his iPhone and clicked "Accept." Every document on the MacBook quickly copied to his phone.

There was no doubt they'd know someone had broken in, but they wouldn't know who. He grabbed the surveillance hard drive, tucked it under his arm, and climbed out of the lab. After putting the table and chairs back in place, he locked the door behind him. In full stealth mode, he crept toward the back fence.

The snarling Doberman barked, charging toward him, only to be thwarted by the short rope attached to his neck and the fence. Rick climbed over the fence, far out of reach of the dog, then made his way over to the animal and quickly cut the rope securing him to the other side of the fence. The dog would surely die of dehydration if Rick left him tethered there, and the animal was only doing its job, after all. He cut the cord attached to the carabiner. The dog leapt toward Rick, biting the fence, doing everything in its power to get to him, but it was no use.

After donning his dive gear, Rick slid back into the water with the surveillance hard drive under his arm. The salt water sealed its fate. He dove down and shoved the hard drive deep into a hidden crevice to rust forever.

Once he reached the dock, he untied the second scuba tank, which had bled out of air by now. Slowly, he ascended and scanned the resort. The door to the scuba class was still closed, but class would be over soon, so he loaded his gear and both tanks on the dock cart and rinsed all of it off. He placed the empty tanks in the tank holders and dried off.

Within a few minutes, he heard some commotion from in the classroom and the door opened. Curtis stepped out, looking over at Rick. He waved at him and gave him the thumbs-up sign. Rick reciprocated and walked toward him.

"Where's your dive buddy?"

"He has an early meeting in the morning, so I rinsed off his gear for him."

"Was it a good dive?"

Thinking quickly, he said, "Yeah, it was awesome. We saw an octopus and several squid."

"Oh, that's great. The squid here are like dogs, eh? They love to come up close to you. Those buggers are very curious creatures," said Curtis with a chuckle.

Jules walked out of class and over to the two men. She kissed Rick on the cheek. "How was your dive, mi amore?"

"Muy bien, chica."

"I do my check-out dive tomorrow and then I'll be certified! I'm so excited." She smiled wide.

"That's awesome, babe. I'm starved. You hungry?"

"Yes, and thirsty," she replied, pulling him toward the tiki bar.

CHAPTER TEN

Rick woke up the next morning with a hangover from hell. He was in a bit of a fog trying to remember the end of the night. Jules was still horizontal, as were three bottles of wine on the floor. As his eyes adjusted, he saw the dry bag sitting on the desk. Gradually, it all came back to him.

Moving slowly and deliberately, he slid out from under the duvet and went to the desk, careful not to wake Jules. She rolled over and never opened her eyes.

Piece by piece, Rick removed the contents of the dry bag. He had a lot of new clues and needed to analyze what he'd discovered. He looked at the photos on his iPhone and decided it was a good time to talk to Emily.

He stepped onto the terrace with his iPhone and wireless headphones, and quietly closed the sliding glass door. After dialing Emily's cell number, he realized it was only 6:00 a.m. back in Houston.

"Hello?" said Emily, her voice hoarse from sleep.

"Hi, Emily. So sorry, I forgot y'all are on central time."

"It's ok, Rick. What's up? I was gonna get up soon anyway."

"I have a couple questions for you. I know we talked about it before, but I want to double check some details," said Rick. "Can you describe the room you were held in during your abduction?"

"Sure," she said, but paused for a second or two and took a breath. "It was a large room with a hospital-type bed in the center. I was facing the door. On my left was a toilet and sink and beside it was an open shower with a glass wall."

Rick scrolled through the photos as she described the room.

"Can you describe the door?"

"Um. Well, it had a one-way peep hole on top and a slot to insert food trays below."

"Thanks, Emily. I appreciate the info. Do you remember where that room was located?"

"You mean in the building?"

"No, the town."

"Oh, I assume it was somewhere in Tampa," she said.

"Would it shock you to know that it is in Grand Cayman?"

"Grand Cayman?! I've never been to Grand Cayman," she exclaimed.

"Trust me, you have. You must've been here. You must've been unconscious on your way there and back."

"I was blindfolded when they put me in the room. I remember hearing crashing waves on the beach, come to think of it, when they walked me from the van to the building. I assumed it was near Clearwater," she replied.

"Do you remember smelling anything?"

After a short pause, she said, "Yes, I smelled flowers. They were sweet and floral, similar to *Light Blue*, a perfume I used to wear by Dolce & Gabbana. I've smelled them before but I can't remember the name."

"Could it be jasmine?" asked Rick, remembering noticing jasmine bushes at the Swiss house.

"That's it! Jasmine! There was a restaurant in Tampa I used to go to for lunch a lot called Jasmine Thai. They had two bushes out front. I never thought much about them until I went there at night and they were blooming. The smell stuck with me."

"Well, that makes sense. That means they took you into the compound at night. I'm all over this," said Rick. "I'll be heading to Houston soon and we can rendezvous and go over the case."

"Ok, I'll be standing by. Possum has been taking good care of me. He's so sweet and a great cook, and I'm enjoying being here."

"That's great to hear. I'll let you know when I'll be heading there. Say hi to Possum for me."

"Thanks, Rick. Talk to you soon."

"Bye, Emily."

Rick stepped quietly back into the hotel room and into the bathroom. He grabbed an aspirin and drank a bottle of water. It was close to 8:00 a.m. and Jules still hadn't moved. After he brushed his teeth, he sat down on the edge of the bed. She slowly opened her eyes and cupped her hand over her face.

"Oh, my head," she said with a groan. "I'm never drinking again."

Rick handed her a bottle of water, kissed her forehead, and gave her an aspirin. She popped it in her mouth and guzzled a big bottle of water.

"Much better," she said almost immediately. She sat up in bed. "So, what's the plan for today?"

"I thought we'd head over to the turtle center and be tourists today. Sound good?"

Her eyes lit up. "I think turtles are so cute. Can we pet them?" she asked, just like a little kid.

"I'm not sure, but we'll find out. You want breakfast in bed?"

"Yeah, that'd be great. Just a bagel or something."

Rick walked down to the buffet and grabbed a couple of bagels with cream cheese, two glasses of orange juice, and a giant coffee. Jules sat cross-legged and munched on her bagel, while Rick sat on the edge of the bed.

"You wanna walk over to the turtle center? It's only about a mile and a half away. It's over by the Dolphin Discovery place we went to."

"Sounds good. Maybe the exercise will help with this hangover," she responded.

They each threw on a pair of shorts and a t-shirt and jogging shoes before heading downstairs.

As they walked out of the resort toward the main road, they noticed several police cars stopped in front of the house Rick had broken into the night before.

It hit Rick like a brick in the face. In his hurry to leave the house, he'd left behind his GoPro tripod. *Shit.* He'd worn gloves, so there wouldn't be any fingerprints, but his name and number were stuck to the side of the tripod on a label he had made. A few years back, he had been given a labeler machine and gone on a frenzy putting his name and number on all of his electronics. It was just a matter of time before they traced the tripod to him.

His heart pounding fast, he touched Jules's arm. "Jules, I'm afraid we need to leave. I'll make it up to you."

"What's wrong?" asked Jules, her brow furrowing in confusion.

"You see those cops over there at that house? Well, they are there because of me and they'll be coming soon." He pulled her back toward the resort doors. "I'll explain on the way to the airport. Can you drive the car? I'll book a flight on my phone on the way."

"I'm scared, Rick. Are we in trouble?"

"No, *you* are definitely not, and if we get out of here fast enough, I won't be either."

They ran back to the room and packed their bags as fast as possible. Rick stowed all of the evidence he'd retrieved from the house in Jules's bag, not to put the blame on her but for safekeeping, in case he was stopped.

Outside, they jumped into the rental and Jules took the wheel, Rick navigated for her as he quickly booked two separate reservations to Houston Hobby.

They topped off the tank, dropped the car at the airport, checked in, and made it through security. Rick was starting to breathe normally again. He figured it'd take some time for the authorities to figure out his name and number matched his reservation at the resort.

The plane was only three-quarters full, and they sat across the aisle from each other. "Don't speak to me until we get to Houston," said Rick in a low voice. She nodded in understanding.

The flight attendants did their usual safety routine but only a few people paid attention. The captain gave his flight plan, and soon they closed the main door. Rick let out a sigh of relief. Soon they'd be in the air. He glanced over at Jules and winked.

Without warning, the door opened. Over the PA, a flight attendant said, "Rick Waters, please ring your flight attendant call button."

Shit. It was too late. There was nowhere to run. Rick knew what that meant. Jules looked over at Rick with fear in her eyes. He gave her a whisper sign over his mouth and then made the phone sign with his hands and quickly sent a text to Possum.

Pick up Jules 7:45pm—Hobby

There was no one in his row, so he tucked his phone in the seat back and pointed at it, making sure Jules saw him. He knew she would grab it once airborne.

He rang his call button. Two men in blue came down the aisle and took his arm.

"Come along with us," they said.

Rick didn't look back as they escorted him off the plane. He couldn't. No one on the plane knew he and Julie were together.

As he was handcuffed and taken out of the airport, the plane taxied to the runway.

CHAPTER ELEVEN

When the plane touched down, Jules was a mess. She didn't know what to do or where to go or why she was even in Houston. As she moved toward the main terminal, a smiling man was holding up a sign with JULIANA in big red letters. She immediately knew it was for her.

"Hi. I'm Possum, best friends with Rick. He texted me to pick you up."

"Oh my God, he was arrested on the plane and taken away. I'm totally freaked out. Is he gonna be ok?"

"I know less than you do, Jules, but I do know Rick, and he has gotten himself out of tougher situations, so don't worry. He's quite squirrely. Are you hungry?"

Possum was wearing a RICE University T-shirt, khaki pants, and a pair of green Crocs. He'd never cared much for fashion.

"I haven't even given it a thought, but all I've had today is a bagel, so yeah, I should eat something," said Jules as she rubbed her flat belly.

"Let's hit Pappadeaux, my treat," said Possum.

She frowned. "You don't have to do that. I have money."

"Any friend of Rick's is a friend of mine, so don't think twice about it," said Possum with a wave of his hand.

Possum pulled into Pappadeaux and let Jules out at the front door while he parked. They sat at the bar and he ordered a Pineapple Mule. "Want one?" he asked Jules.

She let out a long sigh. "I said I was never gonna drink again this morning, but after what happened, I'll take a double."

Possum held up two fingers to the bartender and asked for doubles.

"Ok, Juliana, tell me about yourself. You seem to have Rick wrapped around your little finger and that's a rare thing for him."

Jules tried to make small talk, but she couldn't stop worrying in the back of her mind about where Rick had been taken and if he was okay. After her second drink, she started to relax a little.

"I met Rick in St. Croix at the resort I was working at. We seemed to hit off right away," Jules began, with a half-smile.

"Well, you seem to have captured his imagination. I've never known him to be like that," said Possum, wrapping a palm around his glass.

Jules's smile grew and her eyes sparkled. "I can't hide it, Possum. I love him. I really do."

Possum took a deep swig of his drink and smiled back in acceptance. "Ok, are you calm enough now to tell me what happened, Juliana?"

"Call me Jules. All I know is last night, I was in a scuba class Rick had set up for me, and he went on a night dive with some guy he knew in Georgetown."

"Did you meet the guy?" asked Possum.

"No, as a matter of fact, I didn't. I never saw him," she declared.

"Recon!" Possum said abruptly.

"Recon?" asked Jules, raising an eyebrow. "Well, he did say he was doing a B&E."

"Yeah, most likely Rick went on a night dive alone as a cover to get some intel on something. That's when he broke inside. What happened this morning?" inquired Possum.

"We were walking out of the resort to go to the turtle farm and when we got to the main street, we saw a bunch of cop cars at a house a few buildings down from the resort." Her hand shook a little as she recounted the memory. "Rick grabbed my arm and turned me around and said we had to leave and he'd explain later. But he never got the chance." She bit her lip, fighting back tears.

"It's ok, Jules." Possum patted her on the back. "Did Rick give you anything?"

She thought for a minute, then reached into her purse and handed him Rick's iPhone.

"He also put his dry bag in my duffel bag," she said.

Possum took Rick's phone and typed in four numbers. Apparently, he knew Rick's password. He opened the photo app and scrolled through the most recent pictures. It looked like a lab, lots of surveillance cameras, and what appeared to be an operating room.

"Jules, look at this. Do these mean anything to you?"

She shook her head. "I've never seen them before."

"Ok, this must be inside the house he canvassed last night. He must've been worried he'd be found out by the authorities and wanted to leave to protect you. He's like that," said Possum.

They finished their meals. Jules was too upset to have much of an appetite; she barely ate a couple of bites.

"Look, Jules, I know you don't know me well, but trust me," said Possum, touching her shoulder again. "I've known Rick all my life. He'd be furious with me if I put you in a hotel. You are staying with me; you can sleep in Rick's room, as he calls it. It's really one of my spare bedrooms, but he's the only one who really ever stays in it. You're also gonna get to meet the woman who hired Rick in the first place. Her name is Emily and she's super nice."

Jules just nodded in agreement, knowing it'd be futile to argue.

CHAPTER TWELVE

he jail door flung open as they shoved Rick to the floor of the cell. They had already removed his clothing and frisked him, leaving him in nothing but boxer shorts.

"We don't like thieves in Grand Cayman," growled the officer. "Especially ones who steal from such a prominent part-time resident as Dr. Liam Furrer." He slammed the cell door shut.

That got Rick's attention.

Fuck, why did I put the table back over the trapdoor? These dimwits might not even find the hidden room. They think very highly of this guy. He probably donates big money to the policemen's benevolent fund or some other charity for cops.

Rick sat on his cold stainless-steel bed shivering. It felt like his bones were about to crack from the cold. They had the A/C on full blast.

After a few hours of solitary, a man in a business suit entered his cell. Rick had been interrogated in jail before; he knew the drill and was ready for his twenty questions. The man pulled Rick to his feet. "Turn around," he ordered. He handcuffed him and led him to a small room with a table and two metal chairs.

Here we go.

A large two-way mirror covered the wall and a surveillance camera blinked in the far-right corner of the room near the ceiling. A small hand-held recorder lay on the table.

After he sat Rick down, the detective removed the handcuffs as a gesture of goodwill.

"I'm Sergeant Jefferson. Would you like some coffee?"

"How about a cigarette, too?" Rick suggested sarcastically.

The detective gave him a hard look. "There's no smoking. Why were you in Dr. Liam Furrer's house?"

"Who is Dr. Liam Furrer?" Rick asked, seemingly dumbfounded.

"Oh, so you don't know who the doctor is? We know you were inside there; we found a GoPro tripod inside the house with your name on it," said the detective as he slammed his hands on the table, startling Rick.

A younger detective walked in with a cup of coffee, placed it in front of Rick, and smiled.

"Ok good cop, bad cop, I get it," said Rick, trying to sound nonchalant. "So, you found a tripod with my name on it. That proves nothing. That tripod was stolen from my dive bag three days ago."

That stopped the detective in his tracks. His eyebrows rose a little in surprise. He motioned for the other detective to follow him; they both left the room.

Rick sat in silence for several minutes, assuming the detectives were both behind the mirror observing him and listening. The recorder was still sitting on the table flashing.

Rick knew he had already pissed off the detectives and they were flustered. He was getting to them, so he picked up the recorder and began to sing his favorite Texas swing song by Asleep at the Wheel.

"*I saw miles and miles of Texas, all the stars up in the sky,*

"*I saw miles and miles of Texas, gonna live there till I die...*"

Suddenly, the door burst open and the detective ripped the recorder out of Rick's hands.

"Do you want to be handcuffed again?" asked the detective angrily.

"Oh, sorry, I was just practicing for my audition for *Grand Cayman's Got Talent*," said Rick with a grin.

"Look, I don't like your sarcasm or your attitude. We know you were inside that house and we're going to prove it. I want a confession," he said as he reached down and turned off the recorder.

"I will beat it out of you if I have to," he whispered with his back to the security camera.

"Bring it!" replied Rick.

The detective glared at him. But Rick figured he wouldn't dare with the camera still on him.

"We sent the forensic team to the house. If we find one hair matching your DNA, you're going to be prosecuted for this."

"What house?" said Rick defiantly as he sipped on the coffee.

The detective just exhaled in frustration.

Rick knew they would find his DNA at the house. Even though he'd worn gloves and was very careful, it was highly likely some speck of skin or hair had been left behind. He was now working against the clock.

The young detective came in and took the coffee cup from Rick. His DNA would be on the coffee cup. There was no way around that. That was how they would match it.

They stood him up and spun him around, securing the handcuffs tightly around his wrists. It was go-time.

As they pushed Rick back into the cell, the detective slid his foot in front of Rick's and tripped him. With his hands behind his back, he fell to the floor and his face hit the concrete hard. Blood shot from his nose and his eyes watered up.

"Is that all you got?" asked Rick.

"You should be more careful, Mr. Waters. These floors are slippery," the detective said with a sneer.

He helped Rick up and in one motion threw him against the back of the wall, head-first beside the metal bed. The top of Rick's head hit squarely on the cement wall and sent pain shooting down his spine. Lying on the bed, bleeding profusely, he began to laugh. He laughed as loud as he could, almost sounding insane.

This seemed to take the detective by surprise. He slammed the cell door shut and walked away. As Rick lay there bleeding, he knew there was only one course of action. Escape.

His head pounded and he had a hard time sleeping with the handcuffs on all night. It was fifty-nine degrees in the cell according to the thermostat on the wall. So cold it was hard for him to think. The stainless-steel bed was not accommodating, and his entire body was sore from shivering all night. His face was covered in dried blood and his nose was probably broken.

Finally, the detective walked in and uncuffed him without saying a word. He wiped the blood from his face and took the washcloth with him.

About thirty minutes later, a woman dressed in white scrubs walked in with the young detective. They both helped Rick up.

"Hello, I'm Angela, the infirmary nurse. I understand you tripped and fell yesterday," she said.

"Yeah, something like that."

"Well, let's get you to the infirmary and get you all checked out," she said, holding one of Rick's arms while the detective held his other.

"No handcuffs?" asked Rick.

"That won't be necessary," declared the nurse before the detective could answer.

Rick limped and moaned a little as they walked, trying to seem more injured than he really was, hoping they'd let their guard down.

As they approached the sick bay, Rick surveyed his surroundings. The main door, which the detective locked with his key from the inside, led to a hallway halfway between the cells and the interrogation room. The only way out was through the main lobby, presumably full of cops. It seemed futile, but Rick knew in a day or two they'd match his DNA with something from the house. He had to get out of here and off the island before then.

In the corner by the door was a coat rack, with a white lab coat hanging from it. Next to that was a locked cabinet, presumably with all the meds inside.

The nurse sat Rick down on the exam table and carefully looked at his nose. "It appears to be broken. Are you able to breathe through it ok?" she asked.

"Not too bad," replied Rick, "but it is very sore and my head is pounding."

"Let me get you some Tylenol," she said.

She spun around, pulled out a long set of keys on a retractable chain, and unlocked the cabinet. It was Rick's only chance. He didn't want to hurt the nurse; she was kind and gentle, as well as innocent. The detective would have to be taken out, though.

With the nurse's back to him and the detective staring at his smart phone, Rick rushed the guy. Before he could even look up from his phone, Rick slammed him against the wall and pulled his gun out of his vest holster. Holding the gun on the terrified nurse, he elbowed the detective in the gut, knocking his wind out. When the guy reflexively collapsed forward, Rick hammered him on the back of the head with the butt of the gun, knocking him out instantly.

"Don't move or make a sound—I don't want to hurt you," Rick ordered the trembling nurse.

She just stood there shaking, her hand covering her mouth.

"Walk toward me slowly."

She did as she was told.

"Now, get on your knees next to the detective, and hold out your right arm."

As she did so, Rick took the handcuffs from the detective. He clamped one on his limp left wrist and the other around the nurse's right wrist, securing them both to the base of the metal exam table that was bolted to the floor.

Walking over to the medicine cabinet, he pulled out some self-sticking sports tape and wrapped it around the nurse's and detective's mouths.

"You will both be ok, and someone will find you soon enough. Stay calm and I'll be gone before the detective comes to," Rick told the nurse, trying to calm her down.

She nodded in agreement.

Rick quickly put on the lab coat and slipped off the detective's shoes and pants. They were both a couple sizes too big for him, but they'd have to do. He tucked the gun in the pocket of the lab coat and swiped the keys from the unconscious detective's belt.

Slowly unlocking the door, he peeked out into the hallway. No one was around. He stepped out and walked toward the main doorway leading to the lobby. It was now or never.

As he unlocked the lobby door, one uniformed officer looked up at him, then back at his computer. The lead detective was nowhere in sight. Rick nodded to another officer behind the reception desk and walked right out of the jail.

On the key chain, he found a keyless remote. He pushed the unlock button, and a blue Toyota Camry beeped in the corner of the parking lot. Rick got in and took off. One step done. Now, he just had to get off Grand Cayman. Within minutes, every cop on the island would be looking for him.

A walkie-talkie sat on the passenger seat. Rick turned it on, hearing chatter from other cops on the beat. So far nothing was said about an escape. He needed to ditch the car and find a disguise. He had no money, passport, or credit cards; his only option was to shoplift. He was already in plenty of trouble, so what difference did it make?

He pulled onto West Bay Drive, looking for a shopping center, and found a place called the Funky Monkey. Once inside the store, he grabbed several polo shirts, beige slacks, and a pair of jogging shoes. The young girl working behind the counter paid him little attention as he asked her, "Can I try these on?" She merely pointed to the corner of the shop.

Rick walked inside and quickly undressed, then slipped on the slacks and polo shirt and put the shoes on. Pulling the lab coat back over his clothes, he walked out. The girl never looked up. He still needed to ditch the car and get another, so he drove down toward Seven Mile Beach. Stopping in front of a dive shop and resort, he tucked the car in an inconspicuous spot at the end of the parking lot and dumped the lab coat in a garbage can.

As he walked through the lot, he peered into each car, looking for keys. An older brown Mustang with a magnetic dive shop sign on the door was parked beside the shop, and the windows were down. He looked inside and spotted keys in the ignition. It must've been the dive shop owner's car, and the guy was most likely out on a boat dive for several more hours. He peeled off the magnetic signs and threw them in the trunk.

With the gun tucked behind his back and the walkie-talkie on his waist, he climbed into the Mustang and fired it up. He laid the walkie-talkie on the seat and grabbed a pair of sunglasses from the glove box. His eyes widened when he spotted a wallet. Several credit cards and about a hundred bucks in cash were inside.

Rick hated to take it, but he was in a bind. He'd pay the man back somehow, some way.

His mind raced as he tried to figure out how to get off the island. He glanced back inside the wallet at the man's driver's license. His name was James Hebert, and he had dark hair and a beard. He was heavier than Rick, but with a little luck and disguise, he might be able to pull off this guy's appearance. Without a passport, though, he would be screwed. Then he got an idea.

He turned up the walkie-talkie full blast and drove toward the address on the wallet.

He parked a few houses past the address on a side street. He walked slowly toward the guy's home, looking for any signs of life. It appeared to be empty.

Walking around to the backyard, he opened a small gate leading to the pool and backdoor. It wasn't locked—another sign this guy was too trusting. Using an old burger wrapper from the car, he opened the door without leaving prints.

Once inside, he found a messy office. Tons of papers from the dive shop were scattered across the desk, and a laptop with the dive shop logo was sitting idly by in screensaver mode. He tapped the keyboard, and it came to life. No password. Rick shook his head.

He opened several drawers in the desk, looking for a passport. The third drawer he opened revealed a dark red-colored passport with the same name as the driver's license in Rick's back pocket. He snatched it and looked at the photo. In it, the man didn't have a beard and his hair was longer but still darker than Rick's. It might just work. Rick grabbed a small duffel bag in the closet that had James's nametag on it, and threw in some clothes and socks to sell his persona even better at the airport.

With Mr. Hebert's credit card, Rick booked a round trip flight to Houston, hoping not to arouse suspicion with a one-way flight. As he began to leave the house, he heard an APB come across the walkie-talkie.

"A man has escaped the Grand Cayman jail, assaulted a detective, and stolen a car. Be on the lookout for a 2009 Toyota Camry with government plates."

They were looking for him in the blue Toyota, but they weren't looking for James Hebert in a brown Mustang. This would buy him a little time, as long as they didn't set up roadblocks. Rick slipped out the back door and closed it, then hightailed it through the backyard toward the Mustang.

What he needed was some hair coloring. He came to a roundabout and spotted a Cost U Less. Inside, he grabbed a can of instant hair-color mousse, then a baseball cap. A few more miles down the road, he slipped into the men's room at an Esso Fuel. After applying the color that closely matched the photo on James Hebert's driver's license, he ducked his head under the hand dryer and brushed his hair with his fingers until it was completely dry, then got back on the road.

He drove toward the airport on Esterly Tibbetts Highway, avoiding Seven Mile Beach Road, which could have a roadblock. Staying with the speed of traffic and constantly checking his rearview mirror for blue lights, he made good time.

He exited the main road and took a left on Roberts by the airport Post Office. He hoped he was in the clear. Then he noticed the cars were stopped up ahead.

Maybe it's just a traffic backup.

Police cars lined both sides of the main road to the airport. He had no choice but to continue toward the roadblock. His hands were sweating, but he tried to maintain composure. He prayed none of the cops were the detectives.

No such luck. Two cops were looking in both sides of each car and checking IDs. The one on the passenger side was Sergeant Jefferson. Rick ground his teeth together. *Dammit.*

A police cruiser was parked on the shoulder next to the sergeant with the windows down. Rick bent down and picked up the walkie-talkie.

"*Car Mike Bravo 422, are you receiving?*" he asked, making his voice deeper.

The sergeant walked toward the car, opened the door, sat down and picked up his radio.

"*Go ahead dispatch, loud and clear.*"

"*I have a report of escaped suspect on West Bay Drive near the fire station., white male, six foot, two-ten, blond and blue, break—*"

"*No problem. I'm only a couple of K's away.*"

"*Roger 422.*"

Sergeant Jefferson stood up and waved his hand in a circle. "Follow me, boys, he's been spotted on West Bay Drive," he yelled.

All the deputies jumped in their cruisers and peeled out to follow the sergeant.

"Phew!" Rick sighed as the roadblock vanished. He had a free pass to the airport now. After parking in long-term and placing the keys under the visor, Rick walked to the terminal.

He approached the Cayman Airways ticket counter and looked for an agent with a friendly disposition.

"Good afternoon, ma'am. I'd like to check in for the flight to Houston," said Rick.

"Hello, sir, that's the nonstop to Houston Hobby. That flight leaves real soon, but you won't have time to check any luggage," said the agent.

"That's fine. I only have a carry-on."

"Ok. I just need your passport and the credit card you booked the flight with."

Rick handed her his passport and credit card. The woman behind the counter looked at the passport, then back at Rick and the credit card.

"Ok, you're all set, Mr. Hebert. Please head down to gate 30B."

Rick got in line at the security checkpoint—the last thing between him and his freedom. The agent waved him through after he set his duffel on the belt. The scanner alarm rang out, and Rick tensed for a moment. But he forced himself to relax as he held his arms up with his passport in his hands so the officer could scan him.

The officer patted Rick's chest. He pulled a pen from his shirt pocket. "Oops, sorry about that," said Rick with a sheepish smile.

The officer handed it back to him. "Ok, you're all clear. Have a good flight."

"Thanks," he said, as he grabbed his duffel off the belt.

"Phew," he said again aloud as he made his way to the gate.

He boarded the half-empty flight, took an aisle seat, and shoved his bag in the overhead compartment. All the excitement and adrenaline finally came crashing down on him.

The next thing Rick knew, the plane was on final approach. He had slept through the entire takeoff and most of the flight.

After he stepped off the plane, he approached immigration. The bored Homeland Security agent swiped his passport, barely looked up at him, and waved him through.

Wow, that was too easy.

Now he needed a ride.

CHAPTER THIRTEEN

Rick walked down to the baggage level to find the taxi stand. He waved one down and slid into the back seat.

"Where to, Señor?

"Galena Park," he told him. "I don't have the address, but I can direct you by landmarks."

The cabby set the meter and pulled out to the main road. As they approached Galena Park, Rick pointed out the turns until they arrived on Possum's street.

"It's the third house on the right, just past that Chrysler in the street."

"No problemo. That'll be $24.50, Señor."

Rick handed him thirty bucks. "Keep the change, partner."

Walking up to the front door, Rick knocked it.

Possum opened it, and shock widened his eyes. "Rick, how did you get here? Come on inside. I was just about to fire up the grill. You hungry?"

"Yeah, I could eat."

"I've got a mess of ribs and some chicken wings in the fridge. I put some great rub on them last night."

"Sounds great. Let's sit on the porch and I can tell the whole story as you grill. Where's Jules?"

Possum cracked open a beer and handed one to Rick as he took a swig of his own. "She left late yesterday afternoon after I picked her up. She was upset that she had to leave, but said you would understand and booked a flight. I took her back to the airport. She left you a letter in your bedroom."

Rick went straight to his room and saw the note sitting on his pillow. He sniffed it and could smell her perfume.

My Dearest Rick,

I am so sorry I had to leave. I was so torn. I'm worried to death about you and I pray you will be ok.

After we met in St. Croix, I received a job offer for a position in Brazil to study the pink dolphin. Besides being a gaming dealer, I also studied Zoology and Botany in school. I never imagined I would get the position but it's a once-in-a-lifetime chance to do something I love. I almost turned it down to stay with you, but I was afraid I'd be resentful, and it wasn't fair to me or you.

Rick, it's a three-year stint. I'll be staying in the town of Fonte Boa if you ever want to come visit.

Please don't wait for me. I wouldn't expect that. I love you and always will. Please contact me as soon as you can. Until we meet again.

Jules
Xxoo

Rick folded up the letter and stuck it in his shirt pocket. He swallowed hard and tucked it all away in a corner of his mind as he stepped back into the kitchen and picked up his beer from the counter.

"Possum, I got some great intel in Grand Cayman, but I had to circumvent the law a little to get it and I won't be visiting Cayman anytime soon, if ever again."

"You? Circumvent? I can't imagine. Do tell," said Possum, grinning. His smile faded after a moment. "I'm sorry about Jules. She told me before she left. I'm really sorry, man."

"Hey, we've all got to make a living, right? I'm actually happy for her. I will miss her, though."

Rick told him how he had escaped jail and snuck out of Grand Cayman on another man's passport, including all the details of his amazing trip off the rock. Possum took it all in stride, as he was getting used to Rick's adventures beside and between that law.

"I need to FedEx this guy's stuff back to him tomorrow. I'm going to repay him, with interest, too, and leave him a note about his car at the airport parking garage. His carelessness saved my ass, but I'm no thief and I'm grateful he was so trusting with his keys and wallet. Maybe we both learned a lesson," said Rick with a chuckle.

"Do you think they'll come after you here, in Houston?" asked Possum.

"I highly doubt it. I think they're too embarrassed to follow up and will probably file my report away somewhere in hopes I return one day."

"You're probably right."

Possum piled the ribs in a pan and covered them with foil as he flipped the wings and sipped on his Lone Star.

"Any update on Emily?" asked Rick.

"Oh, yeah. After I took her to that hypnotist, she recalled a little more than before. Let me grab the file. It's on my desk."

"Where is she now?"

"She's in town. She said she needed some stuff from Office Depot, so I gave her my truck."

"How's she doing?"

"I think, all things considered, she's holding up well."

"That's good. When will she be back?"

"She should be here shortly. I asked her to grab some potato salad and a case of beer."

"Great. We can all get on the same page during dinner."

Rick read through Emily's notes as Possum tended to the wings. The case was moving along now, and he was beginning to see a pattern develop between Emily's story and the intel he'd gotten in Grand Cayman. She was definitely onto something big in her lab, and whoever had killed her husband wanted it bad enough to commit double homicide. There were still many pieces of the puzzle to put together, but Rick had a better grip on it now. He hoped after speaking with Emily it would make more sense and he could begin to get closer to solving it.

Emily arrived twenty minutes later. It was perfect timing, as Possum pulled the last of the wings off of the grill. They smelled like heaven. Rick's stomach was growling.

"Hi, Emily, how are you?"

"Hi, Rick." She smiled. "We weren't expecting you. I'm doing well. Possum is an awesome host and I feel right at home here."

"He is an awesome host. Wait until you see these ribs he made!"

"Wait until I tell you what I remembered while sitting at a red light!"

Emily, Rick, and Possum gathered around the old, hand-carved hardwood dining table Possum had picked up on a trip several years ago down in Matamoros. A colorful bull-fighter on velvet painting sat behind Possum at the head of the table.

He raised his glass of wine, and began:

> *"There are good ships,*
> *and there are wood ships,*
> *The ships that sail the sea.*
> *But the best ships, are friendships,*
> *And may they always be."*

"Cheers!" replied Rick and Emily in unison as they all clinked their glasses.

Possum had taken quite a shine to Emily. Rick could see it when he looked at her. And why not? He was single and Emily was widowed. He didn't see anything wrong with it.

As they all chowed down, Rick mumbled to Emily, mouth full, "Spill the beans on what you remembered."

"Well, I had just left the grocery store and I was sitting at a stoplight. It was an excessively long light and there was no cross traffic whatsoever. I was getting frustrated and about to run the light because I thought it was broken. That's when it came back to me—I remembered that when I was in my prison of sorts, one of the nurses would often come in and put an eye mask on me. It was hooked up to a wire, and this bright red light would come on and a series of loud subliminal messages would play in headphones attached to the eye cover."

"What did they say?" interrupted Possum.

"That's not the important part, but they said, *Your name is Patricia Benning, from Mobile, Alabama,* over and over. I guess they were trying to brainwash me into believing that's who I was. What they didn't know is that I reached down the cord attached to headphones and found the volume knob, and I turned it down low so I could hear what they were saying. They assumed the headphones would drown them out. I distinctly recall them saying something about the surgery being a success and the cancer drug being on schedule."

She sighed, clutching her wine glass. "Rick, I was going to release the drug to all drug companies for free. It would've changed the world. Now, only the richest of the rich would be able to afford it. It's a tragedy!" She took a long sip of the drink.

Rick swallowed the piece of rib he was chewing on. "I agree. We have to stop them."

Emily nodded vigorously. "Exactly! This drug could save millions of lives. It's the cure for all cancers. Everyone should have access to it. The big drug companies can keep making money on Viagra and hair loss creams, as far as I'm concerned, but this is too important!"

Something occurred to Rick just then. "Wait, how will they use a faux Emily to announce the launch of the drug if Emily is you, and you are wanted for questioning about a double homicide?" he asked.

"I can't figure out that part, but we need to find this other Emily and stop them before it's too late," she replied.

The idea of a company using what was essentially a clone, albeit in reverse, since they'd actually changed the real Emily to look like someone else, was beyond comprehension. Big Pharma had always been considered to operate on the fringes of the law, out for one thing and one thing only: profit. But generally, it was squeaking by the FDA or fudging the truth of some of the side effects of some new hair-growth drug. This, though? This was straight up immoral and illegal.

Rick needed to get inside NoahTech. Their headquarters were in Escher Wyss, on the outskirts of Zürich. To accomplish this, Rick would need to come up with a plan to meet with the head honcho.

"Emily, what can you tell me about Liam Furrer? What makes him tick?" he asked.

"He's an incredibly brilliant scientist and chemist, not to mention a ruthless businessman who will stomp on anyone to get what he wants."

"What about him personally. Does he have a weakness? Drinking? Women? Anything you can think of?"

After a thoughtful pause, Emily said one word: "Ego!"

"Ego?"

"Yes, he loves to talk about himself and brag about what he's done or what he's going to do. He hates to share a new find with any other scientist, and rumor has it, he paid off a couple of fellow chemists and then fired them so he could take sole credit for several of the new drugs NoahTech developed. He has framed magazine covers in his office with his own picture on them from interviews he has done. He's been on the cover of the New Yorker and Bloomberg. I also know he aspires to be known for his wealth and wants to be recognized for it."

A lightbulb went off in Rick's head.

"Do you think he would meet with me if I posed as a journalist from some business magazine? Maybe interview him in his office and hire a photographer to accompany me?"

"I can almost guarantee it!" replied Emily.

Rick excused himself from the table and pulled out his laptop as Emily and Possum cleaned up and did the dishes. Rick went to Fortune magazine's website and looked up the writers, and clicked on each man's name until he found one who slightly resembled himself. His name was Michael Compagno. His goatee was a little gray, but his height and weight looked close enough to Rick's that he thought he could pull it off. He then went to a website for photographers in Zürich. He found a couple who had done magazine shoots before and fired off some emails to inquire on their fees. It was almost 9:00 p.m. in Houston and Zürich was seven hours ahead. Calling would be useless, so he decided he'd touch base with Liam via email.

"Emily, can you come back to the dining room?"

Emily was drying her hands as she stepped back in. "What's up?"

"Do you have a contact email for Liam in Zürich?"

"Yeah, that's easy. It's liam@NoahTech.com, simple as that."

"Does he personally monitor his email?"

"Oh, yes, he's a micromanager and workaholic. He rarely delegates. He likes to be hands-on for everything. He does have a secretary to screen his calls and schedule meetings, but I know he often emails back rather quickly."

"Thanks, Emily. I've set the trap. Are you sure he'll bite?"

"Hook, line, and sinker!" replied Emily.

He smiled. "I have his secretary's email, too; you might want to CC her. It will look like you did your homework."

"Good idea. What's hers?"

"It's LaraA@NoahTech.com. Her name is Lara Aebi."

Rick needed a Fortune.com email. That would seal the deal. He found a website that generated false email addresses for any company. For $8.99 a month he could create Michael_C@fortune.com. The game was on. He took his time creating the email for Liam, including plenty of compliments and a list of achievements he was known for. He typed it up in Word, then showed it to Emily for proofreading.

Dear Mr. Furrer,

My name is Michael Compagno. I am a senior writer for Fortune magazine. I would like to request an interview with you for the cover story of April's issue. We are a doing a story on Europe's Top Ten people to watch in business. Your name is at the top of the list. Since you were already featured in The New Yorker and Bloomberg, you appeared on my radar and once I read more about you, I was beyond intrigued to meet you and hear what makes such a brilliant scientist/businessman tick. What you have done in the field

*of cancer research is nothing less than spectacular. If
this interests you, please reply and I can come to you.
I will be bringing a photographer with me and I have
the go ahead from the editor-in-chief to use your image
on April's cover.*

Sincerely,
Michael Compagno
Senior Writer – Fortune Magazine

"How's that?" he asked. "Anything I should add?"

She read the email aloud, then commented, "I would add that you are especially interested in his car collection. It will get you into his house. He has a lab in the mansion and my guess is any uber-classified info is held in a safe in his private lab."

"Done."

Rick finalized the email and sent it off. He checked his Sent email, and when he hovered over the email address, it still read Michael_C@fortune.com. It was the best $8.99 he'd ever spent.

Now all he had to do was wait.

CHAPTER FOURTEEN

Possum invited Rick onto the back porch for an after-dinner Cuban and cognac. Emily headed off to bed, leaving the boys alone.

Rick sipped on his cognac and filled Possum in on his plan to interview Liam.

"How'd you like a travel partner, Rick?"

"You wanna go? I could use someone to watch my six."

"I can be your driver," Possum suggested. "They drive on the same side as we do here in the U.S., but the roads are probably about as easy to navigate as London's. The villages in and around Zürich are medieval. They weren't designed for modern traffic. Not to mention I have 450,000 air miles on my American Express card that are getting close to expiring. We may as well go first class!" announced Possum as he raised his glass in a toast.

"Ok, I'm down!" Rick clinked his glass against Possum's. "But what about Emily?"

"What about her?"

"It's too risky for her to go, but do you think she'll be ok here alone if we both go?" So far, it didn't seem like NoahTech was keeping tabs on her, not thinking her a threat to them now that they'd changed her identity and framed her for murder. But that could change.

"Rick, she is one of the most confident, savvy women I've ever met," said Possum. "Not only will she be ok here; she will insist on it. After all she went through in the kidnapping and murder of her husband, it amazes me how together she is mentally. She's already figured out the lay of the land here in Houston and is comfortable driving in the area. She will be a great help to us if we need more intel on Liam and will only be a phone call away in the safety of my home here."

"You're right, Possum. She does seem to have it all together."

Rick's phone chirped, and he glanced down at it. "Holy crap, it's Liam. He replied already. It's almost 5:00 a.m. in Zürich. He's either burning the candle at both ends or a very early riser."

He read the email aloud to Possum:

Dear Mr. Compagno,

I indeed would be pleased to be interviewed for your magazine. My secretary Lara will be in touch with you for a date that works for us both. Expect to hear from her later today. She will email you with the possible dates and you may speak to her to finalize the details. My office number is in the signature below. I look forward to meeting you and your photographer.

Sincerely,
Liam Furrer
President, NoahTech

"We caught a fish, Possum!" declared Rick. "Do you still have that camera you told me about?"

"The Canon 80D?"

"Yeah, the one you bought yourself with all the accessories last year."

"You betcha. I'm getting pretty good at using it, too. I added several lenses since I bought it. Why?"

"Well, I was gonna hire a local photographer in Zürich for the photoshoot, but since you're tagging along, do you think you can pull double duty as a driver and photographer?"

"Oh, yeah, I can swing that." Possum grinned. "I just got a new backpack case for all of it. I can carry it on board. It's quite impressive, and Liam will never know I'm really just a retired professor. I'll be Stefan, staff celebrity photographer. I think I can still do my theatrical persona."

They both laughed and clinked their glasses again.

Rick quickly responded to Liam's email and said goodnight to Possum. Tomorrow was going to be a big day, and he wanted a good night's sleep.

Possum retired to his bedroom as well and soon the entire house was quiet and everyone was off to dreamland.

The next morning, Rick awoke to an email from Lara.

Dear Mr. Compagno,

Mr. Furrer has informed me of your request to interview him. I also saw the CC you sent.

Mr. Furrer is a busy man, but he can open up his schedule at the end of the week if that will work for you and your crew. Can you be here by Thursday? We can have a car sent to the airport and you can stay in the company suite in Escher Wyss. It's a three-bedroom on the top floor of the E2A *Towers, walking distance to NoahTech. It should suit your needs for your stay. Feel free to add a few days over the weekend for sightseeing. Mr. Furrer will have a driver for you and would like to have you over for brunch at his château on Saturday. I look forward to your correspondence.*

Sincerely,

Lara Aebi

Executive Assistant to Liam Furrer

Rick stepped into the kitchen, drawn by the smell of fresh Community Coffee and Possum's famous biscuits and gravy.

"Morning, Possum."

"Morning, Rick. Want a cup of java?"

"Damn straight! I have good news and bad news. The good news is, we are going to Switzerland. The bad news is, we have to leave by Wednesday, so we're gonna need new passports with our new names. Do you know anyone?"

Possum grinned and said, "I know a guy who knows a guy. And I couldn't sleep last night, so I went to the Amex website and checked flights. The weekends were blacked out or sold out, but I did see some first-class seats available for the middle of the week. As soon as we finish breakfast, I can book them for Wednesday. I already told Emily we were heading there soon, and she was fine with it. No time like the present, they say."

Rick sipped on his coffee as Emily came into the kitchen.

"Good morning, Rick," she said with a sleepy smile. "Possum filled me in on your flight plans to Zürich."

"Yeah, do you think we can go over anything else you can think of about Liam that might help me?" asked Rick.

"Sure, sounds like a good plan."

They all ate breakfast on the patio, and then Possum cleaned up while Emily pulled her chair closer to Rick's. She began to tell him about the times she had met with Liam and what she knew of his habits and routine.

"He's a tall, thin man but in great shape. He jogs at least five miles a day every morning at 6:00 a.m. like clockwork. If you need to make sure he's not home, that's your best timeframe. He lives alone but has several servants who live in a cottage at the back of his property. His security will probably be high at the château, especially in the lab. He keeps a video log of everything, including a time-stamped log of every time his security key code is entered. I spent two weeks there working with him and Hans on an immunotherapy drug that never really worked; that's where I got the original idea for the treatment I finally created. Liam gave up and said I was off-base on my theories. At that point, I kept working on his strategy, but I guess he got tired of using his code every time I needed to be in the lab, so he made me a temporary one. I doubt it still works, but you never know. It's 6776. I memorized it right away. Probably because I used it so many times, plus it's a fairly easy number to remember, I guess. I was born in '67, so I just inverted it to make it easy."

Rick stored the code in his iPhone notes app. He also doubted it would work, but there was only one way to find out.

"I left on good terms with Liam, and shortly after that I heard he and Hans had a falling out," Emily continued." When I met with Hans a couple years later in Tampa, I assumed he wanted to catch up on my trials and fill me in on what he'd been up to. I had shared several emails with him on the efficacy of my new drug. That's the day he was shot and I was drugged and kidnapped. My guess is Liam hacked Hans's email. I wouldn't put anything past him."

"Well, I hope to find out more about Liam shortly. This time Thursday, Possum and I will be in Zürich."

"Rick, how many days will we be needing for the trip?" Possum hollered from the other room.

"Let's land on Thursday and head back Monday. Is that available?" Rick yelled back. "Excuse me," he said to Emily before heading to Possum's office.

"Well, what's the deal?" he asked.

"We're booked for a Wednesday flight on Lufthansa from Houston Intercontinental to Zürich with a stop in Newark, first-class, landing Thursday and returning to Houston on Monday."

"Ok, we better pack then. Emily, in case we get side-tracked and have to stay longer, feel free to head back to Destin. You can stay on the boat with Johnie."

"Ok. Thanks. I'll be fine. If I do leave, I promise to stay there."

Rick went straight to his room and began to pack for the trip. He had stayed at Possum's so many times before that he'd kept a few changes of clothes in the closet. Business clothes and a few pairs of jeans—in case they would have time to tour—went into his carry-on suitcase. In his backpack, he loaded electronics and his MacBook Pro. He needed business cards, and fast, so he went online and found an Office Depot nearby. He created cards with the down-loaded Fortune magazine logo and his new assumed name, Michael Compagno, and even added a toll-free number he got from Google that would go straight to his voicemail. He quickly changed his voicemail greeting.

Hi. you have reached Michael Compagno, senior writer for Fortune magazine. At the tone, leave your name and number and I'll get back to you. You can also email me at michael_c@fortune.com. Thanks.

Setting his phone down, he smiled. He had covered all his bases. His cards would be ready later that day and he'd pick up a few more supplies at Office Depot to make him look more like a journalist.

When he arrived at Office Depot, he picked up a yellow notepad, some good quality pens, and two of the latest issue of Fortune magazine. He opened the front cover and saw his name—his new name—Michael Compagno. It made him smile. He wondered what the real Michael Compagno was like and how he'd feel about Rick taking liberties with his name and title. He'd never know, anyway, as the story would never come out.

As he was checking out, his phone rang. It was a +41 43 country and area code.

"Well, hello, Ms. Aebi, this is Michael. How are you doing today?"

"How did you know it was me?" she asked.

"Well, I don't get too many calls with a +41 country code, and Mr. Furrer said I'd be hearing from you. I assume you got my email and our flight information?"

"Yes, I did. I have you booked in the apartment and a town car arranged for you for the entire weekend. Will you be able to attend dinner with Mr. Furrer? He has arranged a small car show at his château with some of his friends in Zürich. Can you attend that as well?"

"Yes, thank you! My schedule is free and I'm looking forward to the day. Would it be all right if my staff photographer joins me?"

"Mr. Furrer will be expecting you both. I'm sure he wants to do a photo beside his new Bugatti. He had it custom built and it's trimmed in twenty-four karat gold. It's truly a sight to behold," boasted Lara.

"Tell Mr. Furrer we'll be there and we are mighty grateful for the invite."

"Do I detect a southern accent, Mr. Compagno?"

Rick had forgotten to watch his southern idioms. "The magazine is headquartered in New York, where I reside, Ms. Aebi, but I'm originally from Texas and I've been down here a couple of weeks doing a piece on a Texas oilman. I guess my old accent reared its ugly head again, being down here with all these good ol' boys," he replied quickly.

"Well, I find it quaint. I do hope we get to meet when you are here. I've never met anyone from Texas."

"You can count on it, ma'am. We'll be seeing ya real soon."

"Fine, Mr. Compagno, have a nice day. *Auf Wiedersehen.*"

"Goodbye."

Rick was glad he had done a quick study on a few common Swiss German phrases. He knew *Auf Wiedersehen* was goodbye and *Grüezi mitenand* meant hello.

As he put his phone away, he wondered what Ms. Lara Aebi was like and if she could be helpful if he got on her good side. He was off on the right foot, at least. At the checkout counter, he grabbed the perfect gift for Lara: a fridge magnet in the shape of Texas. In red, white and blue, it read: *Don't Mess with Texas.*

CHAPTER FIFTEEN

"What would you like to drink, sir? Perhaps a Bloody Mary or mimosa?" asked the flight attendant.

"I'll have a Bloody Mary, spicy if you can. You, Possum?" replied Rick.

"I'll take a mimosa, light on the O.J., please."

Possum and Rick sipped on their drinks and enjoyed some fancy mixed nuts as the rest of the herd loaded in the back of the plane. It was nice to fly first class again. Rick hadn't flown up front since his days working at Delta Air Lines. He was savoring every minute.

"I must say, Rick, you look quite distinguished with the dyed gray on your beard and temples,'" Possum commented, as he took another swig of his tall drink.

"Call me Michael, Stefan," replied Rick with a wink. We need to get into character.

"Ok, be a soldier!" replied Possum, a.k.a. Stefan, in a vivacious manner, holding up a pretend camera and snapping pictures. His theatricality made Rick nearly spit out his Bloody Mary laughing.

"You're so good at playing that character. But we have to remember, no matter how nice and accommodating this guy Liam is, he is also likely a murderer," Rick reminded him.

"Oh, my goodness, you are so wicked, Rick. Of course, I'll remember."

The connecting flight was on time and before they knew it, they were buckled in and on their way. Next stop, Zürich. Rick watched every video he could on the plane's small screen about the city and tourist destinations.

When the plane landed, they made their way to the main terminal. A tall, blond-haired man stood at the exit with a handwritten sign that read *Michael Compagno*. The man had a thick accent as he escorted Rick and Possum to the town car. He spoke a mixture of broken English and Swiss German that was hard to understand, but they got the gist.

"Grüezi, Härr Compagno. Is this your first time in Zürich?"

"Hi, yes, it is. Neither of us has ever been here before," Rick responded. "I'd like to exchange some money. Can you take me to a place with the best rate?"

The man thought for a minute then said, "Ummmm, ja, there is a bank on the way to the corporate apartment. I will drop you and wait by the entry."

The man handed Rick a card with his cell number on it as they stepped into the limo.

"I am here for you twenty-four seven, for motorcar use. Ring anytime."

"Vielen Dank."

"Du sprichst Deutsch?"

"No, not really. I only know a few phrases."

The man nodded in the rearview mirror as he put the car in gear and pulled out of the airport onto the A51 bound for Escher Wyss. Rick and Possum took in the scenery as the car headed south on the A51. As they approached Opfikon, the beautiful roadway became a tunnel with a park above. The cleanliness of the city was something to behold.

Euro-styled wooden benches sat in perfect lined order beneath the broadleaf beech trees. Everything seemed so perfect, everything in its place.

The driver pulled up next to the Credit Suisse Bank just off the toll road. Rick and Possum stepped out and inside the beautiful bank. The both exchanged five hundred US dollars for Swiss francs. The colorful tender seemed like monopoly money to the two Texas boys.

Once they arrived at the corporate apartment, they checked in and put their luggage away, took showers, and made a plan to do a little sightseeing after they made contact with Liam. A huge gift basket sat waiting for them on the main dining table, with a note inside.

Dear Mr. Compagno,

I hope you had a pleasant flight. Please enjoy the wine and fruit I have provided. I took the liberty of making you a reservation at my favorite restaurant, Grüntal Zürich, tonight at 7:00 p.m. in Escher Wyss. You must try the schnitzel. It's the best in the city. I will be unable to attend and if you prefer to make other arrangements, please contact my assistant Lara at the number below. I have scheduled our interview for 10:00 a.m. Friday if that works for you. Please confirm with Lara also.

She has informed your driver of the dinner and meeting
times. Feel free to use the car at your disposal.

Sincerely,
Liam Furrer

"Let's grab some lunch, Stefan."

The sun was warm on their faces and the sky was a stunning, pure blue as they strolled onto the street in front of the
E2A Tower. The district was a mix of residential and indus-
trial. They didn't have any direction in mind and stumbled
upon a take-away Indian restaurant called The Coconut.
Both of them ordered butter chicken with rice, and they ate
in a nearby park. They were feeling jetlagged and decided
to head back to the apartment for an afternoon nap.

Rick laid his head down but couldn't really sleep. He just
stared up at the ceiling admiring the beautiful light fixture
above the bed and the intricate crown molding. He had
dimmed the lights above, leaving just enough to see how to
get to the bathroom. As his eyes began to close, he noticed
the lightning-fast flicker of a tiny red LED in the shadows
of the glass surrounding the light fixture. He frowned and
focused harder at the edge of the fixture. A few minutes
later, he saw it again. Intrigued, he stood up on the bed
and unscrewed the small fastener holding the light fixture
in place.

After gently laying the glass on the bed, he inspected the
bulbs. There were three and one was distinctly different. At
first, he thought it was one of those fancy compact fluores-
cents, but after closer examination, he nearly fell backwards
when he concluded what it was—a bug. A tiny condenser
mic protruded to the center of the bulb. Black electrical tape
had peeled back, originally meant to hide the LED light that

he had luckily seen flash, while looking at the right place at the right time. If that tape hadn't peeled back, he never would've known.

In the living room, he grabbed a Post-it note and a pen sitting by the phone. He tucked both into his pocket, then stepped into the shower, making sure the shower head was not bugged as well. On the Post-it note, he wrote in capital letters: DO NOT SPEAK! He tucked it back in his t-shirt pocket and slowly stepped into Possum's room. He woke him up gently, and then put his index finger to his mouth to emulate SHHHH and held up the note. Possum nodded with wide-open eyes. Rick motioned with his head for him to follow him. The stepped outside to the main street and walked a few blocks without murmuring a word until they got to a loud, bustling street.

"The apartment is bugged. I found one in the light fixture above my bed, I'm sure there are more. There's only one way we can handle this, I think. We need to stay in character, accents and everything, amigo, I mean Stefan!"

"I agree, Rick, er…Michael. This will actually help us sell this if we play our cards right. I have an idea. I'm going to text a friend of mine in Houston who is a part-time actress at Playhouse 1960. I'm going to tell her to act like my agent and have her call me to tell me about a shoot I've been offered at a new play on Broadway. She'll know exactly what to do. They will hear my side of the conversation and it will further help prove I'm a pro photographer."

"Great plan, *Stefan*! From now on, we must call each other by our aliases and talk shop about Fortune. There's no way yet of determining if there are any hidden cameras, but I did notice several mirrors that could be two-way. Luckily, there are none in my bedroom, so they have no idea that we know the place is bugged. Let's keep it that way," replied Rick.

Possum texted his friend from the playhouse and explained to her what to do in twenty minutes. Then they headed back to the apartment, grabbing a bottle of Trojka vodka and some club soda at a corner liquor store on the way. Rick poured a couple of glasses and started up a conversation on how excited he was to interview such a brilliant scientist.

"I am uber-excited to photograph Liam!"

"Calm down, Stefan."

Possum's phone rang, and he mischievously answered it with, "Guten Tag!"

Rick listened as Possum spoke to his friend on the other end.

"Oh, that would be fabulous. I'd love to do a shoot on Broadway. Tell them to count me in. I'll be there with bells on!"

After Possum hung up and filled Rick in on the "offer" he'd gotten to shoot a rehearsal on Broadway for an upcoming play, Rick called the driver's number. He confirmed they would indeed be taking Liam up on the reservations and would pick them up at 6:30 p.m. in front of the apartment. It was almost 5:30 p.m. now, so they both got ready and headed to the lobby.

The restaurant was small and quaint, and they were escorted to a corner table on the balcony with bright red umbrellas. Only four tables were on the balcony, but as small as the place was, it was brimming with customers. Everyone was speaking Swiss German, and the menus were in the same language.

A waiter greeted them with water. "Still or sparkling?"

"Oh, you speak English," said Rick with relief.

"Yes, I do. Most of us here do. We don't get a lot of tourists at this restaurant, but occasionally we do, so it is required," he replied.

"We'll have still, please. I can't read the menu; can you assist us please?"

"I'd be happy to. I was informed you are guests of Liam Furrer. He told my manager to take care of you and set you up with his favorites. I'd be happy to explain the menu or, if you prefer, as I suggest, let me have the chef prepare Liam's favorites and you can both just sit back and enjoy the experience."

Rick closed his menu and said, "Let's do the Liam special!"

The waiter nodded, filled up the water glasses, and left the remainder of the bottle on the table. A few minutes later, he returned with two rocks glasses half-full of a bright neon green spirit. He gently laid a spoon topped with one sugar cube across the top of each glass, then poured cold water slowly over the cube as it settled in the mix.

"Wait two minutes, then stir the mixture together and enjoy," he told them.

"What is it?" asked Rick.

"It is Liam's favorite cocktail, the absinthe drip. You won't get another like this anywhere in the city." The waiter leaned in closer and whispered, "We make it in-house, true absinthe with strong thujone or wormwood, as you call it in the States. It used to be strictly prohibited. I wouldn't drink more than three, though, if I were you. You will see green fairies," he warned, laughing.

They both sipped their cocktails, and soon the waiter set a beautifully adorned plate of what he called *Bergplatte*, which he explained was dried meat, mountain cheese and pear bread.

The combination was savory and rich. After a couple more absinthe drips, Rick and Possum were beginning to feel high. Not buzzed like after drinking vodka or whiskey, but more of a high as if they had both smoked a bit of chronic mixed with shrooms. It was a peaceful feeling.

"I'm digging this absinthe. How about you, Possum?" said Rick.

"I feel fabulouuuuusss!" Possum flung his arms high in the air in exhilaration.

Rick just shook his head and tried not to laugh.

Their main course arrived shortly after their third absinthe drip. A huge portion of perfectly prepared schnitzel with an accompaniment of grilled vegetables and french fries, along with a side of rich, brown gravy.

They ate their meals, rarely saying a word. The meal was incredibly comforting, and they were both overcome with a sense of complete peace, if not almost numbness. Permanent smiles were pasted on their faces. They took the waiter's advice and chose not to have a fourth absinthe drip. Why ruin a perfect feeling?

Once back at the apartment, they both said goodnight and prepared for bed. Rick was asleep in no time and began to dream as he never had before, feeling lucid at the same time.

He was having what felt like an out-of-body experience, as if his soul were slowly rising above his body.

As he looked down at himself peacefully sleeping with a smile on his face, he smiled in his dream state, drifted through the walls into the living room, then stuck his face though the mirror adjacent to the dining room table. Inside the mirror was a camera recording his every move. He playfully waved at the camera and made funny faces, knowing his soul was invisible to the recording device. He began to drift out onto the balcony, looked down at the street, and then moved forward to the skyscrapers near the apartment. As if in an instant, he flew toward the building closest to him, then through it, and shot through the roof toward the stars. After breaking through the atmosphere, he remembered a quote from a book by Richard Bach he'd read as a young adult.

"You will begin to touch heaven, Jonathan, in the moment that you touch perfect speed. And that isn't flying a thousand miles an hour, or a million, or flying at the speed of light. Because any number is a limit, and perfection doesn't have limits. Perfect speed, my son, is being there."

He remembered every word as if it were printed on a heavenly sheet of pure white paper. He flew to Mars at the speed of light, then on to Saturn and Jupiter. His flight was perfect, endless, without effort. Another friendly soul drifted in beside him and joined him on his journey. Together they flew from one galaxy to another, exploring each planet and solar system, and then parted ways without uttering a word. Once he circled all of the heavens, he returned to his body, still lying motionless, at peace. Upon reentering his body with a jolt, he began to race through the veins and organs inside himself, exploring every miniscule cell and his DNA. His inner space was as interesting as outer space.

Suddenly, he awoke. It was 8:00 a.m. He had slept ten hours, which felt like an instant, yet he was completely refreshed and rejuvenated. It was something he had never experienced before and he couldn't wait to compare notes with Possum.

Possum was on the balcony sipping a cup of coffee with a peaceful look on his face. Rick looked at him. "Stefan, I had the most amazing experience last night."

"I know. I was there. That was me flying beside you."

They both stared at each other without saying a word, knowing they had both experienced the same event. Was it lucid dreaming brought on by the absinthe, or a true out-of-body experience? Without speaking, they knew what each other was thinking and nodded in agreement. It was *real*, or the perception of it was. It was something Rick would never forget. He knew one thing for sure: he was an instant fan of absinthe.

Their meeting with Liam was at 10:00 a.m. They needed to be sharp. Rick mentally prepared to become Michael from Fortune magazine, while Possum cleaned his camera lenses and checked to make sure all his SD cards were empty and all his batteries were fully charged.

They walked over to NoahTech, which was only a couple of blocks east of the corporate apartment. After checking in with the receptionist, they waited in the minimalist-styled lobby. Soon they were escorted to an office on the top floor.

"Mr. Compagno, it's nice to meet you in person," said the girl behind the desk. "How was your first day in Zürich?"

"Call me Michael. This is my photographer, Stefan. You must be Ms. Aebi. I have something for you." Rick handed her the *Don't Mess with Texas* refrigerator magnet.

Her eyes lit up. She clutched it to her chest as if she were cherishing it. "Oh, thank you, Mr. Compagno. That is so thoughtful."

"Well, I live in New York now, but as they say, you can take the boy out of Texas but you can't take the Texas out of the boy," said Rick with a smile.

She grinned and stuck the magnet to the front of a filing cabinet beside her desk.

"Perfect!" she said. "Dr. Furrer will see you shortly. He's on a call at the moment."

"No worries, Ms. Aebi," said Rick as he thumbed through a magazine on the coffee table.

"Call me Lara, please, I insist."

"Ok, Ms. Aebi. Lara it is," replied Rick. He had a feeling she was charmed.

"Dr. Furrer will see you now."

She opened the door to his office and formally introduced them to Liam.

Dr. Liam Furrer was a tall man with strong Swiss features. His face was thin and his blond hair, parted perfectly down the middle, was collar-length and straight. He reminded Rick of Karl Vreski, the second-in-command villain from the action film *Die Hard*. They could have been twins.

"Welcome, Mr. Compagno. How was your meal last night?" asked the doctor.

"It was perfect, Dr. Furrer. Oh, this is my photographer, Stefan."

They both shook the doctor's hand.

"Please call me Liam. No need for such formalities. May I call you Michael?"

"Of course. It's a pleasure to meet you in person, and I can't thank you enough for taking care of our meal last night, not to mention the absinthe. It was really not necessary."

"It was my pleasure. Did you see any green fairies?"

"Not green fairies, but my dreams were otherworldly," replied Rick.

"Absinthe can do that. Especially from Grüntal Zürich. Theirs is the finest and they always keep a bottle especially for me and my guests. Ok, let's get down to business, shall we?" Dr. Furrer took a seat behind his desk, and Rick and Possum sat across from him.

Rick noticed several small framed photos of Liam sitting on his desk. A tell-tale sign of a true narcissist.

"Would you mind if I record this while I interview you?" asked Rick. "I don't want to misquote you."

"Not at all. Where do you want to begin?"

Rick made sure his recorder was turned on. "Tell me about how you got interested in pharmaceuticals."

"When I was at university, my original plan was to become a medical doctor, but seven years of medical school seemed like an eternity to me. Then I met a fellow who was studying to become a pharmacist. He told me it was a two-year program, and I decided to change my major and minor in business. While studying to become a pharmacist, I realized the science behind pharmaceuticals was more interesting to me than dispensing them, and the future was in developing them, so I switched my major yet again to chemistry."

"Wow, what an interesting journey," replied Rick.

"Yes, it was. Upon graduation, I went to work in a small lab called Bletzwill, where I met a man named Noah Rechsteiner. We became fast friends. Together, we invented several lucrative drugs, which are still on the market today. Noah's family was very wealthy, and he confided in me his plan to buy Bletzwill and bring me in as a partner. He renamed Bletzwill Noahtech, which eventually became NoahTech, and made an initial public offering on the stock market in 1980. Noah owned 51% and we both signed life insurance policies naming each other as beneficiaries, which is standard in business practice. Unfortunately, Noah passed away quite suddenly, just before we were about to merge with a larger company, which now is under the umbrella of NoahTech. He had no family, and in his will, he left me all of his shares. I already owned 22%, so that brought my stockholdings to 73%. After the merger, the stock rose by two thirds, and I became a multi-millionaire overnight. I took over as CEO."

He chuckled, shaking his head as if he still couldn't believe it. "I never had money like that before and now I was CEO of the strongest drug company in Switzerland. I continued my work here at NoahTech, overseeing daily operations."

"How did your life change after becoming so wealthy? Do you have any hobbies?" asked Rick.

"My daily work life didn't change much, but I did buy a castle—I prefer the term château—and I started collecting cars. As a child, we never had money and I always dreamed of owning a fast car. I thought it was out of my reach to own a fancy sports car, but now I could buy anything I wanted, so I did. I built a huge garage next to and under the château and added a private laboratory. I'd love to show you my car collection. I would be pleased if you could attend brunch on Saturday."

"Of course, we'd be honored," replied Rick.

"Come to think of it, I'm having a few good friends over for dinner tonight. Can you attend both?" asked the doctor.

"Sure. Why not?" Rick smiled. "We have no plans other than to interview you and get some photos for Fortune. Stefan would like to take some here and at your château, maybe one in front of your new Bugatti. Would that be ok?"

Liam's eyebrow rose a little. "You really do your homework, Michael. I just received that car a few days ago. It hasn't even left the garage yet. I'm still having the engine modified for maximum horsepower by my car tech. It's quite impressive."

"Would it be possible to view the private lab as well?"

Liam thought for a moment, then said, "Yes, that's fine. I can show you that tonight if you can stop by before the dinner party. But I must insist on no cameras inside the lab."

"Not a problem."

The interview continued for another hour, and then Possum took a few photos of Liam in his office near the window and in the main lab of NoahTech. They said their goodbyes and planned to meet at 6:00 p.m. at Liam's residence later that day.

As they leisurely made their way back to the corporate apartment, Rick and Possum discussed their unexpected good fortune of being able to visit the château a day early. It would give them time to case the lab and hopefully find a weakness in security, so they could do recon for Saturday morning, while Liam was out for his daily jog.

They had one chance to find out the truth behind Dr. Liam Furrer and NoahTech, and that chance was a mere day away. Everything had to go perfectly.

CHAPTER SIXTEEN

Rick called Possum's house from his cell phone in a café near the apartment. Emily answered on the third ring.

"Hi, Emily, we are in. We are having dinner tonight with Liam at his château. With any luck I'll be able to get into the lab tomorrow morning and try to find some evidence about your case. Can you write a small note to me and send it to me in a text so I can match your handwriting to any paperwork in the lab?"

"You won't need to, Rick. Every single finding and paper I've ever worked on has my initials in the bottom right of each page. If you see an *ED* at the bottom, it's my work. What you need to find is a folder or anything labeled C5X. That's the working name I gave to the cancer drug after trials. It has everything in it. I mean, everything. If you can find that, we may be able to beat Liam to the punch and launch the drug for free and share the news with the media. Once the media has it, there will be no way Liam can claim ownership of it."

"That makes sense. I probably have only one shot at this. If I can bypass his security code and get in, and he does get me on camera, is that something he reviews daily?"

"As I mentioned before, Liam is a micromanager and workaholic. This immunotherapy discovery is so big, it wouldn't surprise me if he kept an armed guard in the lab twenty-four seven. He's also a big fan of redundancy. He owns a home, as you now know, in Grand Cayman, and I remembered him saying one time he had always wanted to buy his own island, so I took it upon myself to do a little sleuthing when you left for Zürich. It turns out he has an LLC called DoppeltKreuz that purchased an island in the Keys near Islamorada for fourteen million dollars, known as Terra's Key. I used an aerial photo from eight years ago, then looked at it again this morning on Google Earth. Besides two purple-colored roofs and a large tennis court in the center, there isn't much else on the property. My guess is that under of those purple roofs is a redundancy lab," said Emily.

"You may be right. I'll keep you posted on what happens Saturday. We gotta go for now."

"Ok, Rick. Talk to you soon."

Rick returned to the apartment and joined Possum on the balcony. Pulled the curtains closed behind them, he opened his laptop. He motioned for Possum to come closer so he could see the screen, and typed: LETS TALK LOUD ABOUT HOW GREAT THE MEETING WITH LIAM WAS BUT LET'S TYPE WHAT WE'RE REALLY TALKING ABOUT SINCE THERE ARE NO CAMERAS ON THE BALCONY.

Possum nodded and said, "I can't wait to do the photo-shoot Saturday with Liam and his car collection."

Rick said, "Yeah, he's very successful. It should make for a great article."

Then he typed: LIAM OWNS AN ISLAND IN THE KEYS, WE SHOULD GO THERE NEXT.

Possum nodded again. "I have enjoyed Zürich, but I can't wait to get back to the Big Apple. There's just no place like home."

"That's true, Stefan. I'm excited about getting Liam's interview down on paper and you getting the best portrait of him for the cover of Fortune," replied Rick, then typed: I WANT YOU TO DISTRACT LIAM TONIGHT SO I CAN DO SOME RECON FOR SATURDAY MORNING.

"I agree, Michael. I need to jump in the shower."

The plan was set, and Possum took a shower and got dressed for the evening's event. Rick stayed on the balcony for a while and tried to do some research about the LLC DoppeltKreuz, but he couldn't find anything. He wasn't quite sure how to spell it. He looked up the island Terra's Key near Key Largo and zoomed in on it with Google Earth. What Emily said was right. There looked like a concrete outbuilding just behind the main house. To his surprise, a road from A1A connected the island to the mainland. He pondered how to get there without being seen, then decided using scuba and a diver propulsion vehicle at night would be his safest bet. It had worked in Cayman, so there was no reason it wouldn't work in the Keys.

Then he remembered the photo Marcy Nobles had shown him of her great-great grandfather in the Florida Keys. Rick had signed a finder's salvage agreement with her to find the infamous Fletcher's treasure, and the last clue had led him to believe the treasure could be in the Keys. Maybe he could multitask while there. The prospect of finding the treasure was always on his mind, regardless of what cases he might be working. After all, he considered himself a treasure finder, *not* a treasure hunter.

Closing his laptop, he showered and got ready for the evening. He ironed his nicest collared shirt and slacks and put a pen in his pants pocket. It wasn't a regular pen but a 1080p recording pen, with a 64 GB Micro-SD card for up to sixteen hours of HD video recording storage and a recording battery life of up to two hours. It looked identical to the black Montblanc he usually kept in his pocket that he had received as a gift from a client; the only difference was a tiny pinhole where the camera was situated in the top of the pen cap. It wrote like a regular pen but with a small twist, recording would begin. He was glad he'd brought it on the trip. The stash of tech gadgets he kept at Possum's was turning out to be incredibly useful. He would bring them both, in case he needed to hide one—the recording pen in his right pants pocket and the nearly identical one in his shirt pocket. He would be sure to make the switch if needed.

The car picked them up and drove toward Liam's château. The driveway alone was nearly half a mile behind the gated fortress. Rick took mental notes of any cameras and possible entries he could access the next morning. To his surprise and relief, there were no dogs on the grounds. The gate used a key code—4376—that Rick surreptitiously observed the driver punch in. That was one step out of the way. He knew how to get in, at least, but getting out might be a different story.

"Do you work fulltime for Dr. Liam?" Rick asked the driver, keeping his voice casual and friendly.

"Yes, he pays me very well. I must be available twenty-four seven for him or any guests. He lets me keep the town car at my residence. He has many guests and usually insists they use his car service. He's a very kind employer."

"Have you lived a long time in Zürich? Oh, I'm sorry, I never got your name. What do they call you?"

"My name is Luca Muller, and no, I don't live in Zürich. I live in Opfikon, which is a suburb of Zürich. We passed it on the way to from the airport to the apartment."

"Oh yeah, I remember that place—the place with the tunnel and beautiful park on top."

"Ja, I live right next to that park—actually in a townhome owned by Dr. Furrer."

"Oh, that's nice. Do you ever get any time off?" asked Rick.

"He usually gives me Saturday and Sunday off, but I'm always on call."

"I see. Sounds like a good job. Do you enjoy it?"

"Ja, I do, very much. I usually go hiking with my kids on Saturday, but I need to pick you up this Saturday for the brunch," replied Luca.

"Tell you what, Luca. I will talk to Liam and tell him I won't need your services Saturday. I planned on renting a car and we wanted to do some exploring before the brunch, anyway. I know you can drive us, but I love to drive. Consider taking the weekend off, unless you have other clients for Liam."

"That is so kind of you. You don't have to do that. It's my job."

"Spending time with your kids is more important than any job. Consider it a done deal. I can be pretty persuasive, and I'm sure Liam won't mind. I'll speak with him over dinner and let you know on the ride back to the apartment tonight. Sound good?"

"Thank you so much, Mr. Compagno. I'm grateful for your offer. I missed hiking last Saturday because of work, and my kids were disappointed but understood. If this works out, I can make it up to them."

The car pulled up to the enormous château. The grounds were immaculate with lots of shrubs and flowering plants. The cobblestone drive was trimmed in yellow and purple ground cress and thyme, and the entire estate looked like a botanical garden. Once Luca let them out, Rick made a mental note that he'd backed the car under a vine-covered carport. He had an idea and would get Possum up to speed after the dinner party. It would be risky but might just work.

Rick and Possum stepped up to the opulent, hand-carved wooden front door, expecting a butler to open it. But before he could ring the bell, the behemoth door opened and Liam stepped out to greet them.

"Welcome to my humble abode," said Liam, sporting a red smoking jacket.

"Humble abode? This is the biggest abode I think I've ever seen," Rick said with a chuckle. "You must have a big live-in staff."

Liam gestured for them to come inside. "No, I like to live alone. I have house cleaners who come a couple times a week, and of course Luca, my trusted driver. But I love to cook, and I prefer my privacy, so I have no live-in servants or butlers in the main house. I do have caterers come in for special events when I have guests, and I do have some groundskeepers in the guest house behind the château. But in here, it's just me and my ugly cat, Felix."

Behind Liam walked a hairless Sphynx cat that intertwined himself in and out of Liam's legs.

Rick smiled. "Oh, he's not ugly, just different."

"I know. I'm just joking. He's a lovely cat and a good companion. Let me show you around before the rest of the guests arrive."

"Sounds good."

Liam pointed out of some the art he had collected. He had a few original Van Goghs and one Picasso. Rick was impressed.

"I can't believe you own a Picasso," he said, walking closer. "I don't even wanna breathe on it."

"Don't worry, it's a lithograph," said Liam with a wave of his hand. "I keep the original in a temperature-controlled high-security vault in Zürich. I bought them all as an investment."

"Ah, good plan. Still quite impressive."

"Vielen Dank."

"You're welcome."

"Now you must see my wine cellar. Besides my car collection, it's my most prized possession. It also leads into my private lab; I sometimes like to mix business with pleasure. You want to see something impressive?"

"Heck yeah!" replied Rick. He fought his instinct to share a look with Possum. This was already going better than he'd hoped.

At the corner of the massive wine cellar, Liam pulled out a bottle of red wine. An automated door opened, revealing another steel door with a key code device on the side of it.

"I don't mean to be rude, Michael, but I need you both to turn around so I can enter the code to show you my private lab. No cameras inside either, Stefan. Sorry."

"No problem Mr. Liam," said Possum as he set his camera bag on the ground next to the large selection of Bordeaux.

"Oh, I almost forgot again," said Rick. "I have a gift for you. I meant to give it to you at the office, but I left it on my nightstand this morning."

Rick reached into his pocket and, with a quick twist, activated the spy pen and handed it to Liam. "It's a Montblanc pen, identical to one given to me when I did a story on a celebrity for Fortune."

As Rick handed the video pen to Liam, he pulled out his own Montblanc to divert Liam's attention from the video pen. He simultaneously placed the spy pen in Liam's smoking jacket as he explained how his own pen stayed tight in his shirt pocket because of the quality of workmanship. Liam pulled the spy pen out of his pocket to admire it more, but Possum deflected his attention.

"How many bottles of Bordeaux do you have here, and which one is the oldest?" asked Possum.

Liam stuck the video pen back in his pocket, thanked Rick for the gift, and began to brag to Possum about his massive wine collection.

"I have one hundred and fifty-six bottles of Bordeaux, and the oldest one is a Château Mouton Rothschild Pauillac Red Bordeaux Blend 1945. It cost $38,000. Would you like to indulge in a glass?"

"Are you serious?" asked Possum, looking rather shocked by the suggestion.

"Why not? I'll bring it out with dinner tonight. This is a special occasion, after all. It's not every day I get asked to be on the cover of Fortune magazine. Ok, again, my apologies. Please turn your backs. No offense, but I need to key in the code for the lab. It's only known by myself and I intend to keep it that way."

"No offense taken," said Rick as they both turned around.

Rick said a secret prayer that the angle of the spy pen would catch the code. All he'd have to do was switch out the pens sometime during dinner. He hated to give up his five-hundred-dollar Montblanc pen, but it had to be done.

Rick heard a beep as Liam input the code, then pulled open the heavy steel door.

"Follow me," said Liam.

The lab was glistening with clean white walls and a shiny white tile floor. Several islands with Bunsen burners sat in the center surrounded by ample workspace, with everything from spectrometers and microscopes to shelves full of glassware and crucibles. A single white lab coat hung on a rack near the entrance. Rick counted four hard-wired cameras. The wires ran along the edge of the ceiling into a closet that most likely held a hard drive. He didn't see any Wi-Fi antennas on the cameras, which was good because that meant they were only feeding the hard drive and not an additional storage space in the Cloud. He didn't see any file cabinets and assumed they were behind the closed door where the surveillance camera hard drives probably were.

"This is my happy place. I still work often in the lab at NoahTech with other chemists and scientists, but if I'm working on a pet project, it's done in here. I have no distractions in my private lab," Liam explained. "I will be making a big announcement of a new development soon. Maybe in time for your Fortune piece. I'll still working out the business side of the new drug with a few investors."

"I'm impressed, Liam," said Rick, looking around. "Your private lab is nothing short of spectacular. You must be very proud of your accomplishments."

"It's not a modest lab, that's for sure. It's up to par with the lab at NoahTech, with the exception of fewer centrifuges. Since I usually only work on one new drug at a time, I only need the one," replied Liam, pointing at it.

"What's behind that door?" asked Possum.

"That's where I keep my folders, main computer, and safe. It stays under lock and key, and I keep the key with me at all times."

Liam pulled a chain out from under his shirt, revealing a gold key. Rick studied the doorframe of the room and the dead bolt. He knew it would be nearly impossible to get that key from Liam, so he'd have to devise another way in. If he could get his hands on a W-Tool, similar to what firemen used to open car doors after an accident, he would be able to spread the door jamb apart and gain entry. The problem was he needed to get his hands on one before 8:00 a.m. tomorrow. He was going to need to borrow one from a firehouse. There was no other way.

"Now that you've seen my happy place, do you want a quick peek at my pride and joy?" asked Liam, his eyes sparkling.

"Sure, what's that?" asked Rick.

"Follow me and you shall see."

Liam walked to the farthest wall and made Rick and Possum turn around again as he keyed in a code to a door.

"This is the fun part," said Liam. He opened the door, revealing a silver pole.

"After me," said Liam as he wrapped his arms around the pole and slid down to the floor below. Rick and Possum followed and landed below in a room full of vintage and newer-model sports cars: Ferraris, Lambos, several Porsches, and a gold-trimmed Bugatti.

"This is my collection—my pride and joy," Liam declared, as he reached for a set of keys on a rack full of other keys and pressed a button. Both doors of the Bugatti opened upward like something out of a Batman movie. "Do you want to hear her purr?"

Possum clapped his hands. "Yes, please!"

"I'd like to do a photo here tomorrow. We can open the garage doors to let in the light from the vineyard. I think if you shoot me here with the vineyard diffused, it will be a stunning photo for your magazine. I will wear my lab coat as well in the shot. How does that sound, Stefan?"

"I love that idea," said Possum, holding his hands in a square U-shape, like the director of a movie pretending to frame it all in.

Liam sat down in the driver's seat and pushed a button on the console; the perfectly tuned Bugatti fired up. It was breathtaking. Rick had heard Ferraris start up, but the tones coming out of the tailpipes of the Bugatti were like music he'd never heard before. Liam revved the powerful engines a few times, then shut it down.

"What's the top speed?" asked Rick.

"It's never been on the open road yet. The Bugatti Chiron holds the world record of 304 miles per hour, but I plan on beating that. Maybe tomorrow I'll take you for a spin." He flashed his teeth. "Don't worry, we won't go any faster that 150 to 175, I promise. In order to attempt the new speed record, I will have to be on a closed track in Germany."

"Wow, I can't even imagine speeds like that. I'm beyond impressed, Liam," said Rick.

"Thank you, Michael. You two are the first to see my new car. She just arrived a few days ago, as I mentioned in my office this morning. Shall we retire to the great room? The other guests should be arriving soon."

"Do we have to shimmy up that pole?" asked Rick.

Liam let out a huge laugh. "No, let's use the elevator like civilized men. It opens next to the wine cellar, then continues up to the main floor of the house. We can stop and grab your camera bag on the way, Stefan."

Possum smiled and nodded as he followed Liam and Rick to the elevator. It was key-coded also, and Rick and Possum turned around as Liam keyed it in. The elevator opened and they all stepped inside. Elevator music played as a voice announced, "Going up," after Liam pushed the numbers two and three on the wall. Rick recognized the music as the soft rock duo Air Supply.

"I thought it would be funny and ironic to make sure I had elevator music playing in my own private elevator," said Liam. "It's a song on a loop that never changes—'Even the Nights Are Better.' I chose it because I mostly work at the lab at NoahTech during the day, but I love to work down here at night. The irony of that song still makes me chuckle."

When the elevator stopped at floor two, Possum grabbed his camera bag and hopped back in. They kept moving up to the top floor. The elevator opened, and Liam slid a wooden panel open just beyond the opening of the elevator. Once they stepped off, he slid it closed again, and the elevator disappeared behind a wall of hardwood. No one would ever know it was there unless Liam showed it to them.

"Let me show you my office, then we can grab a bottle of wine and try a glass before the other guests arrive," said Liam.

His office, like everything else in the château, was impressive. Three large HD monitors sat in a semi-circle on his desk. Liam pulled the Montblanc pen out of his pocket and set it beside his keyboard.

"Thank you again for the gift, Michael. I will cherish it."

"It's my pleasure, Liam."

Rick scanned the room and noticed no cameras in the office. That would make it easier to make the pen switch. He would just need to be stealthy when the time was right and excuse himself from the gathering for a minute.

"From this room, I run my nightly audit of NoahTech and check my holdings, and other boring business matters. Let's get some wine!"

"Can you hold a glass by the stairway and let me snap a few shots in your stunningly fabulous smoking jacket?" asked Possum.

"Sure, Stefan, we have time to snap a few shots. I just want to make sure the cover photo is in front of my new Bugatti."

"Absolutely!" replied Possum.

Liam summoned the main caterer he'd hired for the night to bring three large crystal wine glasses, and then excused himself as he stepped down into the wine cellar. He returned with the bottle of Château Mouton Rothschild Pauillac, Red Bordeaux Blend 1945 he had shown Possum and Rick earlier.

"You're gonna open it?" asked Rick, astounded. He hadn't believed Liam was really serious when he offered it earlier.

"Yes, my good man, we are going to drink it!"

"That's very generous of you."

Liam didn't respond, as he was intently focused on opening the incredibly overpriced fermented grape juice with a gold wine key pulled from his pants pocket. One of the caterers returned with three sparkling glasses on a silver tray. Liam poured three equal amounts of the maroon wine. Liam swirled the liquid around and sniffed it deeply, then raised his glass. Rick and Possum followed suit.

"Here's to good wine, good friends, and good times," said Liam with a wide smile. "May your Fortune article bring us all good fortune."

"Cheers!" replied Rick and Possum simultaneously.

Rick was no wine snob but took a small sip, savoring it on his palate before he swallowed. Suddenly, he felt like a wine snob, and wanted to use phrases he'd heard before, like *remarkably exotic, over-ripe, sweet nose of black fruits, coffee, tobacco, mocha,* and *Asian spices.* The wine was dense, opulent, and rich, with layers of creamy fruit. He'd never tasted anything like it before and was nothing short of blown away by how many different layers he was sensing. The look on Possum's face told Rick he thought the same thing. They both were honored to share such a fine wine with a man who was turning out to be incredibly unselfish and giving. Not anything like Emily had described him, but Rick knew people had many sides and how they acted at home might be completely different from how they truly were when it came to business and greed.

Liam positioned himself in front of the massive winding staircase in his smoking jacket, with the wine glass in his hand. Possum took several photos, instructing Liam to try different poses. Possum did a great job staying in character, and Liam didn't seem to have any doubt he was a pro photographer.

The doorbell rang and Liam greeted his guests personally, introducing them to Rick and Possum as they came inside. He instructed the caterers to begin passing out hors d'oeuvres and taking drink orders. He had a special case of wine set aside in the main kitchen for the other guests. Rick and Possum were the only ones privy to the Rothschild.

Around twenty people arrived for the dinner. Rick met several of Zürich's elite, including a couple of pro athletes and a few descendants of Swiss nobility. It was the fanciest dinner gathering he'd ever attended, and he tried his best to fit in.

After dinner, Liam invited Possum, Rick, and a few other guests to join him on the expansive balcony overlooking the lighted vineyard below in the rear of the château.

Rick excused himself and asked where the bathroom was. As Liam and the others headed to the balcony, Rick quickly stepped into Liam's office and switched out the pens, making sure no one saw him go in or out. For good measure, he stepped into the bathroom and left the door ajar as he washed his hands, making sure the caterer saw him as he walked by and nodded.

Walking back out, Rick joined the others on the balcony. Liam had the caterer bring out a box of fine cigars from Cuba and pass out snifters of cognac that probably cost more than Rick's first car. It was a special evening he would never forget.

Around 10:00 p.m., the guests began to leave, and Rick and Possum said their goodbyes to everyone and told Liam they'd be back around noon for the photoshoot of the car collection. Before they left, Rick pulled Liam aside. "I'm planning on renting a car for a few days, so you can let your driver Luca have the weekend off to spend with his kids."

"Oh, all right, if that's what you prefer," said Liam. "I'd be happy to pay for the rental."

"No, thank you, but that's not necessary. It'll be on Fortune's dime. If I don't use my per diem on each trip, they might lower it," said Rick with a chuckle.

Liam smiled. "Of course, I understand."

Outside, Rick gave the driver the good news once they'd entered the car. Luca beamed at him in the reflection of the rearview mirror.

"Thank you so much, Mr. Compagno. I am so grateful."

"It's my pleasure. Please remember to call me Michael. Mr. Compagno is my father."

Luca laughed and focused on the road as Rick and Possum pounded fists out of view of Luca. They had pulled off the first step of their plan.

CHAPTER SEVENTEEN

Rick opened his laptop on the patio of the apartment and looked up Luca Muller's address. He was listed in the Zürich white pages. Typing the address into his phone, Rick began to go over the plan for the morning. He now knew where the town car would be parked, and he could hotwire it. Luca had a red beard. Luckily, so did Rick, along with several other disguises he had brought along on the trip. He knew Liam would be jogging from 6:00 a.m. to 7:30 a.m. That wouldn't give him much time, and he still needed to locate a W-Tool to open the locked door in Liam's private lab.

He Googled *fire department* and found one a few blocks away. It was a large one, with several fire engines and ladder trucks. He figured the W-Tool would be in one of the smaller trucks.

"Hey, Stefan, you feel like stepping out and grabbing a late-night drink before we call it a night?"

Possum peered through the balcony door. "Sure, Michael. I'm still wired from the party. Let's go."

Rick explained on the way to the fire station that he needed Possum to create a distraction so he could swipe a W-Tool from one of the fire trucks.

"Do you think you can get their attention somehow long enough for me to do a snatch and grab?"

"I'm sure I can come up with something."

Rick and Possum stopped just around the corner from the firehouse and saw a couple of firemen polishing a chrome wheel on one of the trucks. Three of the water trucks were parked inside, with the huge bay doors open. The entire inside of the lower level where the trucks were parked was lit up. Firemen worked split shifts and usually stayed at a firehouse seven days on and seven days off. The night shift was up trying to stay busy; when there were no fires, all they really did was clean the fire trucks and test equipment. Rick counted three men working. The rest were either upstairs in the break room or asleep.

"Ok, Rick, follow my lead," said Possum. "In two minutes, make your move. You'll see a big commotion on the far east side of the station. There are two smaller trucks on the west side parked outside. That's your best bet. If you look closely, it appears several of the cargo bays are open. They must be doing an inventory or testing gear. That's a good break for us."

Rick squinted to get a better look. Several cargo doors were open and unlatched on the logistical support truck nearest them. It was a sure bet they had a W-Tool in one of the cargo doors.

Possum began to walk toward the firehouse. As he got closer, he started to stagger, then moan. He moaned louder, then fell to one knee.

"Help me! I think I'm having a heart attack."

He fell to the ground with a gasp, holding his chest and seemingly writhing in pain. It caught the attention of one of the firemen, who ran over to Possum and waved over the other two. One grabbed an EMT bag. *Possum's becoming quite the actor,* thought Rick as he made his move.

He looked in the first door with no luck, then opened a couple more hatches. On the third cargo door on the driver's side, he lifted the hinged door open and saw it: a large red duffel bag with the words "W-Tool" and "Weddle Tool Company" stitched on the side. This was it. Rick knew this piece of gear was invaluable to the fire department, so he had every intention of returning it as soon as possible.

Possum was still pulling off his Fred Sanford routine as the three firemen checked him. Rick caught his eye and shot him a quick thumbs-up as he escaped into the darkness.

The W-Tool carrying bag stood out like sore thumb; there was no way he could return to the apartment carrying it. It would be a dead giveaway. He spotted a 24-hour drug store, and after stashing the W-Tool in some shrubs, went inside and bought a large, black, rolling duffel bag. Retrieving the W-Tool, he shoved it inside and headed to the apartment.

It was after midnight and there was no telling when Possum would return, so Rick took his laptop back onto the balcony and pulled the curtains mostly closed. After removing the micro memory card from the spy pen, he popped it into the laptop and prayed a little prayer that it had captured Liam entering the key code. As he scrolled through the footage, a text popped up on his phone. It was Possum.

I'm at the hospital for evaluation. You owe me a twelve pack for this one! See ya soon, hopefully.

Although it wasn't really funny, Rick couldn't help but laugh, thinking of Possum hooked up to an EKG machine and being poked and prodded at the hospital. He sure was a team player.

Rick continued to scroll until he found the right spot. He slowed the footage way down, and there it was. The key code was 1982.

Son of a bitch! That's the year "Even the Nights Are Better" was released. Liam truly loves irony.

He continued to scroll though the spy pen footage. It turned out Liam used the same code for the elevator as well.

At least he's consistent.

Rick familiarized himself with the W-Tool as he waited for Possum's return. He finally got a text around 2:15 a.m. saying his friend was being released and would grab a cab back to the apartment. Possum arrived about 3:10 a.m. Neither one would get much sleep, if any, that night, and they needed to be at Luca's place by 5:30 a.m. Possum stepped out onto the balcony with Rick and shut the sliding glass door behind him.

"What happened?" asked Rick.

"Well, they hooked me up to all kinds of machines. They said my EKG was normal and that I did *not* have a heart attack. I explained to them that I had been under a lot of pressure from work and have been feeling super anxious lately. They think I had an anxiety attack. I played them like a fiddle," replied Possum with a grin.

"You sure are quite the actor, dude. Maybe when we get back to Houston you should join that playhouse your friend acts at."

"Nah, I have enough hobbies. Wanna hear something funny?"

"What?"

"They gave me a script for Xanax for anxiety. I ain't about to start taking Benzos!"

"That's hilarious! Possum, the drug addict!"

Possum wadded up the script, shoved it in his pocket, and smiled.

"Ok, so here's the plan," said Rick. "You pick up the rental car and drop me near Luca's place. I'll hotwire the town car and drive toward Liam's château. I have the same style glasses Luca wore and a black suit. All I need is the limo driver's hat. Hopefully, he left it in the car. Once I get what I need, I'll text you and you can pick me up and we can drive to Liam's for the photoshoot as if nothing ever happened."

"Is that all? Piece of cake," replied Possum sarcastically.

"Don't forget your camera bag, Benzo boy."

"Very funny!"

They both took quick showers and lay down, setting their alarms for 5:00 a.m. Even a few hours of sleep was better than none. Rick was too wired to sleep and ready to get it over with. Everything rode on the plan today.

With the red beard, glasses, lock-picking tools, and a few other items he would need in the new duffel bag, along with the W-Tool, Rick stepped into the kitchen two hours later. Possum had already made a pot of coffee. They both swigged down a couple cups of joe, making small talk in character about their photoshoot and the sightseeing they would do later that day, for the benefit of the bugs in the house. Then they proceeded to the lobby, where Rick hailed a cab for the car rental site. His adrenaline was flowing, and he felt invigorated, even without any sleep.

After securing the rental, Possum took the driver's side and dropped Rick two blocks away from Luca's place. Rick cautiously approached Luca's house, closely following his GPS on his phone. Once he got within a few hundred feet, he pulled out his mini-binoculars. He could see a carport with the town car on the left side and the other spot vacant. He hoped that meant Luca had already left with his kids in another car to go hiking. There was no way to tell for sure, but he couldn't see any movement in the townhouse behind the carport and had to take the chance.

With a Slim-Jim already in his coat pocket, he approached the town car, ready to pop the lock. He was about to slide the tool down the inside of the door when he spotted the keys in the ignition.

You've got to be kidding.

He pulled the handle to the town car, and the door opened. Luca's townhouse was in a good neighborhood, but Rick had never dreamed he'd be lucky enough to find the keys in the unlocked car. On the passenger side, to top it off, sat the limo driver's hat Luca always wore when he drove.

Rick pulled the car out of the carport, drove a few blocks away and parked, texting Possum the A-Ok. He donned the red beard and hat, using the rearview mirror. The look was close enough to Luca's that if he was spotted by any staff, they wouldn't give it a second thought. His plan was to drive the town car to Liam's, enter using the code, then park under the same spot Luca had the night before and gain entry into the château. Timing was everything, though, and Liam would only be jogging for an hour and a half.

He made his way to the château and slowed down to a crawl when he neared it. As he approached the main gate, he slammed the brakes and stopped. To his surprise, Liam was jogging right out of the open gate. Luckily for Rick, Liam was wearing headphones and turned sharply in the opposite direction Rick was driving, so he never glanced at the town car. Rick's shoulders relaxed a little. He quickly backed the town car to the side of the road beside the massive wall surrounding the château, pulled a ski mask over his head, grabbed the duffel bag, and sprinted as fast as he could toward the gate. Just as the gate was closing, he turned sideways and squeezed inside.

He texted Possum the change of plans and told him to park close to the château, return the town car to Luca's, and then double back in a cab to the rental car in case Rick needed a fast getaway.

A light fog lay over the grounds. Since the surveillance cameras were on a rotation, he hid behind a tree and bolted toward the mansion, stopping every so often to avoid one of the moving cameras. As he approached the house, he noticed something. The main garage on the side of the château was the best vantage point to gain access to the château. A yellow Lamborghini was parked just outside the middle garage door, and Rick saw a cleaning kit with wax and a buffer rag sitting beside it. Liam must have planned to wax it after his jog.

He approached the garage with stealth. When he got there, he spotted a door with a key code device. He quickly keyed in 1982, and the green light flashed. He was in. Oddly enough, there were no surveillance cameras in the garage. Now, all he had to do was get to the next level, using the elevator, then enter the lab through the wine cellar. Then he remembered the fire pole. If he could shimmy up the pole, it led directly into the lab.

It was no easy feat climbing the shiny, stainless sliding pole up to the next level, especially with the heavy duffel bag wrapped around his waist, but with solid effort he made it to the top.

Now he had to gain access to the storage room in the lab. He secured the W-Tool to the frame of the door and began to crank the hydraulic tool and spread the door jamb. With very little effort, the door began to spread. There would be no hiding that there was a break-in, but he had no other choice. One final crank and the door jamb spread enough that Rick could open the door. The jamb actually didn't look that bent unless you were looking closely at it.

Inside the storage room, Rick quickly spotted the hard drive for the surveillance cameras. Even though he was wearing a ski mask, he wanted the footage gone. Instead of taking the time to delete the last few minutes of recording, he simply unplugged the hard drive and stuck it in the duffel.

He pried open several filing cabinets, looking for anything with ED or immunotherapy written on any of the folders. After going through several files, he found what he was looking for. A large folder holding the cure for the worst disease of mankind's history was now in his hands.

A big computer sat idle on the desk. It had several external hard drives all synced together. There was no time to copy the data to a flash drive. In addition, the hard drives were all four terabytes, and he didn't have a flash drive anywhere near that size, so he unplugged them and put them in the bag with the other surveillance hard drive. Finally, he slid down the pole and made his grand escape.

As he approached the side garage door he had originally entered, he got a little sloppy and opened the door quickly, without taking the time to see if the coast was clear. A large man standing beside the Lamborghini looked directly at Rick as he froze. Stepping out of the château with a large duffel bag and wearing a ski mask wasn't something he could explain away.

The man shouted something in Swiss German, which Rick figured meant something like, "Hey, what the fuck are you doing?" Then the massive guy rushed toward him. He was at least six-foot-five and two hundred and fifty pounds of solid muscle. Rick dropped the duffel bag as the guy slammed into him, smashing him against the wall of the garage. For a big man, he was surprisingly fast. He swung hard, connecting with Rick's body and forcing all the air from his lungs. As he gasped for air, he crouched down and swept the man's legs out from under him.

With a huge thud, the man hit the ground, cursing. He kicked hard as Rick slid away from him. Before he could get to his feet, though, Rick slammed him with the duffel bag with all his might. The W-Tool connected with his torso, knocking his breath out. He rolled over and popped to his feet, then swung at Rick with a right hook that went way over his head. Rick reached down with all his might and hit the man with an upper cut. He had a glass jaw and just like a huge sequoia tree in the forest, he toppled, his face slamming against the hard concrete. He was out cold.

The commotion had gotten the attention of several people working out on the château grounds. They were all running toward Rick. One had a gun pointed in his direction and began firing. He wasn't expecting that. The bullets whizzed by his head only inches from him. *Liam must have security guards he failed to mention*, thought Rick, as he scrambled behind the Lamborghini for protection. The driver's side door was open. He jumped in but there was no key.

Then he saw it. It was on the ground beside the giant Rick had just knocked out. He ran around the car and grabbed the key fob. Bullets exploded bits of concrete next to his feet. He rolled over the hood of the Lambo and hit the start button.

Scrambling back inside, he peeled out of the parking area with the door still open, nearly hitting the man with the gun. He rolled out of the way just in time. As Rick sped toward the main gate, a bullet shattered the rear window and continued into the dash, just to the right of him. Several more pinged the rear of the car as he approached the iron gate. He was going to ram it and pray the car had enough strength to make it through. Then he saw the auto gate opener snugged up firmly in the sun visor. He pushed the button and the massive gate began to open, but it was heavy and wouldn't open in time. *Dammit.* There was no way the car would survive the impact.

He slammed on the brakes and threw the sports car into reverse. With more torque than he'd ever experienced, it leapt backwards toward the guards, who were still firing at him. As the car spun in the opposite direction, he flung the steering wheel hard to the right and simultaneously slammed the vehicle into first gear. He sped directly toward the guards as a bullet barely missed his head and came through the front windshield. The guards leapt out of the way and rolled on the ground. Rick veered to the right, through the bushes, and sped back toward the gate, which was nearly open.

The front of the car went through the gate, clipping the passenger side mirror. It went flying. He took a sharp left, nearly losing control of the vehicle, and spotted Possum in the rental car. Without hesitation, Possum spun around and followed Rick. They drove through a few side streets, and Rick slammed on the brakes on the side of the road, grabbed the duffel bag, and jumped out with the car still running. He bolted toward Possum and dove into the passenger seat.

"Let's go!" yelled Rick.

"Where?"

"Airport! Drive the speed limit now," he said, as he tried to slow his breath.

"Are we flying out?"

"Maybe. I'll know by the time we get there."

Rick peeled off the red beard and ski mask and tossed them out the window into a stream. He was still breathing heavily, and the pain in his ribs from being slammed by the giant body guard was now apparent. He'd be sore but didn't think any were broken.

CHAPTER EIGHTEEN

Possum pulled the rental car into short-term parking, and they both walked to the main terminal.

Rick's phone rang. He exhaled, still trying to get his breath and heartbeat back to normal, before he answered. "Hello?"

"Hello, Mr. Compagno, this is Lara from NoahTech. There's been a problem at Liam's estate."

"Oh, no. Is Liam ok? What happened?"

"Someone breached the walls of the château and stole one of Dr. Furrer's Lamborghinis."

"Oh my God! Was anything else taken? That's insane."

"We're not sure yet. The police have been dispatched and the car has already been located. It had a LoJack GPS tracker on it, like all of his cars. They found it sitting on the side of the road, still running."

"That's incredible. I assume Liam wants to cancel the photoshoot?"

"Oh no, he still wants to do it. He's actually still out on his morning jog. He told me to ask you if we could move it back thirty minutes so he could speak to the police and call his insurance company."

Rick looked over at Possum in disbelief, covered the phone with his hand, and whispered, "This guy is unflappable."

Putting the phone back to his hear, he said, "Ok, let Liam know we'll be at his place around 12:30 for the shoot, and also tell him how sorry we are that some scumbags tried to steal his car."

"I will, Mr. Compagno."

"That's better. Talk to you soon, Ms. Lara. Ciao for now."

Rick hung up and continued to walk toward the main terminal. He needed to put this duffel bag in secure spot. As they entered the terminal, he noticed storage lockers that could be rented.

"Perfect!"

Rick chose a large locker that the duffel bag would fit inside. It allowed storage for up to seventy-two hours.

"Ok if we're still here in three days, we'll have to move lockers. But I think we're out of here tomorrow," said Rick.

Possum nodded in agreement.

"Let's switch cars just in case any surveillance cameras or witnesses spotted this rental. No sense in taking any chances. How did the drop at Luca's go?"

"I parked the car right where it was when you nabbed it and left it unlocked with the keys in the ignition. The hat was still sitting on the passenger seat."

"Ok, good. If we leave now, we should have time to swap out rental cars."

Possum pulled up to the Sixt car rental as Rick waited outside. He soon pulled around from the back in a classy black Range Rover.

"This is way better than that Dodge Maggot you rented," replied Rick as he slid into the passenger seat.

"Yeah, I told the girl behind the counter that the air wasn't cooling properly and she felt so bad she gave me a free upgrade. Maybe we should stay a few extra days and cruise in style," Possum said with a wink.

"We'll see. Let's head to Liam's."

Rick took off his black jacket and stuck it under the seat. He was now wearing black pants and a dark button-down shirt, the sleeves of which he rolled up to look a little less formal.

As they arrived at Liam's château, the police were just leaving. Liam opened the gate for them via the intercom, and Possum parked next to the damaged Lamborghini now parked in the main driveway.

Liam was standing beside the car. He waved Rick over. Pointed at the missing passenger mirror and long scratch along the door, he said, "The punk who stole my car crashed into the gate."

"Who shot at them?" Rick asked, observing the bullet hole in the front windshield and the completely shattered rear window.

"One of my security guards. You probably never noticed them when you were here before, but they are always around. I have lots of enemies," said Liam. "The guy I use to detail my cars got into a brawl with one of the punks who broke in. He's at the hospital now with a concussion. He said he got a few blows in before he slipped and bumped his head."

Yeah, right, bumped his head.

"It was not his responsibility to guard my cars," said Liam, shaking his head. "He's just an auto detailer."

"He sounds like solid guy. How do you know there was more than one person?"

"I really don't. I just assume there was because the cops think it was a two-man operation."

"Was anything else stolen?"

"The police and I did a quick search of the grounds and château. The code to the lab wasn't ever breached, so we left that room alone. There's no way anyone could get in there unless they were a monkey."

"A monkey?"

"Yeah. Without entering the key code, the only way in would be to climb up the fireman's pole. Impossible."

"Oh, I see," replied Rick, trying not to smirk. "Are you sure you still want to do the shoot today?"

"Absolutely. Let's walk to the garage. I have the Bugatti all shined up and the garage doors open. It's a beautiful day, and the vineyard will look great in the background," said Liam.

He opened a closet door and pulled on a lab coat over his clothes.

"That looks fabulous," said Possum. He went straight into character and had Liam take many poses in front of the immaculate Bugatti.

"Can you make the vineyard blurry or out of focus?" asked Liam.

"Oh, you mean the bokeh effect. I can do anything."

Rick stood there with his arms crossed, watching Possum work.

"Well, that should do it. Do you want me to print a contact sheet for you, so you can choose the best shot?" asked Possum.

"That's not necessary. Just email them to me." Liam opened a drawer in a desk in the corner of the garage, pulled out a business card, and handed it to Possum. "I cancelled the brunch because of the break in, but would you to like to join me for lunch?"

"Here?" asked Rick, not really wanting to hang around.

It was 1:45 p.m. now, and he was famished but didn't want to be anywhere near the château once Liam discovered the lab had indeed been breached.

"No, I thought we'd dine at my other vineyard in Wangen. It's beside Obersee Lake and the views are stunning. We can take the Bugatti. I told you I wanted to take you for a spin. It's a two-seater. Stefan, would you mind following us in your rental?"

"No problem."

"Actually, let me write the address on the back of my card. You'll never be able to keep up with us," said Liam with a chuckle. "Just give me a few minutes to get changed. I'll meet you back here momentarily. Please stay and feel free to sit in any of the cars if you want a closer look. There's water, seltzer, or Duvel in the refrigerator. Help yourselves."

"Duvel?" asked Rick.

"It's a beer brewed in Belgium, and it's wonderful. Please try one."

Rick smiled. "I'll take you up on that offer."

He hoped a couple of beers might calm his nerves, as he was antsy to get far away from the château. Liam took the elevator up to the main part of the house to change, and

Rick popped open a couple of Duvels. The sweet nectar of the gods was pleasant to his palate. Like everything else in Liam's life, the beer was exquisite. Rick downed the first one in just a few swigs, then grabbed another to savor it. His nerves were calming down. Still, he'd feel a lot better once he and Liam were on the open road away from the château.

Liam returned wearing freshly pressed dark blue jeans and a golf shirt. "Shall we? What do you think of that beer?"

"It's probably one of the finest beers I've ever tasted," replied Rick. Possum nodded in agreement after taking a big chug.

"Here, let's grab a couple for the road," said Liam. "If you like this, just wait until you taste my new red blend at my other vineyard. I mixed several different grape varietals from France to achieve it. It's nearly my finest work, next to my new cancer drug I'll be launching next month. Oops, I was supposed to surprise you with that news." He grinned. "I'd like you to get the exclusive story on my discovery. It's your scoop, Michael, if you want it."

"If I want it? I'm beyond honored."

"I can't go into great detail until the ink dries on the sale of the drug to several other big pharmaceutical companies, but it will change the world. That much I can tell you. Michael, I've created the cure for cancer. All cancer. I will go down in history because of this development."

Rick gaped at him, hoping his shock came across in a convincing way. Possum slapped a hand over his mouth. "I'm speechless, Liam," said Rick. "Are you certain?"

"Yes, we've completed all clinical human trials and it has 99.99% efficacy. As with any trial, there were some deaths that had to be accounted for, but from the findings, all deaths were unrelated to the drug."

Rick and Possum shared a look of amazement. "That has to be the world's biggest scoop and the greatest achievement in modern chemistry," said Rick.

"Agreed. Let's roll!"

Liam and Rick climbed into the Bugatti as Possum climbed up into the Range Rover. Liam fired up the mighty, finely-tuned engine, and popped the tops on the Duvels before handing one to Rick. They clinked them together.

"Here's to the end of cancer as we know it!"

"I'll drink to that!" replied Rick.

Liam slowly pulled out of the garage and set his beer in the cup holder, then clicked the gate remote and gunned it closer to the main road. He slowed until the iron gate fully opened, then took a right and smoked the tires as Rick's head hit the back of the seat.

The car was insanely fast. In less than a heartbeat, they were traveling over 140 kilometers an hour. Rick quickly did the math in his head and realized they had gone from zero to eighty-seven miles an hour in what felt like less than two seconds. This was the fastest car he'd ever ridden in, *period*, including the Lambo he had stolen earlier that morning.

"Just wait until we get to Highway 3. This is just a side street."

Liam took another sip of his beer and spoke to the car.

"Take me to Vineyard Obersee."

A fifteen-inch screen with a detailed GPS road map slowly rose in the center of the dashboard. A pleasant voice came over the car speakers. "Scenic or quickest, Liam?"

"Quickest."

"The car knows your name?" asked Rick.

"I had it programmed. That's the least it should do for what it cost."

"I don't even want to ask."

"It's ok, I don't mind sharing," said Liam with a wave of his hand. "I paid the equivalent of 5.5 million US dollars for this car."

Rick took a hard gulp and said, "Damn!"

Liam weaved in and out of traffic with little to no concern for police as the pleasant voice in the car spoke a few times and warned him of radar ahead. Small police cars popped up on the screen, and Liam slowed just enough not to be tagged. Then he floored it again. The power of the car was indescribable. It could hit a hundred miles an hour in a few seconds and drop down safely to thirty with ease, then back up again.

Once on Highway 3, Liam got in the passing lane and told Rick to hold on. Rick looked over at the digital speedometer several times, noticing speeds over 250 kilometers an hour, well over 150 miles per hour. The car had no shake or vibration at those high speeds. It hugged the road and actually felt as if they were doing more like a mere sixty or seventy in any other car. *This is insane*, he thought.

Before he knew it, Liam was pulling into the vineyard. He parked in a spot with his name on it, and the wing-like doors opened as he turned off the massive engine.

"Well, that was fun!" said Liam matter-of-factly. "Let's eat. It'll be about thirty minutes before Stefan arrives. I'll pre-order some goose pâté and caviar while we wait. We can eat once he arrives. Let me show you around the vineyard."

The beautiful, sprawling vineyard reached all the way down to tranquil Lake Obersee, which separated Germany and Switzerland. It was dotted with several sailboats and a rowing team training near the bank. Liam explained that the lake actually had three names, Lake Obersee, Lake Bodensee, and Lake Constance, which it was most commonly referred to. The Lake Constance Basin was a popular tourist destination where Switzerland, Germany and Austria met. Liam chose Obersee as the name of his vineyard because it was what his grandfather called the lake when Liam was a child. The lake had a special place in Liam's heart, as it was the legacy left to him by his grandfather. And what was a run-down, dried-out vineyard had now been transformed into a world-class vineyard and restaurant.

"My grandfather bought this property when it was worthless. He grew grapes but wasn't successful. In his will, he gave it to me because I used to come down here and sail his tiny Norseboat with him. He taught me how to sail. Now, that's my sailboat," he said, pointing down to the water where a beautiful sixty-four-foot Hallberg-Rassy sailing yacht was docked. "The Norseboat is hanging from the high ceiling in the restaurant."

After an entertaining and educational tour of the vineyard, Liam got a text that Stefan had arrived.

"Stefan's here. I've instructed my head vintner to accompany him to the winemaking room. We'll meet them there for a quick wine tasting and mini-tour," said Liam.

"That sounds awesome, Liam, thank you. It's all very interesting to me."

Liam and Rick strolled to the winemaking room. Liam occasionally stopped and plucked a few grapes off the vines, testing their firmness and consistency.

"Hello, Stefan, how was your drive?" he asked.

"Uneventful. The rental is brand new and floats like a dream on the highway."

"Too bad it's so slow," replied Liam with a sarcastic grin.

Possum nodded and gave an agreeable laugh. The vintner began his explanation about how wine was made for Rick and Possum. They both tasted several different varietals as well as the new blend Liam was so proud of. About ten minutes into the presentation, Liam got a phone call and excused himself. He stepped away just out of earshot, then began yelling in his native language. By his body language, it was clear he was upset. Rick could barely concentrate on the vintner.

Liam briskly returned, red in the face.

"I apologize, Michael and Stefan, but I must leave. Please stay and enjoy lunch, but I must return to the château. My head security guard has found another breach at the property and I must attend to it."

"Someone else broke in again?" asked Rick, frowning.

"No, I believe the people responsible for stealing my Lamborghini also broke into the lab as well. I wish could stay longer, but I must leave at once."

"I understand," said Rick. "I hope everything is ok. Keep me posted."

Liam rushed out as Rick and Possum made their way to the dining area of the vineyard. They sat down at the table. "Let's get out of here, Possum," Rick murmured, and Possum nodded.

As soon as the waiter stepped back into the kitchen, Rick pulled aside another waiter and explained they had to leave early for a work emergency. "So sorry for any inconvenience we may have caused," he said.

On their way out, he spoke to Possum under his breath. "The jig is up; we need to leave the country. There will be hell to pay once Liam figures out his hard drives and files were stolen. We need to go back to the apartment, get our stuff, and head straight to the airport."

They quickly packed the Range Rover and headed for the airport. Rick pulled up their flight reservations and changed them to the earliest flight. It would leave in two hours. The only fast flight back they could get that was even close to Tampa was to Miami with a plane change in Washington-Dulles. At least it would get them out of Zürich. Once Liam reviewed the video from the apartment, Rick had no doubt he would begin to suspect him of being involved in the robbery. Even though they'd been careful, Liam would stop at no length to find the culprits who'd taken his cancer cure. He was sure of it.

They dropped the car with a valet, tipped the guy to return it to the rental location, and raced into the main terminal.

Possum posted up near the edge of the storage lockers with a newspaper someone had discarded on a bench seat. He scanned the area as Rick glanced over occasionally to wait for Possum's signal. Possum folded the paper abruptly and flapped it as they had planned earlier, and Rick stepped up to the lockers. He put the key into a locker a few feet from the correct one and waited. No one approached, so he moved to the locker with the evidence inside, opened it, and headed for the self-service ticket kiosk. They were flying first class. Possum tagged the bags and put them on the X-ray belt, then strolled to the gate after they cleared.

On the plane, Rick eyeballed the door of the massive 747. His nerves were on full alert. The flight attendant offered them a glass of champagne. Possum accepted one, but Rick declined and asked for a glass of the best whiskey they had on board instead.

"Make it a double," said Rick.

The flight attendant returned, and Rick guzzled it and motioned for another. She quickly returned with an even larger fill in the glass. Rick sipped it as the door to the cabin was closed and secured. He let out a deep sigh as the flight attendant made the usual safety announcements in several languages, with English being the last.

The captain came over the PA and gave the flight plan and weather for Washington. Rick started to feel a small sense of relief but couldn't completely relax until the wheels were off the ground. As the plane taxied on the tarmac, Rick looked out the window and counted the planes ahead of them.

Soon the captain came on again. "We are number one for take-off. Please enjoy your flight, and thank you for flying Lufthansa."

As the wheels left the ground, Rick's shoulder sank into the soft first-class seats. He sipped on his whiskey, then slowly looked over at Possum as they clinked glasses together. Rick burst into laughter. It sounded like laughter from an insane person, like in the scene in *Anger Management* where Jack Nicholson laughed beside the stoic Adam Sandler, but maybe it was a little insanity mixed with a sense of release. Possum just stared at him and grinned his devilish grin. He could read Rick so well. They had pulled it off and now it was time to celebrate.

"Salud!" said Possum, as he tapped his glass against Rick's.

Once they were airborne and leveled off, the flight attendant returned with two more drinks, and they did the haha, clink-clink.

Rick pulled out the duffel bag with the hard drives. Whatever was on there would be the key to solving this case. He was sure they would be encrypted to the highest degree and thought long and hard about who he could contact to break the code. It would have to be someone he trusted, who also had access to the highest cryptanalysts.

"Carson!" he blurted out.

Rick logged into the airplane's Wi-Fi–. Being in first class, he got free text messaging. He pulled up Carson's contact info.

> Top Secret — Do you have a contact in the FBI you trust who can crack an encrypted hard drive? Rick

A few minutes went by, then his phone whistled.

> Yes, it will take a few days, bring them to me and I will get on it.

> I will FedEx them to you
> from Miami tomorrow. Thank
> you.

> My pleasure.

Rick showed Possum the texts, while Possum displayed a text from Emily.

> Hi Possum, I was lonely in
> your big old house all by
> myself, so I flew back to
> Destin to stay on the boat
> with Johnie and Chief. I can't
> wait to see you when you get
> back. Tell Rick I'm safe on
> the boat.

"We have a few days until we hear anything back, and since we're Miami-bound, why don't we rent a car and head down to the Keys?" asked Rick. "When I did some research about NoahTech, I found they have a lab in Islamorada. We can kill two birds with one stone. You up for a little treasure hunt? Fletcher's gold!"

A huge grin came over Possum's face. He didn't even have to answer for Rick to know he was all in.

CHAPTER NINETEEN

After an uneventful plane change and trip through customs and immigration, the plane touched down in Miami. It was a muggy 89 degrees when Rick and Possum stepped onto the curb under the rental car shuttle sign. You could've cut the air with a knife. A far cry from Zürich.

Rick called Johnie as they waited. He was anxious to see how things were going in Destin.

"Hello, Nine-Tenths Charters. Johnie McDonald here. How can I help you?"

"Wow! I'm impressed, Johnie. That sounds very professional. It's Rick."

"Oh, Rick, I just grabbed the phone fast and didn't even see it was you. I can't read my little flip phone without my readers on anyway. How's it going?"

"Good, Johnie. We're in Miami. It's a long story, but we had to leave Zürich fast. I'll explain it all later. How's Chief and Emily? Everything good with the boat?" asked Rick.

"Oh yeah, it's all fine and dandy down here. Chief has been his joyous self lately. I ordered him a new outdoor cage and play tree and assembled it all on the flybridge. That way, no one will be tempted to mess with him anymore while he's outside enjoying the sun. From his vantage point, he can see way down Destin Harbor Walk and always gets super excited when kids approach. I booked a couple of charters after I invited a family on board and let them take a photo with Chief on the flybridge. He's quite the salesman," said Johnie.

After picking up their rental, Rick and Possum drove to the closest FedEx store. Rick double-padded the hard drives with bubble wrap and paid for next-day early morning delivery to Carson, who was semi-retired from the FBI as a profiler. They had met on a previous case. He still had good connections to the Feds and was always helpful.

"How about a conch fritter?" asked Rick.

"You read my mind, amigo."

At the end of the turnpike, they stopped in Florida City at a Shell station and grabbed a couple of roadies for the trip down to Alabama Jack's. The dive bar was a legend. It had been opened shortly after World War II by Jack Stratham, who ironically was from Georgia and not from Alabama. But "Alabama Jack" became his nickname after he worked a job on the Empire State Building, when the other workers couldn't tell the difference between an Alabama accent and one from Georgia. The name stuck.

They picked a table next to the water and stared out over Florida Bay. It was about as peaceful as a place could be. A country band was setting up, but they wouldn't be starting for a while, so Rick and Possum enjoyed the peace and quiet. Alabama Jack's was known for two things—conch fritters and real, traditional country music.

"Hi guys, what can I get you?" asked the cute waitress who approached their table.

"I'll have a rum runner with a floater, and we'll take two orders of conch fritters," said Rick.

"And I'll take a piña colada," said Possum, kicking back and propping his feet up on the chair next to the water's edge.

"I'll be right back with your cocktails. There are alligators in the water, so be careful," said the waitress.

"Sweet! I love gators," replied Possum with a chuckle.

She brought their drinks back, and the conch fritters followed shortly after. They ate in silence, savoring every delicious, greasy morsel. The fritters were loaded with more conch than corn meal, and were fried to perfection.

The band was tuning up as Rick and Possum were preparing to leave, so they decided to stick around for a few songs and ordered a second round. The same band, aptly named The Alabama Jack's Band, had been playing there for what seemed like forever. Rick had met the fiddle player once. He'd told him he also taught violin at the University of Miami.

"They're not bad," said Rick.

"Yeah, you can't go wrong with Willie or Merle. I just wish they'd play some George Jones," replied Possum.

As if he had sent that message telepathically to the band, they played "The Race is On." A huge smile came across Possum's face.

"Wow, you must be psychic, Possum."

"Well, I do have ESP...N."

They stayed for a few more songs, paid their tab, and took Card Sound Road down to where it dead-ended into County Road 905. If they took a left, they would end up at Ocean Reef, a high-end community where the elite, like Oprah Winfrey and Jimmy Buffett, had second homes. They took a right bound for Key Largo.

"Where we gonna stay?" asked Possum.

"Where do you want to stay?"

"I'm easy."

"Well, you want easy or sleazy?"

They settled on the Playa Largo Resort & Spa on the Gulf side of A1A. The resort featured a massive pool and waterfront dining.

"Maybe you can get a massage from one of the cabana boys, Stefan."

"Shut up! A massage wouldn't be bad, though. You should get one too."

"Ok, but we're not getting a couples massage."

Possum just smirked at Rick and went back to gazing at the calm, clear water on both sides of the road. The Keys were a magical place. Each key had such a different vibe. Key Largo was the diving mecca, and Islamorada, just little way down the road, had an artist's appeal. Key West was a whole other animal, though. It had become a fast-paced tourist trap full of overpriced hotels and t-shirt shops. Still, it had its own charm.

They pulled into the resort, and Rick checked them in as Possum handed the bags to the bellman. Rick chose the bayfront suite with two queens and an ocean view. It sat over a two-story bungalow because of the view. Once they stepped into the room and out onto the balcony, Rick knew he had made the right choice. The view was spectacular.

They both settled in and picked their beds out. Rick took the one closer to the balcony and Possum took the one closer to the A/C.

"Well, let's get down to business, Possum."

Rick pulled out the riddle poem he'd found at the original Fletcher's gold site and read it aloud to Possum on the balcony.

> *You are a lucky man to find the treasure*
> *But only two bars did you seize*
> *The rest was moved into a box*
> *But you will need the Keys*
>
> *To find the box, travel south*
> *Beyond the Seminole*
> *For at the bottom where railway starts*
> *It's deep inside a hole*
> *Fletcher*

Rick handed the riddle over to Possum.

"See how the *Keys* is capitalized?" asked Rick.

"Yeah, that's definitely a clue, plus *Beyond the Seminole, for at the bottom where railway starts, it's deep inside a hole*," replied Possum. "What do you think '*it's deep inside a hole*' means?"

"I thought a lot about that. You see, it's signed *Fletcher*, but it's not Fletcher. He was dead long before the Overseas Railroad. It's Fletcher, Jr., his son," said Rick, handing him the copy of the photo Marcy Nobles had given him.

Possum studied it intently, focusing on the background. Flagler was clearly visible in the old railcar behind him. He closed his eyes and then sat up abruptly.

"Do you think Fletcher, Jr. is referring to a sinkhole? I read that there's a sinkhole off of Key Largo that has filled with sediment over the years. Back in the day, there were no scuba rigs. Diving hadn't even been invented, but they could have anchored a boat above the old sinkhole and lowered down the bounty with ropes and pulleys. Even if it was boxed in wood, the gold would have easily made it sink to the bottom."

"Wow, we're gonna need a boat with GPS, scuba rigs, and probably a towed sonar. Where can we find all that down here?" asked Rick.

"Um, don't you have a boat and all that stuff in Destin?" asked Possum.

Rick laughed. "You're right. What was I thinking?"

He pulled out his iPhone and called Johnie again.

"Hello. Nine-Tenths Charters. Johnie McDonald here. How can I help you?"

"Hey, Johnie, it's Rick again. At least you're consistent. Listen, we are in Key Largo."

"Can I put you on speaker? My hands are full of grease," replied Johnie.

"No problem."

"I was just changing the fuel filters."

"Staying busy, that's good. I have a mission for you. Listen up and after I finish, is Emily around?" asked Rick.

"Yeah, she's sitting in the salon. She's actually been helping me on the boat on some charters. She's quite a good stew. She makes the drinks, appetizers and lunch and is a far better cook than I'll ever be. We've been getting several five-star reviews on Yelp. Plus, she's freed me up from those duties, so I can focus more on finding the fish. It's been going gangbusters. We've been booked solid. Next week we do have a cancellation, though, so I'm trying to fill it."

"So, you have no bookings next week?"

"Not yet, but I can probably fill them," replied Johnie.

"Block out the calendar. How quickly can you get the boat down to the Keys?"

"Hang on. Let me get out a chart."

Rick held the line for a few minutes as Johnie did some calculating.

"Ok, it's in the ballpark of 400 miles. It looks like the best route is to head straight to Venice and refuel, then go down to Key Largo. I can call the Marina Del Mar and see if they have any transient slips. Is that close to where you are?" asked Johnie.

"That's perfect. It's about two and a half miles from here. We passed it on the way to the resort. I'm gonna rush-order a towable JW Fishers Pulse 12 Metal Detector. That'll give y'all a full day tomorrow to get the boat ready for the trip. Also, make sure there are at least three full scuba rigs on board. We can rent tanks here. Ask Emily if she's up for the trip."

"Hang on, Rick."

A second later Johnie got back on the line.

"She's super stoked. Apparently, Chief is too. He's hopping up and down in his cage and his crown is raised. I think he heard your voice through the phone. Anything else I need to get?"

"If I think of anything, I'll text or call you. Tell Emily I'll call her later. I need to run some errands and do some recon."

"You got it, boss. Talk to you soon."

They hung up. Rick turned his attention to his MacBook Pro, where he placed the order for the metal detector on Amazon.

"Recon time, Possum."

"I'm way ahead of you, Rick." Possum spun his own laptop around with the address of Terra's Key.

Rick grinned. "You read my mind. Let's roll. Bring your camera and your longest lens."

Terra's Key was near mile marker 79.7, and also known as Teatable Key. Rick pulled it up on Google Earth. It was exactly how Emily had described it. He zoomed in and saw the water around the island seemed very shallow. If they were going to approach on scuba, it would have to be at night. Then he noticed a channel leading from Teatable channel to the island right next to A1A and up to a boat lift. That would most likely be the best point of entry.

Rick closed his laptop, and he and Possum jumped in the rental, bound for Terra's Key. It was south of them, closer to Islamorada. The afternoon sun was slowly making its way toward the horizon. They parked the car a few yards north of mile marker 79.7 and hiked toward Terra's Key on the Gulf side.

As Rick waited for an opening in traffic so they could cross, he pulled out his tactical binoculars and scanned the island. He couldn't make out any movement. They crossed A1A, and Rick stood with his back to the island. Possum aimed his camera toward Rick but was focused on the island. Rick did his best to act as if he was getting tourist photos taken.

Once Possum had enough shots, he winked at Rick and they headed back to the car. They decided to drive into Islamorada and actually be tourists for a while. Rick spotted a sign that said, *Florida Keys Brewing Company*, so he quickly turned in.

"You wanna try some local brew?"

"Twist my arm."

A solo guitarist was singing on the stage. He dubbed himself the Barstool Sailor. His songs were all about the local characters of the Keys. Rick and Possum enjoyed the music as much as the beer.

During his break, Rick dropped a twenty in the man's tip jar and introduced himself. "Hi, I'm Rick Waters. I really enjoyed that set."

"Well, thank you kindly, Rick. My name is Micah Gardner."

"Can I buy you a beer, Micah? Would you like to join us on your break?"

"Sounds good, mate. What brings y'all to the Keys, and who's your friend?" asked Micah.

"Oh, I'm sorry, this is Possum."

Micah shook Possum's hand. "Possum. Huh?"

Possum smiled. "Long story."

"We're just down for a few days and might want to do some fishing," said Rick. "Do you know the waters very well?"

"Mostly the mangrove creeks. I do a paddle-board tour that explains a lot about the local flora and fauna as well as the Keys' best-kept history secrets."

"You sound a lot like us. Possum is a professor and he studied anthropology. We both consider ourselves to be amateur treasure finders."

"Treasure finders? Don't you mean treasure hunters?"

"Nope, we find stuff. Don't just hunt for it," said Rick with a smart grin.

"I get it," replied Micah. "As I mentioned, I know the creeks well, but the real water guy is sitting over there on that stool at the end of the bar." He gestured with his beer in the man's direction. "His name is Bobby Rogers. He works for Contender Boats and has been here for more years than he probably cares to admit. Let me call him over."

Micah got Bobby's attention and waved him over. He grabbed his beer and sat down next to Micah.

"Bobby, these are my two new friends, Rick and Possum. They seem like good guys. Can you answer some questions about the local offshore waters?" asked Micah.

"Sure, Micah. Any friend of yours is a friend of mine. What would you like to know?"

"Well, I've heard a rumor that there's an old sinkhole somewhere under water on the ocean side," said Rick. "I guess over the years it has filled in with silt and sand. We'd like to dive the edge of it and take some photos of any fish or crustaceans that inhabit the area, and see if there are any fossils there."

Bobby nodded enthusiastically. "Yeah, I think I know where that is. It's back on my GPS on my boat. Do y'all like to fish?"

"Hell, yeah. I'm having my Viking delivered here in a couple of days. Do you do charters?" asked Rick.

"Sure do. I'm open tomorrow if y'all wanna go explore the area and do some trolling. Since you're friends with Micah, I can do a half-day for the locals' price—$375, if you're interested."

Rick looked at Possum, who said, "I'm in."

"What time and where?" asked Rick.

"It's a Contender 39 with triple Yamahas named *Reel Fast*. Just be at Bud N' Mary's Marina tomorrow at 7:30 a.m., ok?"

"We'll see ya then."

"I gotta get back on stage," said Micah, standing up. "Short break."

"You wanna join us tomorrow, Micah? My treat," replied Rick.

"Done! See y'all mañana."

Micah went back on stage and started playing a song he'd written called *Sunshine Billionaire*. It was a catchy tune and Rick could relate to it well. They stayed for another half a set and then headed back to the resort.

In their room, Rick and Possum went over their game plan concerning the unexpected next-day charter.

"We have to play it cool," said Rick. "We can be treasure hunters/finders, but we need to keep it on the downlow somewhat. This guy could be a wealth of information, but there's no need to bring him into the mix too much."

"I know a lot of these guys don't like to share the hot spots they have saved on their GPS, so I think once we get there, let's make it clear that we probably won't be back for quite a long time," replied Possum. "He will probably let his guard down. I'll grab the lats and longs on my handheld Magellan when he's distracted."

Rick nodded. A yawn split his face. "We should hit the hay. It's been a long day and we have to rise with the chickens."

"You're right, and to be honest, either the jetlag or the local beer hit me hard." Possum rubbed his temple. "I feel like I just hit the wall."

"Ditto, amigo. Hasta mañana."

Rick lay in bed and stared at the ceiling fan. Sometimes late at night when he was tired, or at least his body was tired, he couldn't turn off his brain. This was one of these nights. He thought about NoahTech and Liam, the crazy escape from Switzerland, and pondered why Emily hadn't just been killed instead of transformed. It still didn't make sense.

His mind drifted off, and the next thing he knew his alarm was going off. It was as if he hadn't even gone to sleep. In typical Possum fashion, he was up before Rick making fresh coffee.

"Mornin', amigo," said Rick.

"Café con leche?"

"Indeed!"

They both sipped their coffees on the balcony and enjoyed the sunrise over the beautiful blue ocean. The water was flat and flashes of silver broke the surface of the water as bait fish raced for their lives from their aggressive schools of predators. Probably jacks or mackerel.

Rick threw on his John Deere ballcap as Possum laced up his boat shoes. They stepped outside and locked the door, ready for a day of exploration and relaxation.

"Today's the day," said Rick, referencing the famous Mel Fischer saying.

CHAPTER TWENTY

The wispy rib-like clouds were high in the stratosphere. No red or orange colors, just white against a light blue sky. The water on both sides of A1A was dead calm. There wasn't a ripple to be seen. The occasional school of bait fish broke the surface, and hog-nosed ray leapt into the air.

As they pulled into Bud N' Mary's Marina, deckhands were putting gear on all the sport fishers. Tourists and fish heads, as they were known locally, were climbing on board.

Rick found the Contender boat and pulled the rental car directly in front of it. Bobby waved them over as his deckhand tended to the trolling rigs on the stern.

"Good morning, y'all. You ready to catch some fish and do some exploring?"

"You betcha," chirped Possum.

Just then, Micah stepped out on the stern from the salon. He looked a little worse for wear.

"Hey, Rick, after my gig I stopped off here and drank a few more Jaegers than I should've," he said with a chuckle.

"It was just easier to sleep on board. I would've never made it."

"I don't blame you." Rick laughed.

Micah took a big swig of water and chewed on some saltines. "I'm a pro, though. I'll be fine. If I feel too bad, I'll kill my hangover with a start-over."

"Hair of the dog is sometimes what it takes."

As soon as Rick and Possum stepped on board, Bobby fired up the outboards. They purred like peaceful kittens.

"Hi, I'm Paul. I'm first mate and master baiter," said the deckhand with a smile.

"Haha. Nice to meet you. I'm Rick and this is Possum."

"Possum?"

"Long story."

Paul untied the stern and spring lines as Bobby slowly pulled away from the dock. There was a magical electricity in the air. To Rick, there was nothing like heading out early in the morning on a magnificent boat. The anticipation of catching fish and excitement of the crew when the reels screamed and someone would yell, *Fish on!* was more than just excitement; it was primal.

As the beautiful Contender roared out of Bud N' Mary's Marina, the torque of the outboards surprised Rick. The finely-tuned Mann diesels on his Viking were far more powerful, but these outboards were indeed impressive.

The line of boats heading out to the Atlantic sort of reminded Rick of the massive jets on the tarmac lined up, waiting to be cleared for takeoff back in Switzerland all headed to different destinations. Each boat this morning had a different goal: fishing, diving, or just plain sun and fun.

The deckhand, Paul, baited the lines with fresh pre-rigged ballyhoo and began to slowly let out the line on each of the four rods. Possum sat comfortably in the fighting chair as Rick chatted with the captain on the helm. Micah kept drinking water and eating saltines, trying not to chum.

They motored out to the deeper water, then took a turn to the north, moving parallel with the shore at a steady six knots—trolling speed.

Captain Bobby scanned the waters ahead with binoculars, looking for birds or baitfish breaking the surface. He handed Rick the binoculars a few times and told him what to look for.

The still water was a deep blue, almost black, as they slowly trolled with a following fan club of seagulls and a lonely frigatebird. Suddenly, Rick heard a tick on one of the reels, then another, and then the reel whizzed at high speed.

"Fish on! You want it?" Paul yelled as he pointed to Possum.

"Hell, yeah!"

Paul set the hook and tightened the drag before he handed the rod to Possum, who had just cinched himself tight in the fighting chair and shoved the rod in the gimballed fishing belt. The rod bent, and Possum pulled back and reeled. The mighty fish gave up a little line, then took it all back.

"What is it?" asked Rick.

"Not sure," said Paul, squinting. "Maybe a big bull dolphin, but it hasn't broken the surface yet."

As if the fish heard what Paul said, it leapt into the sky in a brilliant flash of iridescent blue and silver. The captain slowed the outboards to a one-knot idle as Possum fought with all his might against the powerful billfish. It was big sailfish by Keys' standards.

"It might top seventy-five pounds," yelled Paul, as he moved to the port rail of the boat wearing special gripping gloves.

The beautiful fish leapt into the air, violently shaking its head in an attempt to dislodge the hook from its mouth. Over and over, it launched out of the water, spinning and tossing its head side to side. Twenty minutes had passed already; Possum was covered in sweat, and Rick knew he must've felt like overcooked spaghetti. Every time he would gain some ground on the sailfish, it would whiz his reel and he'd lose more line. But Possum was starting to win the battle as the fish jumped less and less and was drawn closer to the boat. After nearly forty minutes, the fish was alongside the Contender.

"Grab your camera, Rick," said Paul, leaning over the rail of the boat and grabbing the bill of the sailfish. He pulled her up, measured and weighed her, and then pulled the exhausted fish on board as Possum unstrapped himself from the fighting chair.

He stood beside Paul as he instructed him how to pose for the shot. Rick took several shots with his iPhone and then grabbed Possum's Canon 80D and snapped several more photos and a video. Possum was grinning from ear to ear.

"It's my first sailfish!" he boasted.

"She's a beauty, man, and her weight is a whopping 83.7 pounds. That's a monster around here," replied Paul.

Paul took back control of the fish, leaned over the rail, and held her just below the surface, pulling her back and forth to force water back over her gills. The beautiful fish's colors began to return. Suddenly, she started to move her tail side to side. Paul released her, and she swam slowly away, still exhausted but healthy and safe.

"Sailfish are strictly catch-and-release here," said Paul. "In Mexico, they kill them for cat food—makes me sick! They are too beautiful to execute and aren't good-tasting to eat, to us, anyway. If you want to get a trophy wall mount of your catch, Possum, you can head over to Gray Taxidermy in Miami with the photos, length, and weight, and they can create a mold out of fiberglass that will represent your fish in every detail. It's much more humane that way. Costs a pretty penny, though, probably about eight hundred to a thousand bucks. It's something to think about."

"I might just do that," exclaimed Possum.

No sooner had Paul rebaited Possum's rod than a reel on the starboard side started screaming.

"Fish on! Your turn, Rick," shouted Paul.

Rick strapped into the fighting chair, and Possum handed over the fishing belt.

"This is different, Rick. Not a sailfish," Paul declared, as he pointed behind the boat. "It's a big wahoo, I'm guessing in the fifty-pound range. Y'all are gonna have some tasty seafood for dinner tonight! Wahoo is Ono in Hawaiian, which means delicious. They are truly one of the best-tasting fish in the ocean. I'm a big fan."

Micah was finally feeling better, so he grabbed his guitar and strummed some fish-fighting music for Rick. He started out with a funny rendition of "Eye of the Tiger," then played "Kung Fu Fighting," but changed the words to "Wahoo Fighting."

Everyone laughed as Rick cranked on the huge, gold Penn reel, trying to land the speedy fish. After nearly twenty minutes, he got the fish next to the boat. Paul gaffed it on the first try and pulled it on board.

"Oh man, what a perfect wahoo!" said Paul. "Fifty-eight pounds. Damn, that's a big one for these waters."

Possum snapped a few shots of Rick and his catch before Paul threw the big wahoo on ice. They continued to troll for a couple more hours and caught a few more keeper-size dolphins and one barracuda. Rick and Possum were pretty whipped and thought it'd be a good time to explore the sinkhole Captain Bobby had told them about.

"We can do some bottom fishing over the hole," suggested the captain. "Might snatch up a couple snappers or groupers."

"Sounds good to me," replied Rick. "Can I snorkel over the spot to get a closer look?"

Captain Bobby smiled. "I can do you one better than that. I have a submersible motorized camera. We can send it all the way down, and I can email you the footage for your crustacean research. I'm sure there are some spiny lobsters there, but who knows. Could be some varieties of shrimp or crab as well."

"Sweet. Now I'm excited," Rick replied as the wind rustled his hair.

It took about an hour to reach the spot where the hole was. It couldn't be seen from the boat, but Captain Bobby knew exactly where it was by his GPS.

"How did you find this hole? I can't see anything," asked Rick, squinting down at the water.

"Well, I was flying my ultralight inflatable one day and flew directly over it. I happened to have my handheld GPS in my pocket, so I immediately tagged the location. I've found all sorts of structures for bottom fishing doing this. It gives me an edge over other fishing charters."

"That's clever. How insane is it that you have a flying boat? Is it safe?"

"I've never crashed it and I have no plans to. I only fly on perfect days. It also helps me meet women. Sometimes I'll land near Jimmy Johnson's Big Chill after a few flyovers. The girls flock to the inflatable as I tie up to the dock beside the pool. It's a chick magnet, I swear." Captain Bobby chuckled.

"I can only imagine, you sly dog, you."

Bobby just grinned as he powered down the outboards and instructed Paul to drop the hook.

Paul opened up a Pelican case and began to assemble the submersible camera. It looked like something from outer space: a yellow manta ray-shaped UFO with a huge window in the front housing the camera. He tethered it to a long cable and hooked it up to a color TV monitor, then launched it gently over the rail. As it dove toward the sinkhole, several schools of yellowtail snappers darted in for a closer view.

A large sinkhole over fifty feet in diameter soon became visible as the camera descended to the bottom. The edges were covered in sand and silt, and the hole was only sunken down about three to four feet below the rest of the bottom. It had been filled in by sand from dozens of hurricanes over the years. Sea fans and other soft corals grew in abundance. The occasional sea slug sat motionless on the bottom.

Paul handed the controls over to Rick. "Have at it, Rick. Try and keep it a few inches off the bottom. We don't wanna scratch the lens cover."

"Copy that. How deep can it go?" asked Rick.

"The manual says two hundred feet."

"Is that because of the length of the cable or because of water pressure?"

"I think water pressure, but that's not even the coolest thing about it. It doesn't need to be hooked up to the cable. It comes with a waterproof GPS watch you can wear that allows it to follow you around while diving. I only hooked it up to the cable since we were staying on the boat."

"No way!" exclaimed Rick. "Possum, we have to get one of these!"

"You're damn straight, amigo!" replied Possum.

Rick piloted the amazing underwater drone for a while, then turned the controls over to Possum.

While steering the machine on several lobsters and crabs he spotted, Possum boasted, "That's what I was looking for."

After forty-five minutes, an alarm went off, showing the drone had only about fifteen minutes of battery life left, so Possum called Paul over to bring it home.

Rick reeled in the cable as Paul steered it toward the boat. Once it was close enough, Paul grabbed it and rinsed it off with fresh water. He opened it up and pulled out an SD card.

"Did you bring a laptop in your backpack by chance, Rick?"

"I have my MacBook," replied Rick.

"Oh, even better. I'll just pop the card into my MacBook and AirDrop it to you."

"Perfect. I didn't bring an SD card reader with me, so that will work just fine."

They both opened their laptops and in short order all of the video footage was on Rick's hard drive. Possum had already discretely stored the GPS location of the sinkhole. Rick was pretty sure Captain Bobby would've given it to them, but there was no sense in making him curious as to why they wanted it. After all, while lobster and crabs were delicious and a source of scientific query for Possum, it was really just a cover for what might really lie beneath the surface of the hole—Fletcher's gold.

Paul rigged up a couple of rods with heavy weights and fresh-cut bait. As soon as each line hit the bottom, the reels sizzled. Each time, they brought up a healthy red snapper. After several reds, a yellowtail took the bait. They tossed the yellowtail back. In less than thirty minutes, they had pulled fifteen red snappers on board.

"Well, boys, ready to head back? We have some fish to fillet and some beer to drink!" said Captain Bobby as he cranked up the trip outboards.

"Let's roll!" said Rick.

As soon as the boat was tied off back at Bud N' Mary's Marina, Paul began to fillet the fish. Curious tourists lined up to take pictures, and Captain Bobby took full advantage of it by handing out discount coupon flyers for upcoming charters. He booked a couple of charters right on the spot.

"Works every time, Rick. There's no better way to book a fishing charter than to bring fish to the marina," said Captain Bobby.

"I gotta cruise, y'all," said Micah. "I have a gig tonight at the Lorelei. Stop by if you can. Thanks for the trip, Rick, it was a blast."

"Maybe we'll see you there later," Rick told Micah, patting him on the back.

After Paul finished filleting all the fish and bagging it with ice, he put it in the back of Rick's rental. Rick and Possum thanked Captain Bobby and Paul and tipped them both generously.

"If y'all go see Micah later, the Lorelei will cook your catch," said Captain Bobby. "It's a great deal. They'll prepare it several ways and include sides. It's a good time."

"Sounds like a plan. Possum?"

"Let's do it, hombre." Possum grinned. "Y'all should join us too."

"We might just do that, after I clean the boat. I have an errand to run but I should be able to get there by sunset. They have amazing sunset views there," Bobby told them.

Waving goodbye for now, Rick and Possum hopped in their rental and headed toward the resort to chill for a bit and clean up.

CHAPTER TWENTY-ONE

Nine-Tenths was making steady progress toward Venice as Johnie, Chief, and Emily were all up on the flybridge. The seas were calm and the boat was performing perfectly. The beautiful, frothy-white wake behind the boat looked brilliant against the deep blue Gulf. If all went according to plan, they would arrive in Venice by sunrise, top off the tanks, and bolt to the Keys. Johnie was stoked about getting back to the Keys. It had been quite a while since he'd been down there.

Emily seemed excited as well, although Johnie could tell her current situation always lingered in her mind and kept her anxiety up.

Chief was right at home on the flybridge and sat on top of his cage, occasionally playing with the hanging wood Johnie had secured to the perch.

"You want to steer for a while?" Johnie asked Emily.

Her eyebrows lifted in surprise. "Really?"

"Yep. Just keep her pointed due south and don't bump into anything. I'm gonna get some shut-eye," said Johnie, borrowing a line from the movie *Captain Ron*.

He was joking, of course, and had no plans on sleeping. This trip was too important, and Emily didn't have the experience to be on the helm alone. If she did well, he thought he maybe could at least rest his eyes a bit as long as he used his spotting scope to scan the horizon for other boats first.

Emily seemed like a natural as she steered the 55' Viking on the calm Gulf of Mexico. She was composed and showed no signs of fear. Johnie took full advantage after scoping the sea and plopped down on a bean bag, his hat pulled over his eyes. The sun was setting as he drifted off for a minute, but he hopped up fast when he heard a loud thud. Chief had pulled the wood off the chain, and it had slammed on the deck.

"So much for resting my eyes," said Johnie. "Thanks, Chief!"

Chief cocked his head and fluffed up his crown. The bird already had his sea legs from previous trips and seemed at ease on his play perch atop his cage. He just bobbed up and down as the deep-V hull sliced through the slow-rolling seas. A slight ray of light began to appear on the horizon. The oranges and blacks slowly turned to yellow as the sun peeked above the water. They would be in Venice in less than two hours, according to the chart plotter.

After Johnie took over the helm again, Emily drifted to sleep on a bean bag beside Chief's cage. She awoke as the big Viking engine lowered down to an idle. Johnie steered them into the inlet. Large pelicans sat on the rocks of the north jetty, catching Chief's attention. He bobbed his head up and down and squawked a few times to let them know of his presence.

"Good morning, sunshine," said Johnie, as Emily rubbed her eyes.

"Morning. How far inside do we have to go for fuel? I could use some coffee. Want me to make some?"

"Nah, we're just to the right of Snake Island. It's super close to the entrance. That's why I picked it. If you want to run up to the bow and pull out the bow and spring lines, I'll call the marina and ask for docking assistance. We can grab coffee and some breakfast there," replied Johnie.

"Sounds good."

Emily scurried to the bow, pulled out the lines, and got ready while Johnie made the phone call.

"Hello. Crow's Nest Marina, how can I help you this morning?" said a voice on the other end.

"Good morning. We are a Viking 55 and would like assistance tying up and fueling."

"Perfect timing, Captain. We just had a big charter leave. Come on in and I'll meet you at the end of the dock. I'm Mitch and I'll see you when you get here. How far out are you?"

"I'm just approaching Snake Island."

"Oh, I see you. Just come in to starboard side. See you in two minutes."

"Thanks, Mitch. See ya soon."

Emily tossed the heavy bow line to Mitch, and then the spring line, as Johnie used the powerful twin engines to draw the stern slowly toward the dock. As the starboard edge of the boat slowly touched the dock, all the fenders kept the shiny hull from getting scratched. Johnie climbed down to the stern and handed the line to Mitch, who tied it off to the oversized cleat on one of the pilings.

Chief was barking like a coon dog and jumping up and down, demanding to come down. Johnie climbed back up to the flybridge, shut down the engines, and put Chief on his shoulder. The bird was very excited about something. Johnie took the fuel pump handle from Mitch and began to pump diesel into the tanks.

"Can we get some coffee at the restaurant?" asked Johnie.

"The restaurant doesn't open until 11:30 a.m., but Cheri, the general manager and co-owner, is inside doing inventory. Just tell her I sent you. She always has coffee on and you could probably grab some pie or something like that for breakfast."

With Chief on his shoulder, Johnie strolled beside Emily down the dock toward the restaurant. Suddenly, Johnie realized what Chief was so excited about. A large cage sat beside the marina office with a green head parrot inside. A sign reading, *Hi, I'm Pepe the parrot*, sat atop his cage. Chief was like a bull in a china closet. Johnie took him off his shoulder and held him a few inches from the cage. They both looked at each other, shook their heads, and bobbed and weaved like a couple of welterweight boxers. Chief raised his crown high, trying to assert his dominance and opened his wings. Emily giggled at the sight.

After a long minute of bird egomania, they both calmed down and Johnie continued to the restaurant. The rear door was ajar. He lightly knocked and opened it up.

"Hello, anyone home?" he asked.

"Hi—good morning. We're not quite open yet, but how can I help you?' replied a woman with long brown hair.

"Are you Cheri? Mitch said we might be able to get some coffee."

"Hi, yes, I'm Cheri. Come on in. Oh, you have a cockatoo. Did you meet Pepe?"

"Yeah, this is Chief. They seemed to be mesmerized with each other."

Cheri reached up, and Chief stepped onto her hand. She snuggled with him. It was obvious she had a lot of experience with exotic birds. After a minute of snuggling, she returned Chief to Johnie.

"Let me grab y'all a couple of large to-go coffees."

"Do you by chance have any pie available? I can pay cash if it will make it easier," said Johnie.

"You're fueling up outside, right? Don't worry about it. It's on the house," replied Cheri.

"Thank you. That's so nice of you."

Cheri returned shortly with two huge stainless-steel coffee mugs with the Crow's Nest logo printed on the side, and an entire key lime pie, plus a cup of walnuts for Chief.

"Oh, that's too much for free. Please let me pay you."

"It's fine. The cups are free advertising. Just take care of that beautiful bird and pay it forward one day," said Cheri with a smile.

They all said their goodbyes and stepped out of the tavern. Mitch had already finished fueling and handed Johnie the bill, which he settled with the company credit card. Chief and Pepe continued their bromance until they untied from the dock, swung the boat around once again, and headed offshore.

Suddenly, a white van pulled to the side of the boat and two men jumped out. The van blocked Johnie's view of Emily on the stern. A scream came from the boat.

Johnie dropped the coffee mugs and pie and quickly set Chief on top of Pepe's cage. He ran toward the boat as Emily screamed again. She was struggling with the men as they tried to drag her from the boat toward the van. She grabbed the hand rail tight. One man pulled her legs, and the other one fought to free her clenched hands from the port rail.

"Hey, what's going on?" yelled Johnie. The men looked up. One pulled a hand gun from his waist and fired at Johnie, barely missing his head. He hit the deck with a loud thud.

"Call 911!" shouted Johnie. He rolled to his left behind the van, then sprinted toward the fuel office.

Mitch was already dialing as Johnie bolted inside.

"Do you have a weapon? Two guys are trying to take Emily off the boat."

"Here!" Mitch handed Johnie a flare gun from his top desk drawer. "It's all I got."

Johnie ran back behind the van as sirens blared in the distance. The men gave one last pull on Emily, but she didn't budge. She had managed to wrap her legs around the fighting chair post. The sirens drew closer, and the two men jumped from the boat. One climbed into the driver's seat. The other one ran around the front of the van and jumped in, as Johnie slid behind the van, just out of his view. The van squealed the tires and a floom of smoke wafted over him as they sped from the parking lot. Johnie bolted to the boat.

"Are you ok?" Who were those men?"

Emily was crying as her hands shook. "I—I don't know. I'm okay," she said, her lips trembling.

She rubbed her wrists. They were red from the struggle. "I think Liam sent them. When you screamed at them, one guy said, 'Scheiße!' which is German for 'shit' or 'damn.'

I've heard Liam say it hundreds of times when he gets flustered. That's when the other man took a shot at you."

"Let me see your wrists."

She held them up toward Johnie. He could already see an impression of fingers in a bruise on her arm.

"We need to get you to the hospital."

"No, I'm okay. A little shaken, but I don't need to go to the hospital."

"Are you sure?"

"Yes. I'm sure."

A police car pulled up next to the boat, and a deputy jumped out.

"What's going on here?" he asked with his hand over the holster on his belt.

"Someone, well two men, tried to abduct Emily," said Johnie. "One of them fired at me. They peeled out when they heard the sirens."

"Are you okay, ma'am?" asked the deputy. 'Do you need medical assistance?"

"No. I'm fine. A little freaked out at the moment, but physically I'm ok."

"Do you know the men who tried to snatch you? Did you get a good look at them? How about their vehicle. Did you get any of the license numbers? Either of you?"

Johnie shook his head. Emily began to describe the men to the deputy. Johnie walked back to the fuel office, and Chief hadn't budged from his spot on top of Pepe's cage.

Mitch had picked up the coffee mugs and set them on his desk.

"Is she okay?" he asked.

"Yeah. She's gonna be all right. She's giving her statement to the deputy. I need to call the boss and tell him what happened."

"Do you wanna use the office phone?"

"No, that's all right. I have the company cell phone."

Johnie called Rick and quickly told him the story.

"She won't go to the hospital, so I guess we'll be heading your way as soon as she's done with the deputy. I ain't never been shot at before and I'm ready to get the hell out of dodge in case they come back."

"Alright, y'all be careful. Tell Emily I got her back. We're gonna sort this out soon enough."

Back outside, the deputy gave Emily a card and asked Johnie several questions, then left the parking lot.

"You sure you're all right?" he asked Emily.

She nodded. Her hands had finally stopped shaking. "Yeah, I'm okay. We should get going. I'll call the deputy tomorrow and see if they found the guys or made any progress. I know in my gut that Liam sent those guys. How they knew I was here is beyond me, though."

"Did you have a phone when you woke up in Tampa?"

She stepped inside the cabin, reached into her purse and pulled out an Android phone. "This phone was in my purse when I was first released. It's a pay-as-you-go phone. I used it a few times."

"Can I look at it?"

She unlocked it and handed the phone to Johnie. He scrolled through the apps until he came to one called "Battery Saver." He double clicked it, and a password and ID sign-in form popped up on the screen.

"Okay. This is a tracker app. I installed them on all my company phones when I had a race team. I used them to track my employee cars. They work great and no one knows what they are. Does this phone mean anything to you?"

Emily frowned. "No. I don't even have any numbers stored on it."

Johnie tossed the phone into the water.

"They won't be tracking you now. We can get you another phone in the Keys."

"Whatever you think is best, Johnie. I'm actually not surprised and I should've known better." She sighed, shaking her head. "I completely forgot about the phone, and never considered that they might track me with it."

"We should get going. Last chance. Hospital?"

"No. I'm positive. I'll be fine." She gave him a tight smile.

Johnie went to say goodbye to Mitch, who had refilled the coffee mugs and gotten him a new pie.

"I called the owner and told her what happened," said Mitch. "She had just left to get some produce for the kitchen. She's on her way back. She'd like to speak to you."

"Thanks, but we really need to get going. We're on our way to the Keys today. She can call me later if she needs to."

Johnie handed Mitch a card, grabbed the mugs and pie, and set Chief on his shoulder before heading back to the boat.

As they exited the channel, Johnie pushed the throttles almost all the way up. The big hull dipped at first, then began to rise before it planed out. They were soon headed due south, Islamorada bound.

The sun was high a couple hours later when Johnie spotted the towers in Marathon. He headed east-southeast to avoid the shallow water near Islamorada. Once he got to the intercoastal waterway, he kept the boat in the center of the channel, not taking any chances of running aground. He then passed under the Snake Creek Bridge that had opened on the half-hour. Once he was on the outside, he turned north and dead-headed for Marina Del Mar, which was about fourteen nautical miles away. Before lunchtime, they had tied up to the slip and Johnie stepped onto the dock and pulled out his cell to call Rick.

Before he could dial, he heard a familiar voice.

CHAPTER TWENTY-TWO

"Welcome to paradise, Johnie! How was the trip, other than the incident in Venice?" Rick yelled, approaching his boat and his friend.

"How the hell did you know we were here?" asked Johnie in disbelief.

"I installed a Simrad BoatConnect GPS tracker on the boat. I've been keeping an eye on y'all all the way here. Pretty sweet," replied Rick with a grin. "We were just talking about that. Whoever originally took Emily had installed a tracker app on her phone. I chucked it in the channel."

"Good idea! How are Chief and Emily?"

Johnie pointed at the cage on the flybridge. Rick could see Chief munching on a grape. The bird hadn't spotted him yet.

"Emily's down below, changing clothes. We were about to grab lunch. I look forward to meeting this Possum."

"Great minds think alike, Johnie. Possum is holding us a waterfront table over at Sharkey's. We can walk over. It's right next door."

"I'll let Emily know," said Johnie.

Rick and Johnie stepped onto *Nine-Tenths*, and Rick climbed up to the flybridge to see Chief.

The bird almost jumped out of his feathers when he saw his best friend. Rick took him out of the cage and kissed his beak. "I missed you, Chief!" The bird was overly affectionate and clung to him like Saran Wrap. "I guess I can bring you to the restaurant with us. I'm sure they won't mind."

He heard someone coming up the stairs and turned to see Emily.

"Well, hello, Emily. How was the trip across the Gulf?" he asked.

"The water part was pretty much perfect. The part in Venice was a different story," she said with a light laugh.

"Johnie filled me in on the whole thing. You gonna be ok? You ready for some lunch?"

"Yeah, I'm good. I'm ready for a huge drink with an umbrella stuck in it, though." "Well, you are in luck. We're heading over to Sharkey's and that's one thing they can do great: strong, fruity drinks."

While they were all strolling toward the restaurant, Rick's phone pinged. It was a message from Carson.

Rick, I need to speak with you ASAP. Can you get to a quiet place?

Rick texted back that he could be alone in two minutes.

"Hey guys, go ahead and order me a Bloody Mary. I'll be right back," Rick told the group.

He stepped out to the parking lot in front of Sharkey's beside a tall palm tree and dialed Carson.

"Hi, Rick, you alone?"

"Yep, what's up?"

"Ok. I had a friend at the FBI break the encryption on the hard drives. There data on there is incredibly scientific. There's a detailed formula and results of animal and human trials on a cancer drug that is not only interesting but could be a breakthrough mankind has never seen."

"So, it's true? The possible cure for cancer is on those hard drives?"

"It appears so. There are several chemists involved. Liam Furrer and Emily Davis seem to be the main chemists, and their initials are all over the findings. There's also a person with the initials T.O. involved. We don't know what T.O. stands for yet. We are still deciphering all the data. I would like to keep the original encrypted hard drives and study them more. I've arranged to make copies of them without encryption, and I can FedEx them to you. There are hundreds of photos on the drives too, and you know the faces better than I do, so that may help you," said Carson.

"Ok, thanks so much. Can you put the drives in portable enclosures with USB-C ports?"

"That's exactly what I did. Possum told me you were an Apple guy, so I had those done already with lightning ports. I can send them today," replied Carson.

"Ok, just send them to the Playa Largo Resort & Spa, care of my name."

"I'll head over to FedEx as soon as we hang up. Be careful, Rick. This is the biggest medical discovery and worth trillions of dollars. Whoever was involved with stealing it is capable of murder and probably already has killed."

"Ok, I'll be safe. Talk to you soon," said Rick.

After hanging up, he made his way back to the table and took a big drag of his spicy Bloody Mary. Chief sat on his shoulder, fully content. Rick handed him an olive.

"What's up, Rick? Any info on the case?" asked Possum.

"Yeah, I'll tell you later. Where's Emily?"

"She stepped into the ladies' room. She'll be right back."

"Ok, let's order some food. I'm starved. We need to check out the lab on Terra's key. Liam owns that little island, and one way or another we need to see what's in those buildings. It could help the case."

Rick ordered a double cheeseburger with bacon, and Possum and Emily decided to split an order of nachos and churrasco steak. Chief got a taste of everyone's dish and was in hog heaven.

"Y'all wanna do some sightseeing?" asked Rick.

They all replied, "Yes," at the same time. After Rick paid the bill, the group hopped in the car bound for Key West. It was a perfect day. The sky was blue with a few lazy, puffy white clouds occasionally drifting by. The water was crystal clear, in many shades of blue. Rick popped in a CD he'd picked up from Micah called *Sunshine Billionaire*, and they listened to it three times before they arrived in Key West. They had all the words memorized by then.

He parked just off of Duval and they did the Duval crawl for the next two hours, a nickname given to the sport of bar hopping in Key West. Their first stop was Captain Tony's, a true dive bar with dollar bills covering the ceiling. To their surprise, Micah was standing by the entrance strumming his acoustic.

"Micah! What's up?" asked Rick.

Micah stopped playing, gave him a man hug, and told the bartender to take special care of them. They all sat on barstools and drank rum punch while they listened to Micah play. After four drinks, Rick shoved a couple of twenties in Micah's tip jar, and they headed back out to Duval Street.

Their next stop was Sloppy Joe's, probably the most famous of all Key West bars. They imbibed a few more drinks and listened to a local keyboard player.

"I think I've had enough liquor for a bit," said Rick. "I still have to drive back. Y'all wanna go see Mel Fisher's museum?"

They all nodded and followed Rick out the door. The group slowly strolled toward Greene Street and finally made it to the museum. Both Rick and Possum were enthralled with the exhibits. They spent two hours talking with the staff and examining the finds from the 1622 fleet. Possum bought a gold coin on a beautiful gold anchor chain, all made from the *Atocha*—the mothership of the big treasure find. It cost a pretty penny, but he had to have it.

Rick had sobered up quite and bit and they decided it was a good time to head back. "Emily, if you want to stay at the resort with Chief, Possum and I are going on a night dive tonight. You can use the facilities or order anything you like. Just sign for it."

"Thank you so much! That would be great, Rick. Does it have a spa?"

"Sure does. I'll call ahead and add your name to the room so you can use the room key to get into the spa."

"Thanks, Rick. I appreciate it. Maybe I'll get a massage."

Rick pulled into the resort, and Emily headed straight for the spa with an extra key. He handed Chief to Possum and told him he'd be right back. He and Johnie drove to the yacht so Rick could grab Chief's travel cage and some bird pellets. He returned to the resort while Johnie stayed on board and got the boat and dive gear ready for the night's adventure.

"You ready?" Rick asked Possum.

"Damn straight, I am. I wanna breathe some air under-water ASAP!" replied his friend.

Rick put Chief in the travel cage and fed and watered him. "See ya soon, buddy. Be a good dog."

Chief cocked his head and mimicked a laugh as if he knew what Rick meant. As Rick closed the door behind him, he could hear barking coming from the room. He laughed on the way to the car.

Crazy bird!

When he got back to the boat, Johnie was doing diagnostics. He had already topped up the fuel and loaded several dive tanks in the holders on the starboard side, with two complete scuba sets, two underwater propulsion vehicles, and the new drone camera Rick had ordered with a fresh, empty SD card installed, plus two Pulse 8X metal detectors.

"You are one hell of a first mate, Johnie!"

"Thanks, boss!"

Rick and Possum untied the lines from the dock. Johnie backed *Nine-Tenths* into the center channel and slowly began to spin the huge sport fisher toward open water. Possum climbed up to the flybridge to share the GPS location with Johnie from his iPhone. It was a short trip to the sunken hole.

As they slowly approached it, Rick scanned the surrounding area for other boats using his night vision binoculars. "Run invisible for the last half mile," he told Johnie.

Once they reached the edge of the sinkhole, Johnie dropped the hook, assisted by Possum, while Rick fired up the drone and donned his scuba gear. Possum joined him shortly and they both did quick safety checks of their gear. Johnie had affixed two huge LED lights to the top of the drone, and once the two divers did a backwards roll into the ocean, Johnie used his remote control to light up the drone just underwater. With a quick ok to Johnie, they began their slow descent. Johnie would monitor the live video feed from the drone.

Underwater, fish darted everywhere and tiny, translucent shrimp danced in the lights. A curious cuttlefish came close to the camera lens, as if to say hello, and stayed with the drone all the way down. Both Rick and Possum began round-square sweep patterns with the metal detectors. After several passes and finds of old beer cans and various shards of rusted metal from old boats or nails from old docks, Rick got a huge hit.

He waved Possum over; they both scanned the area and got the same reading. An object was buried at least six feet beneath the sand and silt. Rick grabbed the drone, looked directly into the camera, and shook his head to let Johnie know it was too deep.

Johnie used his remote to flash the lights of the drone three times, indicating Rick should surface. Possum stayed down and put a marker over the spot. It lit up the detectors like the fourth of July.

Back on the surface, Rick reached out as Johnie passed him what looked like a small vacuum cleaner hose. Attached to the other end was a hookah rig with a gas motor attached to an innertube and separate hose that led to a catch bag.

"Where did this come from, Johnie?"

"Amazon. I thought it might come in handy," Johnie told him.

"You're a freaking genius."

Rick once again descended to the bottom and showed the hose to Possum, who looked wide-eyed in surprise. It was like an underwater vacuum cleaner. Rick laid the nozzle on the silt right where the detectors had gone off. It worked like magic. Possum used his hands to move larger pieces of old, dead coral and other rocks out of the way as Rick continued to vacuum. They were only in about twenty-five feet of water and had plenty of air and no worries about getting the bends at that shallow depth.

After nearly thirty minutes of sucking sand from the bottom, a huge, encrusted object clogged the end of the nozzle at nearly six inches long. Rick grabbed it and examined it. He then pinpointed his handheld over it, and the metal detector started beeping again. Possum waved his detector over the hole and got no response. They both gave a thumbs up and began to surface.

Once on board the boat, they ripped off their dive gear. Johnie set up a large rectangular tub with some sort of solution in it.

"What's in the tub?" asked Rick.

"It's a special chemical mix I made that eats away concretion. Just lay that thing in the solution and we wait. Don't get any on your hands."

Rick placed the cylindrical treasure find in the solution, and the liquid began to bubble and boil.

"Let's find a safer spot to let this stuff do its magic," said Rick. "Head toward Teatable Key, but don't get too close. Let's just hold a mile away and change tanks. We have another dive to make."

Johnie fired up the twin engines and began to slowly motor toward Teatable Key. Once they arrived at a calm, clear spot, he idled the engines and set the navigation system to hold. The boat was equipped with a global dynamic positioning system and would hold the boat in place as long as needed with no one at the helm. The technology was quite impressive.

Rick put on his head lamp and long rubber gloves, and began to peel away the years of concretion that had grown around their find. It took a few minutes before they could tell what it was—a glass jar. Once he got enough of the growth off it, he tried to open the top, but to no avail. He laid it on a towel, dried it off thoroughly and picked up one of the dive weights from his gear bag. With one quick blow, he shattered the glass.

After removing the large shards of glass, he slowly pulled out an old, yellowed piece of paper that had been held in place with a gold ring. He slid the paper out of the ring and examined the side of the ring with his readers on. The initials J.F. were engraved there. Inside the ring was an inscription that read *One More Step.*

Rick's heart began to race. Possum and Johnie were hunched over his shoulder to the point that he could barely move.

"Calm down, boys. Let's step into the salon for some better light," he said.

Johnie laid a large towel over the dining table, and Possum began to film the entire event with his Canon 80D for historical purposes.

On the table was a shiny gold ring. Rick picked it up and tried it on. It fit perfectly, so he left it on and winked at Possum. He knew Possum would let him keep it. After all, it was Rick's forensic research and dogged determination that had gotten them this far to begin with.

Rick carefully unrolled the delicate paper and placed a pair of salt and pepper shakers on each corner to keep it in place, then began to read. It was a poem.

What you have found is grand indeed
The ring comes from my father's steed
The markings inside the ring are old
To lead you to the mass of gold
You found the hole and that is true
But the proper hole is known as blue
To find the right one I'll be clear
It's in the waters that quench the deer
The smell at low tide can be rank
But it's just like money in the bank
So, search the pines both big and old
That's where you'll find the mother lode
JF II 1912

Rick, Johnie, and Possum stood there silently, re-reading the words.

"Oh my God," shouted Rick. "This is John Fletcher's son's ring, and I think I figured out the poem!"

"You did?" asked Possum.

"Yes, I think so. I believe he's talking about Blue Hole Lake on Big Pine Key. It's a freshwater lake that all the little Key deer drink from. I've seen hundreds of them there. The whole thing makes sense. His father's steed is referring to the horses that led the wagons he used during the original burial of the treasure. Remember I found two gold bars in saddle bags. Also, 'steed' can be a reference to a machine, like a motorcycle or, in this case, a train. The smell at low tide refers to the dead seaweed that rots on the banks there. It's pretty bad at times. And money in the bank? That's simple. That's where the term 'bank' came from originally, from pirates who used to bury treasure on the steep banks of rivers. Boys, we are getting close."

Rick polished the ring on his pinkie with his thumb and stared at it with pride. He was grinning from ear to ear—they all were. But he knew they needed to get ready for the second dive. This would be a stealth dive and it could be dangerous.

Johnie ran with no lights and used the navigation to get him within three hundred feet of Teatable Key. Once in place, he killed any semblance of light on board and they scanned the houses on the key with night-vision head gear. Convinced that no one was on the island, Rick filled a dry bag with several tools, a .38 special, two pairs of night-vision goggles, and a special camera with dual macro and micro lenses.

"You ready, Possum?" asked Rick.

"Let's roll."

This time they stepped gently off the dive platform into the water and descended to the bottom. Rick used his compass, set his dive headlamp to red, and they made their way to the east shore of the island. They ditched their gear in a pile on the beach and crawled toward the largest house—it looked more like warehouse than a beach house. They were both wearing black ski masks and night-vision goggles, to make it hard for anyone to identify them. As they rounded the corner of the main building, Rick pointed at the two cameras on the east and west sides of the building. Possum nodded and shrugged. Cameras were not as big of a worry as the security alarms. There was no way to disarm them, so it would need to be a smash and grab job.

Rick used a large crowbar to jimmy open the huge metal door. Once it popped open, he expected a loud alarm to go off, but nothing happened. Possum and Rick stepped inside slowly and closed the door behind them. Rick flicked on the light switch. Nothing. There were no lights. He tried another, then realized how hot it was inside. The electricity was off. To their luck, they had arrived during a blackout. There was a rusty old generator at the rear of the building, but it wasn't running when they approached it. This was a huge break for them.

Rick removed his mask and nodded for Possum to do the same. The put their night-vision goggles back on, and Rick pulled out the camera and a spotlight from his dry bag. The building had no windows, so he turned it on and the entire place lit up like the sun. Rick began to open file cabinets and snap photos of all the documents. He was moving fast and just making sure it was all in focus, not paying attention to the details; he would read them later.

Possum used a small camera he'd bought and focused on taking pictures of any photos, awards, or documents hanging on the walls or on tables. All the computers had been removed, but the filing cabinets and a few items remained. It was as if the lab hadn't been used in quite a while, or it was in the process of being eliminated. Either way, there was still quite a bit of documentation that they would have to sort out once back at the resort. They had gone through as much as they could find and scanned it all into their phones and cameras, so they decided to exit while they were still ahead of the game.

Rick made a circular motion after pointing at his eyes, to let Possum know he was going to take a look around the other buildings. They never spoke a word in case there were any battery-driven audio bugs around. Rick pointed at his watch and made a ten with his hands.

Rick was a few feet in front of Possum crouching as he peered around the corner of the building. He was confident they could head back to boat now.

A shot rang out, exploding masonry just inches from Rick's head. Possum ducked down and pulled out his Sig.

"Are you hit?" asked Possum.

"No. Run!"

Possum and Rick ran toward the beach where their dive gear was sitting. *Pew! Pew! Pew!* Shots rang out from a gun with a silencer, kicking up dirt near their feet. Rick turned and unloaded his pistol toward the gunman. Several more shots flew at them from the other side of the building.

"There are two shooters. Let's get out of here."

"I'm hit, Rick."

"What? Where?" Rick looked at him in shock, his eyes running over his body for signs of blood.

"It's just my leg, but I've lost a lot of blood."

"Put pressure on it. Do you have any bullets left?"

Possum tossed Rick his Sig and wrapped his dive belt around his calf just below the knee. The bleeding slowed.

Rick crouched down beside Possum and fired toward both buildings. He heard a loud grunt.

"I hit one!"

With his night goggles, he could see one man helping another man to a van. They climbed in and the van sped off.

Rick took a closer look at the wound on Possum's calf. The bullet had passed clean through. He pulled some thick black tape from his dry bag and wrapped it tightly.

"This will stop the bleeding, but we'll need to dress that wound back on the boat. Can you dive?"

"Yeah. I can do it. It's a short dive back to the boat."

"Don't get too close to me. You're nothing but shark bait now." Rick grinned, hoping his humor would take Possum's mind off the pain of his injury.

It worked; Possum laughed a little. They donned their scuba gear and descended again, heading for *Nine-Tenths*. It was more of a snorkel than a dive as they were barely a few feet below the surface.

"What happened? I thought I heard shots," said Johnie as Rick approached the swim platform with Possum in tow.

"Help me get Possum onboard. He's been shot."

Johnie jumped over the stern, and they both pulled Possum aboard. They helped him to the galley and laid him on the settee.

"Johnie, please grab me a wooden spoon and the first aid kit."

Once Johnie came back with the supplies, Rick turned to Possum and handed him the spoon. "Put this between your teeth. I'm gonna take look. I need to make sure there's no lead still inside ya."

Possum bit down hard on the spoon as Rick peeled back the tape and studied the wound.

"There's a clean exit hole. It just caught the back corner of your calf. Mostly skin, just below the surface. They weren't using hollow points and based on the size of this, I'd say it was a small caliber weapon. Maybe .25 or .22. You're lucky.

If this had been a .45, you'd be missing half of your calf muscle. Now, fair warning, this is gonna hurt."

Blood was trickling out both ends of the bullet hole but had slowed down considerably. Rick cleaned the wounds with Safewash, then peroxide, and wrapped his leg up with fresh gauze and taped it. Possum clenched harder on the spoon handle.

"Okay. I'm done. You're gonna live, but you're gonna be sore as hell. Probably way too sore to dive tomorrow. Johnie can take your place."

"If I can dive tomorrow, I'm gonna do it. We'll see how it feels tomorrow and make that call."

"Whatever you say, Possum. It's your leg. Can you stand up and put weight on it?"

Possum slowly rose from the settee and held the edge of the counter for stability. He put some weight on it. "It's not too bad." He took a step.

"I don't think it hit any muscle." "You may be right, amigo."

"What did you find on the island?" asked Johnie.

"We got some good intel," said Rick, "but I didn't have much time to get a good look at most of it. Let's head back to the marina. We can all meet at the resort for breakfast and go over the plan for Big Pine Key tomorrow." Both Johnie and Possum smiled, and Rick knew they could smell gold. In spite of the pain Possum was in, the excitement in the air was palpable. If they found Fletcher's treasure, it would be the culmination of years of research, planning, and big dreams. Rick glanced down at his dive watch as the time changed from 11:59 p.m. to midnight. He raised his over-sized watch so they both could see the time.

"Today's the day, boys!"

CHAPTER TWENTY-THREE

Emily rose before everyone else, and her noise in the kitchen and the smell of fresh coffee brought Rick out of slumberland.

"Good morning, Emily. How did you sleep?" he asked as he cuddled with Chief, who was clinging to his chest.

"I guess I slept like a log," she said. "I didn't even hear y'all come in last night. What time did you get back? Any luck? I can't wait to hear all about it."

Possum was yawning loudly in the other bedroom. Rick peeked in and saw that he had slept on the pullout couch in the same room Emily slept, and was folding the bed back into the couch.

Such a gentleman.

"Did you hear what happened?" he asked her.

"Possum got shot last night."

"What?!" Emily turned in alarm to Possum.

"Are you ok? You got shot?" Rick lingered in the doorway to let them have a moment.

"It's just a flesh wound," replied Possum in an exaggerated Monte Python voice.

Emily didn't seem to think that was funny. She crossed her arms and gave Possum a serious look.

"But seriously, I'm fine," he said. "It's a tad sore, but I can walk on it. I'm a little gimpy, but I'll survive."

"Did you see who did it? Did they get away?"

"Rick winged one, but they sped off in a white van."

Emily raised an eyebrow.

"Was it a Ford van by any chance?"

"Umm, yeah, I think so. Why?"

"The guys who tried to take me in Venice were in a Ford van. Coincidence? I think not."

"Neither do I."

"You need to rest and take care of that leg today."

"I wish I could, but Rick needs my help today. I want to help him."

Emily rolled her eyes. "Okay, Mr. Hard Head. Do what you gotta do." She turned to Rick. "Did you guys find much at the lab last night?"

"Not a whole lot," said Rick. "And honestly, we got out of there so fast we didn't really have time to go over any of it. I'm planning on doing that tonight and tomorrow morning. We have a bit of a treasure hunting to do today. You wanna come?"

"I'd love to, but I have a friend coming over to the resort today that I knew when I worked in St. Pete. She moved down to Marathon and gave up corporate life to become a bartender at Dockside Tropical Café. She loves it. If it's ok with you, I can just hang here at the resort. A little downtime and girlfriend talk would do me some good. I can cancel if you need me though," replied Emily.

"No, that won't be necessary. Do your thing. Did you tell her about your appearance? I mean, she's got to be quite shocked, no?" asked Rick, raising an eyebrow.

"Well, I told her I went naturally gray. We haven't seen each other in over ten years, so I'm sure she will look different as well."

"That's true. People do change."

Rick texted Johnie to come to the resort and bring all the metal detectors, diggers, and anything else he thought they'd need. He ordered an extra-large Uber to pick him up.

Possum went straight to making breakfast after giving Emily a peck on the cheek and a light butt slap when he must've thought Rick wasn't looking. Rick smiled to himself. They were really starting to like each other, he could tell. He hadn't seen Possum this happy in a long time.

They all sat on the balcony and ate breakfast. Chief sat on the edge of the table and delicately nibbled on Rick's pineapples. He had made French toast with pineapples drizzled in rum. The alcohol burned off from the heat of the skillet, but the flavor remained and Chief, along with everyone else at the table, loved them.

Johnie arrived just after breakfast, and Emily made him a quick plate that he gobbled up like a ravenous wolf. Rick and Possum geared up, went over notes and re-read the poem again. All the guys said goodbye to Emily and got in the car, including Chief in his travel cage. He was up for an adventure.

As they pulled to the main stoplight on A1A in Big Pine Key, Rick turned right on Wilder Road, took the split to the left on Key Deer Boulevard, and soon Blue Hole Lake came into view.

Rick kept Chief in his travel cage after spotting a couple of lazy gators basking in the sun on the bank. Donning his scuba gear, he waded into the water. Possum handed him his Pulse 8X and fins, and Rick descended to the bottom. The lake was small, more like an oversized pond. Once Rick got to a certain depth, he could see saltwater layered under the fresh water that had a familiar haze he was used to while diving the cenotes in the Yucatán Peninsula. The lake was actually an abandoned limestone quarry that had been used to help build Henry Flagler's Overseas Railroad.

Rick did a round-square sweep pattern, and his detector picked up a few small pings that turned out to be fishing hooks and a couple of beer cans. He started in the center of the lake and continued outward until he reached the bank. It was like trying to find a needle in a haystack.

After an hour of metal detecting, he returned to where he'd started and asked Possum to bring the poem out of the trunk in his go bag. Rick dried off and read it aloud again, hoping that would make a difference somehow.

"Wait, what if 'pines big and old' refers to actual pine trees and not Big Pine Key?" asked Rick.

They all looked at each other, then back at the lake. Several large pine trees grew along the shore. One in particular caught Rick's eye. It was the largest one by far, leaning over the lake at an odd angle.

Grabbed his land detector, he sprinted along the bank to the tree. This part of the bank was higher than the rest and didn't slope down, but had a ledge that was a sheer drop of about three feet. As Rick peered over the side of the ledge, he saw it continued straight down into the water until it reached the bottom. This side of the man-made lake was also deeper along the bank than any other.

"Quick, grab my mask, fins, and Pulse 8X," shouted Rick. He put on his equipment and made a giant stride off of the ledge into the lake, and almost hit the bottom. Once his eyes adjusted to the light, he scanned the lake floor and did a fast sweep of the area. Nothing made the needle move on the detector. Getting frustrated, he swam back to the bank slowly.

That's when he saw it. There was a cavern on the side of the ledge about four feet below the surface. It was too small to swim through with scuba gear, on but just big enough to squeeze into by skin diving.

Rick surfaced and swam to the edge of the ledge. He held his head above the surface and shouted to Johnie, "Did you bring the Spare Air 600? I found a small cave."

"Yeah, I brought two of them but didn't attach them to the BCs. They're in your gear bag. Let me go grab them."

"Please get my dive light too," Rick added.

"Gotcha, boss."

When Johnie came back, he handed Rick both of the Spare Airs and his dive light, along with some nylon cord on a reel. With one scuba tank fastened to his waist, he held the other one under his right arm. After several fast, deep breaths to eliminate some of the CO_2 in his lungs, Rick descended toward the opening of the cavern. On a large rock, he tied the nylon cord and took his first breath from the Spare Air. He then slid the two tanks into the cavern and used his free arm to pull himself inside. There was no more than an inch or two around his body as he manipulated his torso through the opening.

It was pitch black once he got through the hole. He fumbled to find his dive light, hanging from his waist. The hole in the cavern opened up, and once he turned on his light, he could see it was about ten by twelve feet in size and the ceiling was about three feet high above the water. He surfaced and slowly took a breath.

The air smelled a bit off but breathable, so he decided to save his Spare Air for his exit. Scanning the edge of the cavern, he saw tiny white crawfish crawling just under the surface. At the far-left edge of the cavernous room was a flat ledge sitting half a foot above the water's surface. A large, almost perfectly rectangular-shaped piece of limestone sat in the very corner. It was about four feet high and three feet wide, and it looked like it didn't belong there. There was no way Rick could move it by hand. The entire cave seemed to be natural except for the rectangular limestone boulder. Just underneath the water's surface, he saw a large rectangular hole the same size as the boulder. It had silted up a bit, but the shape was the same. Whoever had found this cavern had also cut out that limestone wedge.

Rick hyperventilated a few times, then squeezed back through the small cave opening to the main part of the lake. He surfaced and ripped his mask off in one quick movement.

"I think I found something," he told the others. "It could mean nothing but might be everything. Johnie, can you please take the car over to Ace Hardware? Buy the biggest come-along they have, a couple of those tourist Flagler railroad spikes, and a large hammer."

"I'm on it," replied Johnie.

"Possum, grab your dive light, mask, and gloves. I'm gonna need your help. Chief can stay in the front seat with Johnie while he makes his run. I've got a good feeling about this."

Johnie returned in about thirty minutes with everything Rick had asked for. He handed the gear to Possum and set Chief on the hood of the car in his travel cage, with a towel over the top to block the heat of the day's sun. Chief was running back in forth in his cage, wanting to come out and play, but there were far too many gators in the area, not to mention birds of prey and huge iguanas.

Possum lowered himself into the lake and took the second Spare Air from Rick. They both descended, and Rick pulled himself though the opening once again. Possum followed close behind. It was a tighter fit for him, but hc managed to get through. He handed the come-along, hammer, and spikes to Rick on the other side.

They both surfaced inside the cavern and hung their masks around their necks.

"I guess that second helping of breakfast wasn't a good idea," said Possum with a chuckle.

"Is that a self-deprecating fat joke?" Rick asked.

"Haha. No, just a fact," replied Possum.

"Ok, I'm gonna pound a spike as deep as I can into the limestone floor on the opposite side of the cavern," said Rick. "See if you can find a good, flat spot on the side of that rectangular boulder. I'll be right over with the other spike."

"Gotcha, amigo."

The limestone was soft but still dense enough to hold the spike firmly. He left the end of it sticking up to wrap one end of the cable of the come-along to it, then swam back to the other side. Possum had climbed up to the boulder. When Rick arrived, he reached out and handed him the hammer and spike.

Possum drove the spike into the side of the large rock, sparks flying off the metal with every blow. It echoed loudly in the cavernous room. Rick handed him the other end of the come-along, and Possum attached it firmly to the spike.

"Ok, here goes everything," said Rick. He began to winch the come-along, and it started to tighten up. Still, the stubborn limestone didn't want to move, though he was cranking as hard as he could.

A creaking sound came from the big rock, and it moved about an inch closer to Rick. Possum shined his light in. "Can't see anything yet," he said.

Rick continued to crank with all his might, slowly inching the boulder away from the wall. Once it was about a foot away, Possum stuck his head inside and shined his light again. He reached in and grabbed something.

"What do you see?" shouted Rick.

Possum turned off his light and handed something to Rick. It was smooth and heavy.

"I don't see a whole lot, just a bunch of these," replied Possum.

He turned his light back on and shined it directly at the object in Rick's hands. It was a solid gold bar. Possum grinned.

"Oh my God! How many are in there? Did we find what I think we found?" Rick asked, barely able to get the words out.

"It's hard to say how many," Possum decided, after a pause. "If I had to guess, I'd say all of them. Rick, you did it. You found Fletcher's treasure. You found the motherlode!"

"We did it, we did it! I'm about to drown holding this heavy-ass bar."

Possum stuck out his hand, and Rick grabbed it as he set the gold bar on the floor. He climbed up and peeked into the man-made hole behind the limestone boulder. As he shined his light inside, he could see stacks and stacks of gold bars and an empty bottle with a cork in it, sitting atop them all.

He jumped back in the water and wrenched more on the come-along until the opening was big enough to step inside. Out of courtesy, Possum waited and let Rick crawl inside first. There was just enough room for him to barely fit inside and grab the bottle off of the stacks of gold. He was hyperventilating and feeling as if he were in shock. Or maybe it was a dream or déjà vu. Whatever it was, it was surreal, to say the least.

Rick crawled out backwards and set his light down so he could pull the cork out of the bottle. Possum held his light toward Rick as he unrolled the tattered paper inside. He read it aloud.

> *You are the finder of bars of gold*
> *A Texas treasure of riches untold*
> *The story ends who reads this script*
> *For you have found the sacred crypt*
> *Never again a treasure hunter*
> *To move the gold, you'll need a shunter*
> *You title now is a real reminder*
> *For you are now the treasure finder.*
> *JF II 1913*

"This is it! We did it! We found Fletcher's treasure," hollered Rick, laughing with joy. "What the hell is a shunter?"

"Oh, I got that one," said Possum. "A shunter is a small locomotive used to move rail cars to different tracks. I think it's a metaphor, since the gold is here in the Keys near the Flagler Railroad. He probably meant you found so much gold it will take a train to get it all out of here. I guess they even spoke sarcasm in the early 1900s. But seriously, how are we gonna get all this outta here? Each bar weighs 400 Troy ounces, or the equivalent of about twenty-seven pounds."

"Ok, you're freaking me out. You're too damn smart. You know I hate math. Like I told you before, four out of three people have trouble with math," Rick said, winking at him. "Maybe it wasn't a metaphor. Maybe a shunter is just what we need. I don't mean a real locomotive but the equivalent. Johnie can go buy an electric winch, and we can place some aluminum siding along the floor of the opening of the cave. You can be on one side and I can tie a few bars at a time to the end of a pulley. We can put at least three to four bars in a heavyweight dive bag and pull them out, and have Johnie load them all in the trunk. We'll need full-size scuba tanks; these Spare Airs won't do. I can stay inside and you can slide a tank and regulator to me. What do you think?"

"I think it might work. I'll squeeze out and let Johnie know," said Possum.

"Aw, hell no, I'm coming out too. I wanna see his face when you hand him that gold bar just like you did to me. That will be priceless," said Rick, smiling bigger than he ever had before.

They both squeezed through and climbed up the bank.

"Any luck?" asked Johnie anxiously.

They both looked toward the ground disappointed, and then Possum handed him the gold bar wrapped in a cloth he had in his goodie bag.

"Nah, we just found a few hundred of these," said Possum with a shrug.

Johnie unwrapped the cloth and almost fainted when he saw the shine of the gold. "A few hundred? Are you saying what I think you're saying?"

"Yes, we found it! It's real." Rick patted Johnie on the back and made a quick list of what they needed to retrieve the gold from the cave. "Go get everything on this list and get three—no, make it four—bottles of champagne. I want one to pour over my head and one for my gullet."

"Make it six. We should all do it!" added Possum.

"Good thinking," replied Rick.

"I'm not sure I can find an electric winch. They are usually attached to Jeeps," said Johnie.

"Ok, then buy a Jeep with a winch. I've always wanted a Jeep."

"Are you serious?" Johnie was astounded.

"Serious as a heart attack. I added your name to the business account, so just stop at Bank of America and get a cashier's check. I saw a used car lot on Big Pine that had several nice, four-door Wranglers."

Rick pulled Chief down from the hood so Johnie could drive back into town. He let the bird out of the cage, held him tightly to his chest, and danced around in a circle, singing a song.

"*You are my lucky bird, little white bird, oh, my lucky bird.*"

Chief flapped his wings and raised his crown in approval. Rick picked up the gold bar to let Chief examine it. He seemed uninterested and was probably hoping for a grape instead, so Rick texted Johnie.

> Grab some grapes and three jerk turkey subs at Winn Dixie.

Johnie responded,

> Will do, boss. I found a 1974 Jeep with a lift kit and a huge electric winch at the lot. He wants $8900. Will that work? It's a two-door.

Get it, texted Rick, as he continued to dance around with Chief clinging to his chest for dear life.

CHAPTER TWENTY-FOUR

Johnie returned in a snazzy red 1974 Jeep CJ5 with Pro Comp A/T Sport off-road tires and Weld Racing rims. It was tricked out and Rick loved it.

"I told the guy at the lot we'd swing by later and grab the rental car," said Johnie.

"Perfect!" replied Rick.

"You ready to make that shunter, Possum?"

"Choo fucking choo!"

Rick leapt into the lake. Possum handed him the scuba tanks, regulators, and goodie bags, then reeled out the stainless cable from the winch on the Jeep. With that, Rick dove down and shoved one of the scuba rigs into the cavern opening. He slid the shiny aluminum panel into the cave and secured it to the bottom of the hole. It was almost a perfect fit. He resurfaced and waved for Possum to come in. Possum secured the tank to the edge of the ledge and waited for Rick to pass him the first load of gold bars.

With three quick tugs of the stainless cable, Johnie would roll in the winch as Possum guided it to the end of the opening. Once each bag, weighing in at over a hundred pounds, reached the end of the opening, Johnie guided it to the top of the bank, loaded the bars in the back of the Jeep, and covered them with a moving blanket he'd also picked up at Ace Hardware. It took nearly three hours to get every bar out of the cavern.

When it was over, Possum and Rick surfaced, handed Johnie the winch cable and all the gear, and climbed up the ledge to the top. Rick walked over to the Jeep and peeled back the moving blanket. He snapped a few shots with his iPhone, then propped the phone up on the Jeep mirror and pushed the video button.

With Rick, Johnie, and Possum each holding a gold bar in one hand and champagne in the other, they toasted, hooted, and hollered as they poured the champagne over each other's heads and shook the bottles. They made a royal mess and soaked Chief, but luckily, he didn't seem to mind; the bird was caught up in all the excitement. Popping open the second bottles, they chugged them. Rick even gave Chief some, but he shook his head in distaste and settled for a fresh grape.

They all climbed into the Jeep, which was sitting very low in the back from all the weight of the gold bars. Chief sat atop a fortune of gold in his travel cage, as they headed back to the car lot. Johnie followed them back to *Nine-Tenths*, where they began the arduous process of transferring the gold bars to the yacht, placing each bar under the settee, then covering them all with towels and tackle boxes. The sun had settled, and no one was paying attention to what they were doing.

"Let's head back to resort. I can't wait to tell Emily we hit the jackpot. We also need to go over all those photos we took in the lab," said Rick.

Emily was in the shower when they arrived back at the resort.

"Honey, we're home!" yelled Possum.

He went to make Cadillac margaritas at the bar, and Rick began to thumb through the documents they'd photographed at the lab. Emily toweled off, put on a robe, and joined the crew in the kitchen. Possum's back was to her when she walked in.

"Well? What happened? I'm dying to hear," asked Emily.

Possum spun around with a huge margarita in his right hand and a gold bar in his left. The look on Emily's face was priceless when she saw the treasure.

"Y'all found one?"

"No, we found them all!" Possum told her, handing her the margarita.

"Oh my God, are you serious?"

Rick walked over and showed her the photo he'd snapped from the back of the Jeep. "Dead serious."

"How much is it worth?"

Rick looked over at Possum who was staring at the ceiling, obviously doing math in his head.

"Oh, at current gold prices, just over a hundred and fifty million dollars," Possum finally said.

Emily held on to a chair as if she was about to faint, and took a huge swig from the margarita. They all clinked glasses together and laughed aloud.

"Oh Possum, you got a delivery from Amazon," said Emily. "It's sitting in the corner by the balcony."

"Oh sweet, it's my new spear gun. Four bands and a razor-sharp spear that could drive through an elephant's head. I was hoping we can have some R&R this week and do some spearfishing."

"Amigo, we can do whatever we want as long as we continue to work on this case," said Rick. "We need to clear Emily's name and get this drug to market before NoahTech buries it."

"True dat!" said Possum. "That reminds me—I snatched a few pictures in the frames off of the wall. I was getting too much glare while trying to snapshot them, so it was easier just to throw them into the dry bag." He stepped into the bedroom, then returned with the dry bag and handed it to Rick.

"Are y'all game for some macadamia nut-encrusted grilled wahoo topped with fresh pineapple-mango salsa for dinner tonight?" asked Possum.

"I'm telling you, Possum, you'd make a great husband!" Rick smiled and winked at Emily.

"Emily, you wanna run to Publix with me?" asked Possum.

"Sure, let me throw on some shorts and a blouse," she said with a smile. "Let's get some New Zealand sauvignon blanc too."

"Great idea. It's time to celebrate."

The was a knock on the door. Possum looked though the peephole before opening it.

"Wazzup, treasure finders?" said Johnie.

"I'm studying the stuff from the lab and Possum and Emily are heading over to Publix shortly to get some side dishes for dinner," said Rick. "Have a seat."

"What's in the long box?"

"That's my new spear gun."

"You want me to assemble it for you while y'all are at the store? I'll make sure all the parts are there and it's ready to slay some fish," said Johnie.

"Yeah! Thanks so much, bud," replied Possum.

Emily and Possum headed out, and Rick continued to study the documents they got from the lab. At the bottom of several clinical trial papers were the initials E.D., L.B. and T.O. Rick still had no idea who T.O. was, but he was determined to find out. He planned to ask Emily if she knew who it could be when they returned from the store. He used a magnifying glass and carefully scanned every photo for some kind of clue. When he reached the middle of the stack, he found a vacation request approved by Liam for Tammy O'Neil.

That's T.O.!

Upon further inspection, he figured out that Tammy O'Neil was an assistant at the lab and not a chemist, but she was very detailed and helped Liam with the organization. It was time to call Liam and pray he never figured out who broke into his lab in Zürich.

Rick punched in Liam's number and crossed his fingers. On the second ring, Liam picked up.

"Michael, how are you? You left so fast, I assumed you had an emergency, Is everything ok?" asked Liam.

"Yes, I had a family emergency. I apologize profusely for not saying goodbye. I'll make it up to you. A dear friend had taken ill, but it's all good in the end."

"That's good to hear, Michael."

Rick could hear caution in Liam's voice, as if he wasn't sure he believed him.

"I have a question, Liam. I'm almost finished with the story for Fortune and you *will* be on next month's cover. My question is, who is Tammy O'Neil?"

Silence fell over the line, and then Liam cleared his throat and spoke.

"Tammy was the best lab assistant I ever had. She had a strong background in chemistry but didn't have a degree. She was there during all the human trials of my new drug, which I plan to launch in ten days. Sadly, she died in a tragic auto accident and was burned beyond recognition. I still mourn her."

"Will she get any credit on the cancer launch, at least posthumously?" asked Rick.

"Yes, I owe her that much. We actually had a falling-out right before her crash. To be honest, she got a little greedy and wanted to get a percentage of the discovery. I refused and she walked out angrily, and that was the last time I ever saw her."

"I'm truly sorry for your loss, Liam. Did you want me to mention her in the article?"

"That would be perfectly acceptable. Please describe her as a valued lab assistant, not a chemist."

"I understand. Wait? Didn't someone break into the lab and steal your findings?"

"I have one word for you, my boy: redundancy. All my hard drives were backed up to the Cloud. In addition, the hard drives were encrypted and I keep a flash drive on my keychain of my latest trials. Technology is amazing. It's hard to believe that the little flash drive has more storage than my first desktop by twenty-fold."

"Ah, I see. That's great news. I'll send you a copy the story before we go to print so you can proof it for any errors."

The clock was ticking now. Rick needed to beat Liam to the punch or the drug might never get to the masses.

"Thanks, Michael. It's getting late here and I have an early meeting in the morning. Can we chat tomorrow if you need to?"

"Sure, but that probably won't be necessary. I'll email you your article and we can talk after that, all right?"

"Perfect, Michael. Auf Wiedersehen."

"Ciao, Liam."

The mystery was getting more complicated now. Rick did a search online for Tammy O'Neil but came up with nothing. He did find an article in a Zürich newspaper about her death and copied it into Google translate, but it was more of an obituary than anything about the accident, and there were no photos.

Rick went back to the photos he had, then pulled out the framed wall pictures Possum had snatched from the lab on Teatable Key. He looked at the pictures and nothing stood out to him. Then he saw a photo of a dark-haired woman with her arm around Liam. In the background, on the far right, was a gray-haired woman in a lab coat. She was a little out of focus but looked familiar. Rick opened the back of the frame and pulled out the photo. On the back, writing in pen said: *Liam, Emily, and Tammy.* Rick pulled out his magnifying glass and focused on the woman in the back. She resembled Emily. Not the Emily in the photo but the Emily that was at Publix shopping with Possum.

No way, that can't be.

Rick did an image search on Google of Emily and found several photos of her receiving awards, and even found a few with Liam. The Emily online was taller than the Emily at Publix and had dark black hair, almost blue-black, but she'd explained how they had changed her look in Grand Cayman. Rick was beginning to feel uneasy.

Johnie continued to fiddle with the spear gun as Possum and Emily came through the door of the resort with arms full of Publix bags. Possum laid out all the groceries on the kitchen counter while Emily made another batch of margaritas for everyone and put the wine in the fridge. Rick continued to study the papers from the lab, spotting T.O. on many of the trial findings.

"Where's the gold, Rick? Did you put it in a safe place?" asked Emily.

"Of course." He smiled. "It's worth more than anything I can even imagine. Half of it goes to Marcy Nobles, the rightful heir to half of the find, and some goes to the state. For that part, I'll do some creative accounting."

"So, where is it actually?" asked Emily.

"Why so curious? You gonna steal it?" said Rick sarcastically.

She laughed. "I'm worth way more than that once you solve this case. I was just being a curious cat."

"Well, it's on the boat and I have cameras everywhere."

"That's good."

There was a knock on the door. Rick peered through the peephole and saw it was a FedEx driver with a package.

"Rick Waters?"

"Yes."

"Can you please sign here?"

Rick signed and took the padded package from the driver. He sat back down at the kitchen table and ripped open the package.

Inside were two new hard drives in enclosures, and a note from Carson.

Rick,

These are the unencrypted versions of the hard drives you sent me. These findings, if approved by the FDA, could literally mean the end to cancer as we know it. Safeguard them. I have the originals in my vault at home. We have to tread lightly. I understand the weight of these findings. I don't want the government to bury this. It must be released in a big way that can't be stopped. Think Snowden.

Carson

"What's that, Rick?" asked Emily.

"It's what we've all been waiting for—the unencrypted copies of the hard drives with the cancer cure you developed," he told her.

"Are you certain?"

"Without a doubt."

Emily moved over to the bar and put her purse over her left arm. Grabbing her margarita, she approached the kitchen table.

"Cheers, Rick! Thank you."

"Cheers!"

Emily stepped away from the table and set her drink down on a small sideboard as she studied the beautiful painting of sailboats on the wall adjacent to the kitchen table. "Do y'all think I'd look good on one of these boats?"

"You'd look good on a skiff!" piped up Possum.

"I agree, Tammy, or should I say T.O.?" Rick responded.

Emily reached into her purse and spun around, simultaneously pulling out a small caliber handgun and pointing it straight at Rick's face.

"I'll take those hard drives, Rick!"

You could hear a pin drop as she made her unexpected move. Rick was already prepared.

"What are you doing?" yelled Possum.

"Shut the fuck up, redneck," she snapped. "Those hard drives are my destiny. I deserved to be regarded as more than assistant during those trials. I should have been included in a big cut of the profits!"

"So, let me get this straight," said Rick. "You were a lowly lab assistant with a background in chemistry who was paid extremely well by Liam, and you want to take all the credit?"

"Fuck you, Rick. You have no idea."

"I tend to disagree. Let me tell you what I think happened."

Rick took a deep breath, and then said it all without inhaling again.

"You assisted Liam and Emily in the lab in Zürich. You were greedy and jealous. During the meeting in Florida, you killed Hans Larsson with the help or hire of three masked men, if they even existed. Then you killed Emily and her husband and burned down their house, impersonated Emily, re-zoned her house, and turned it into a parking lot. You planted the hairbrush with your own hair you dyed black. You left some money in the lab coat to corroborate you story even more. Once in Destin, you laid the whole thing out for me about being transformed from Emily Davis to Patricia Benning and, being the kind, open-hearted, empathetic man I am, I believed you, as crazy as it sounded. You even created those X-rays and faked your way through the hypnosis session. You are nothing more than a petty thief, a liar, and a murderer. Does that cover it all, or did I miss something?"

"Nice job, Rick, but you did leave out one detail." She smiled coldly. "I have the gun. It's pointed directly at your forehead, and thanks to your honesty, I also know where the gold is. I'm gonna kill the three of you losers, shoot myself in the arm, and say we were attacked by home invaders. Then I'm gonna take the hard drives and the gold, burn down the yacht, and live the good life from now on. I think I'll drown that stupid bird of yours in the hot tub for good measure. Does that cover it all or did I miss something?"

"Yes. Fish on!" shouted Rick.

Emily looked at Rick with a confused stare and even tilted her head a little, the way Chief did sometimes. Rick bumped his knee into Johnie's leg under the table and gave him a sly look.

Faster than the flash of a hummingbird's wings flapping, Johnie pulled the trigger of the spear gun. A stainless, razor-sharp spear launched like rocket and drove deep through the shoulder of the faux Emily and impaled her against the wall, directly into the jib of the sailboat in the painting. The pistol dropped from her hand and bounced close to Rick, who picked it up and shoved it against her temple.

"Game over, Emily, Patricia—uh, I mean, Tammy!"

She writhed in pain as blood dripped down the wall. It was a perfect shot, so she would survive. Possum, in shock, dropped his head in disgust as Rick dislodged her from the wall and affixed some tight dressings on both sides of the wound to stop the bleeding, then tied her hands behind her back.

Rick called Carson as Johnie and Possum kept an eye on her. "Hi, Carson. It's Rick. I got the hard drives and I sorted out the case. Can you send a couple of Feds here to take the perp away? I don't trust the local yokels here. This crime is too big and complicated. She'll need medical treatment, but she'll be fine. I'll type up all the details and email you a pdf. She committed at least two murders and attempted to steal the world's most valuable cancer therapy."

"Ok," said Carson. "I'll call some of the boys in Miami—I think I can still call in some favors. They can be there in a couple of hours."

"All right. I'll put a copy of the report on a flash drive and give it to the agents when they arrive."

"Sounds good. Great job, Rick. Talk soon."

Carson hung up, and Rick patted Possum on the shoulder.

"Come with me, Possum. Keep an eye on her, Johnie," said Rick as he handed the gun to Johnie.

Rick led Possum down to the pool bar and ordered two mojitos.

"Here, man, drink it down. I'm really sorry she fooled you," said Rick. "Hell, she fooled all of us. I know you were starting to have feelings for her."

"Yeah man, I'll be all right. I did have feelings for her, but she was just playing a part, so I really just had feelings for the actress she was." He shook his head. "I hate fake people."

"Amen to that."

"What are you gonna do now? Are you giving the drug therapy back to Liam?"

"Yes and no," replied Rick. "Yes, I'm gonna give it back to him, but the late Emily also deserves credit for the discovery, and no, as it's too valuable for any one company to own the rights to it. That's probably why Emily had set up the meeting with Hans in the first place. If NoahTech were the only drug company with the cure for cancer, they could charge any price they wanted and only the richest of the rich could afford it. I have an idea and I plan to execute it shortly."

When Rick returned to the room, he typed out all the details of the crime, emailed one copy to Carson, and saved one to a flash drive. He'd left Possum at the bar. He figured his friend wanted to self-medicate for a while and try to get over the painful ruse Tammy had inflicted upon him. It was obvious he had truly cared for her.

After a couple of hours, an unmarked black van arrived at the resort, and three special agents took Tammy and the flash drive away.

Rick, Johnie, and Chief joined Possum at the bar. Rick ordered a mai-tai and gave Chief the pineapple wedge. Johnie ordered an IPA and pulled out three cigars.

"Hold that thought, Johnie," said Rick. "I need to go to the business office and get some padded envelopes and a permanent marker."

Rick bought several padded envelopes and a Sharpie. Then he went back the room and loaded several flash drives with the formula Liam and Emily had developed at NoahTech. He addressed one to the New York Times, one to Fortune Magazine, and four more to the big pharma companies: GlaxoSmithKline, Johnson & Johnson, Lilly, and Pfizer. He printed FedEx labels back at the business center, taped them to the envelopes and gave them to the girl working the front desk.

"Can you please have FedEx pick these up in the morning?" asked Rick.

"It would be my pleasure," she replied with a smile. "We have a pickup already scheduled for tomorrow morning for another guest. I'll add it to the outgoing mailbox."

Rick thought a lot about how Liam had merely been a pawn in Tammy's game. He wasn't a bad guy but maybe a tad too self-absorbed and greedy. The discovery was far too great for any one man or company to control. By sharing it with the media and other big pharma companies, Liam would get the credit he deserved and his ego would be stroked, but at the same time, the cure would be more available to the population at a reasonable cost.

When Rick returned to the gang at the resort bar, Chief was still sitting on Rick's chair, munching on another pineapple wedge the bartender had given him. No other guests were sitting at the pool bar.

"Where were we?" asked Rick, sitting down and propping Chief on his knee.

Johnie pulled out the three cigars again and handed one each to Rick and Possum.

"Would you mind?" Rick asked the bartender.

He looked around and said, "Be my guest. Y'all are the only ones here."

Rick put Chief back on the chair, and they all moved to a high-top table a few feet away so the smoke wouldn't bother the bird.

"Let's celebrate, boys!" said Rick as he raised his glass to toast.

"Here's to another case solved and making this world a better place."

They all clinked their glasses together.

"Are these Cubans?" asked Rick as he bit the end off and lit it up.

"Nah, these are Dominican. But you know we're only ninety miles from Cuba," replied Johnie.

"Are you thinking what I'm thinking?" asked Rick, raising one eyebrow.

"My mojito in the Bodeguita del Medio and my daiquiri in the Floridita?" replied Possum with a grin.

"Yes, Havana daydreamin'," said Rick. "Havana day-dreamin'."

The End

ABOUT THE AUTHOR

Eric Chance Stone was born and raised on the gulf coast of Southeast Texas. An avid surfer, sailor, scuba diver, fisherman and treasure hunter, Eric met many bigger than life characters on his adventures across the globe. Wanting to travel after college, he got a job with Northwest Airlines and moved to Florida. Shortly thereafter transferred to Hawaii, then Nashville. After years of being a staff songwriter in Nashville, he released his first album, Songs For Sail in 1999, a tropically inspired collection of songs. He continued to write songs and tour and eventually landed a gig with Sail America and Show Management to perform at all international boat shows where his list of characters continued to grow.

He moved to the Virgin Islands in 2007 and became the official entertainer for Pusser's Marina Cay in the BVI. After several years in the Caribbean, his fate for telling stories was sealed.

Upon release of his 15th CD, All The Rest, he was inspired to become a novelist after a chance meeting with Wayne Stinnett. Wayne along with Cap Daniels, Chip Bell and a few others, became his mentors and they are all good friends now. Eric currently resides in Destin, Florida with his three exotic birds, Harley, Marley and Ozzy.

Inspired by the likes of Clive Cussler's Dirk Pitt, Wayne Stinnett's Jesse McDermitt, Cap Daniels Chase Fulton, Chip Bell's Jake Sullivan and many more, Eric's tales are sprinkled with Voodoo, Hoodoo and kinds of weird stuff. From the bayous of Texas to the Voodoo dens of Haiti, his twist of reality will take you for a ride. His main character Rick Waters is a down to earth good ol' boy, adventurist turned private eye, who uses his treasure hunting skills and street smarts to solve mysteries.

FOLLOW ERIC CHANCE STONE:

Website:

www.EricChanceStone.com

Facebook:

www.facebook.com/RickWatersSeries

www.ingramcontent.com/pod-product-compliance
Lightning Source LLC
Chambersburg PA
CBHW060527260626
47161CB00003B/791